STEPHEN OSBORNE

Dreamspinner Press

Published by
Dreamspinner Press
382 NE 191st Street #88329
Miami, FL 33179-3899, USA
http://www.dreamspinnerpress.com/

Wrestling with Jesus

Cover Art by Anne Cain annecain.art@gmail.com
Cover Design by Mara McKennen

ISBN: 978-1-61372-450-7

Printed in the United States of America
First Edition
April 2012

eBook edition available
eBook ISBN: 978-1-61372-451-4

For Liz Rapp

CHAPTER
ONE

THE folded chair hit the back of Kyle's head with a resounding thud that could be heard at the top of the bleachers. Kyle flew forward, hitting the ropes. His opponent, a rather good-looking Hispanic kid who went by the unlikely name of El Toro, swung again and slammed the chair into the center of Kyle's back. Kyle collapsed to the canvas, seemingly dead to the world, as the crowd cheered.

Randy Stone, sitting far up in the bleachers in an attempt to distance himself from the more rabid wrestling fans in attendance, winced in sympathy. "I don't care what he says. That's got to hurt like a son of a bitch."

Randy's companion, a raven-haired beauty and card-carrying fag hag named Debbie Jacobs, munched on her popcorn. "I can't see what attracts you to the guy. If you ask me, he's got a hot body, but that's about it. He's got the brains of a split pea."

"You haven't even met him yet," Randy replied, the tension in his stomach mounting to Huge Fucking Butterfly levels. He'd been worried that Debbie would be skeptical about his blossoming romance with a professional wrestler, but he'd hoped she wouldn't start off with quite such an openly negative attitude.

"He just got hit by a chair. Twice. And he let the guy do it. Believe me, he's got the brains of a split pea, and that's being insulting to split peas. Don't get me wrong, I'm sure this Kyle guy is fine for a quick fling, but you've been acting like he's The One, and I just can't see that."

"He's sweet," Randy replied. "He's just a really nice guy, and he treats me like I'm Einstein."

"Compared to him, you are."

"I admit, at first it was his hot bod that attracted me, but it's developed beyond that. I'm really falling for the guy."

"Seems like you might fall quite literally. I'm betting he'll want to body slam you before sex or something like that. He looks like he's got that gorilla mentality." Debbie chewed more popcorn. "How on earth did you ever meet up with this guy? Didn't you say he was a closet case? You didn't meet up at a club, then. And I'm pretty sure he isn't a customer at your bookstore. That guy never progressed beyond *Hop on Pop*." She found a kernel that hadn't popped and spit it back into the bag.

"Would you give him a chance?" Randy pleaded. "I really like this guy, Debbie. I want the two of you to get along."

An older gentleman near them was staring not at the ring but at Debbie, or more precisely at Debbie's chest. She caught him and flashed the guy an angry glare. "Hey, Gomer, the action is down there in the ring." The man flushed and shifted his gaze back to the middle of the gym.

In the ring, the tide of events had turned. Kyle Temple had managed to kick El Toro in the genitals without the referee catching him. After several punches to El Toro's face that would, in a real fight, have resulted in the Hispanic boy suddenly sporting at the very least a bloody nose but instead simply gave El Toro a stunned look, Kyle leaped up and dropkicked the handsome kid right out of the ring.

"So violent," Debbie muttered.

"It's not real," Randy reminded her.

"Well, duh. That poor little bastard would have been wheeled out of here on a cart minutes ago if these blows were actually landing full force."

"It's like playacting," Randy continued, picking up on Debbie's condescending attitude toward his new beau's chosen profession. "They're enjoying themselves and entertaining the crowd. What's wrong with that?"

A grimy teen seated in front of Randy turned around, a sneer on his pimpled face. "You can't fake that shit, dude. Say that any louder and Kyle Temple will come up here and pound the fuck out of you."

Randy shrugged. "He pounded the fuck out of me pretty good last night, actually."

Debbie laughed, nearly choking on her popcorn.

The teen frowned in confusion before turning back to watch the action in the ring.

Sweat was making Kyle's long light-brown hair stick to his face and neck. He took a second to pull some strands out of his eyes before hoisting El Toro over his shoulders for the Torture Rack finisher. El Toro screamed his submission, and the referee quickly called for the bell to ring.

"I don't suppose he did that last night," Debbie said as Kyle unceremoniously dumped his opponent's body onto the canvas.

"Can't say he did. But then, I wasn't putting up much of a fight, either."

The referee held up Kyle's hand in triumph as the crowd booed loudly. El Toro was lying at Kyle's feet, curled up in a fetal position. For good measure, Kyle kicked the beaten wrestler in the stomach before climbing out of the ring.

Debbie shook her head. "I don't get it. He won. Why is everyone booing?"

"Kyle's the heel. He's the bad guy. The crowd is supposed to hate him. If they cheered he'd actually be upset, since that would mean he wasn't presenting his character correctly."

Narrowing her eyes at Randy, Debbie said, "It worries me that you know all this. This is a side of you I've never seen before. You didn't grow up putting your friends in headlocks and half nelsons, did you?"

Randy helped himself to a small handful of her popcorn. "Kyle's been explaining it all to me. It's really quite fascinating. It's a world unto its own, kind of like a circus in a way. And yes, I grew up putting my friends in headlocks and half nelsons. It was the only way I knew to get some body contact with them."

The announcer climbed into the ring as Kyle and, more slowly, El Toro made their way out of the gym. With the usual announcer gusto, he introduced the next bout. Two more wrestlers entered the ring, climbing in at their appropriate corners.

"I see what you mean," Debbie said, staring forward. "About it being like the circus. Oh. My. God. They're midgets."

Randy's cheeks reddened. "Yeah, I guess they are. Although isn't the current politically correct term vertically challenged individuals?"

"They're midget wrestlers."

"I'm sure they—"

"Your new boyfriend works with midgets. Midgets who wrestle. Do you see what I'm saying here?"

"Debbie," Randy said, giving her his best puppy dog look, "I really want you to like Kyle. I want you guys to get along. It's important to me."

Debbie's glare melted somewhat. "I'll try," she promised, "but it's not going to be easy. I mean, look at the people watching this shit. That kid"—she indicated the dirt-streaked teen in front of Randy—"hasn't had a bath this century, and the last book he cracked open had things pop back up at him."

The kid in question turned. "Hey, fuck you, lady. I had a bath last week."

The look Debbie returned was stony. "I stand corrected."

Randy grabbed her elbow. "Come on. We don't have to stick around for the rest of the show. We can go find Kyle and go out and get something to eat." Randy wasn't actually eager to get his best friend and his new boyfriend face to face, but he knew Debbie's penchant for picking fights, and he wanted to get her away from the teenager as quickly as possible.

Debbie stood, brushing popcorn remains off her blouse. "I guess we can get something to eat. This Kyle does eat something other than squirrel, doesn't he?"

As they passed the teen on their way down the bleachers, he looked at Randy challengingly. "Hey, mister. Were you serious? Is Kyle Temple a fag? Did he really fuck you last night?"

Randy stopped in his tracks. He hadn't actually paid much attention to what he'd been saying, having spent most of his life blurting out whatever was on his mind regardless of who was present. Remembering Kyle's closeted status, he looked around to make sure no one but the kid could hear his reply. "Yeah. Yeah he is, and yeah, he did."

The teen looked thoughtful. "Next time he plows your ass," he said, "can you ask him for an autograph for me?"

As THE show was at a high school, the wrestlers were using the boys' locker room to change. Just being in the vicinity of a high school locker room brought back fourteen-year-old memories to Randy. Having been tall and thin even while attending Thomas Jefferson High School, Randy had been one of the favorite victims of the more athletic set, led by a towering bulk who'd been nicknamed Mongo after the Mel Brooks character.

Mongo and his cohorts terrorized several people, some much worse than Randy. Randy mainly remembered gym class as the time one was chosen last for basketball and for games of dodgeball that left nasty red welts on his arms and legs.

Standing in the tiled hall waiting for Kyle to emerge, Randy found himself feeling anxious and not a little uncomfortable. The ghost of Mongo seemed to be hanging around, taunting Randy. Debbie, however, seemed bored. She started to light up a cigarette.

Randy smiled weakly. "I'm pretty sure you can't smoke in here."

Debbie took a long drag and exhaled the smoke slowly. "I'm pretty sure I won't get detention or anything, either. Hell, I smoked in high school ten years ago when I was a student. I'm certainly not going to hold back now."

The locker room door opened and El Toro came out, dressed in a T-shirt and jeans. He carried a large gym bag. As he passed Randy and Debbie, he gave them a searching look.

"We're waiting for Kyle Temple," Randy explained. "We're friends of his."

The wrestler smiled. "Oh, he's still in the shower, I think. He shouldn't be too much longer, I guess." He moved down the hall, giving them a cheery wave as he approached the exit.

Debbie eyed him as he disappeared from view. "El Toro's got a nice butt. Very muscular. You could bounce a quarter off that ass. Maybe he's single and we can both date wrestlers."

"It would make for some interesting double dates. Can you blow your smoke the other way? I feel like I'm at a gay bar at closing time with the smoke in my eyes like that."

Debbie was still gazing after the now-vanished El Toro. "He's probably gay, though." She leaned back against the wall and sighed. "I mean, why would a straight guy be interested in professional wrestling? Putting on little shorts and boots and jumping all over some other half-naked guy. You can't get much gayer than that."

"I can't figure it out, either," Randy replied, "but apparently most of them are straight. Extremely straight, even. Construction worker straight. Stanley Kowalski straight. I think they turn a blind eye to the homoerotic aspect of pro wrestling and just don't think about it."

"They hit each other in the crotch. How can they not think about it?"

Randy shrugged. "Honey, if I could figure out straight men, I'd be one happy faggot."

The locker room door swung open again, revealing a huge black man with a heavily scarred forehead. Randy recognized him from the evening's opening match. The man had been announced as The Black Death, which had made Debbie snort with laughter.

"No autographs," he growled as he strode past Randy and Debbie.

When he was out of earshot, Randy asked, "I don't recall asking for one, do you?"

Debbie blew out more smoke. "I don't know. I would have like to have gotten one just to see what he'd write. I mean, what can he put? 'Have a great life. Love, The Black Death'?" She tossed her cigarette down and stomped on it.

Kyle finally emerged. His long hair was still wet from his shower, but that only made him look sexier in Randy's eyes. The ass-hugging jeans and the tight black T-shirt certainly didn't hurt. Kyle's short beard and mustache couldn't hide his youthful baby face, and the full, red lips were tantalizing. Randy slapped his new boyfriend on the arm. "I thought you did great tonight. You're not hurt, are you?"

Kyle shook his head and grinned. "Naw. Pete's boot smacked me right in the nose at one point, but luckily it didn't break this time. Got a nasty bruise from that chair, though."

"Pete?" Randy asked.

"Yeah, the guy I was wrestling. You didn't think El Toro was the name on his birth certificate, did you?"

Debbie discreetly cleared her throat and Randy, taking the hint, quickly made the introductions.

"I've heard a lot about you," Kyle said warmly, shifting his gym bag out of the way so he could shake her hand. "It's nice to finally meet you."

If Randy had thought Kyle's boyish charm would win Debbie over, he had been mistaken. While Debbie smiled as she greeted his new boyfriend, Randy could tell she was still reserving her judgment.

"I've heard a lot about you as well," she replied. "I have to say I was expecting someone bigger, though. What with the wrestling and all. I figured you'd be more the Hulk Hogan size."

Kyle nodded enthusiastically. "It's a common mistake. We're not all big guys anymore, especially in the independent circuits. Even then, we fudge a little. I'm really around 185, but they announce my weight at 210. It sounds more impressive."

"I can understand that," Debbie said. "I'm 140, and I usually announce myself at 125."

DEBBIE wanted to go dancing, but Kyle refused to go to a gay club for fear that he might be recognized. This did nothing to raise the wrestler in Debbie's eyes, and as soon as Kyle was out of earshot, she hissed at Randy, "As if anyone would recognize him anyway! Christ, he's acting like he's a celebrity instead of a grotty little small-time wrestler."

Desperately, Randy suggested they head to the Witch's Brew, a downtown Indianapolis coffee house. The Brew wasn't strictly a gay hangout, but its close proximity to several of the dance clubs made it a natural hangout for Indy's homos. Randy hoped the presence of dozens of coffee-slurping twinks and club kids would soften Debbie's mood.

"You don't understand," Kyle said as they found a booth near a window. "I can't possibly come out. You saw the people who go to wrestling shows. I mean, some of them are okay, but there's always a sort of redneck feel in the air."

Debbie grudgingly nodded. "True. I would say that they had an IQ of about 70, and that was all of them put together."

Kyle took the lid off of his hot chai and blew into the cup before taking a tentative sip. "I'm out to my mom, and a couple of my friends know, but that's really as far as I can go. If anyone else knew, my wrestling career would be over."

"There are other things to do than wrestle, though," Debbie said. "You don't have to work in such a homophobic environment."

Kyle took another sip and then smoothed out his beard and mustache. "Not for me. It's all I've ever wanted to do. I mean, I always wanted to grow up to be a wrestler. That or an astronaut."

Randy grinned weakly and tried to change the subject before Debbie could reply to that statement. "My chai tastes kind of weird. Does anyone else's chai taste kind of weird?"

"Surely you can't make all that much money at these small promotions, though," Debbie went on, "and I'm sure it's hard on your body, getting kicked and hit with chairs. You won't be able to do this forever. You'll have to find something to fall back on, like accounting... or ditch-digging."

"Debbie," Randy warned through gritted teeth.

Kyle didn't seem fazed. "I don't plan on doing small promotions all my life. I'm only twenty-one. Eventually I want to wrestle for the UWE. That's the Universal Wrestling Extravaganza," he added by way of explanation.

"Yeah, them I've heard of, seeing as how they're on TV something like three times a week." Debbie blinked and looked at Randy. "He's over ten years younger than you."

"Say it a little louder. I don't think some of the people at the next table caught that," Randy said, frowning. "My chai really does taste funny. Does anyone else's chai taste funny?"

"That's my dream," Kyle said, again blowing into his cup to cool off the liquid. "I want to wrestle in the UWE. My dream match would be against Crusher Phillips. I could die a happy man if I could get a match with Crusher."

"That's a dream?" Debbie asked, incredulous. "To get a chair crashed over your skull by a guy named Crusher?"

Kyle smiled broadly. "It'd be a privilege to get hit with a chair by Crusher."

Debbie nodded slowly and then eyed Randy. Very slowly she mouthed the words "Dump him!"

Kyle took another sip. Frowning, he said, "Maybe we should go somewhere else after all. This chai tastes a little off tonight. Anyone else notice that?"

CHAPTER
TWO

THEY were in Randy's king-size bed, enjoying a moment of post-coital bliss. Well, Randy was enjoying it. Kyle, after climbing off Randy and collapsing against the pillows, seemed nervous and jumpy. Randy snuggled close, laying his head on the wrestler's still-heaving chest. "You okay?" he asked.

Kyle began anxiously twisting strands of Randy's thick black hair. "I need a smoke. It's so hard to shoot a wad and then not light one up."

"Oh, thanks. That's always what I've wanted to hear after a heavy banging session. Not 'That was fantastic. You rocked my world,' but 'Wow, I've shot my wad. Now I need a smoke.' Very romantic."

"No," Kyle protested, "you don't get it. It was so great that it makes me want to smoke. Nonsmokers just don't understand."

"You haven't had a cigarette for a week. You don't want to slide. Just think of something else."

Kyle's fingers began twisting Randy's hair faster. "Okay, I'll give that a try. Are these sheets silk? They feel like silk."

"No, they aren't silk."

"They don't feel like my sheets is all," Kyle said, the nervousness still in his voice.

"Well, for one, these sheets are clean."

"Yeah, there's that. What, are you saying you don't like fucking in my bed?"

Randy kissed Kyle's chest. "No, I'm not saying that at all. I had a great time the other night. One of the all-time great fucks, in my opinion.

It's just that my face was buried in your pillow and there was a stain right by my cheek that seemed to be moving."

"You didn't complain."

"I couldn't, really," Randy said. "We were going at it so hard I was nearly swallowing the bedsprings."

Kyle reached around to rub at the nicotine patch on his left bicep. "This thing doesn't seem to be working. Maybe I need to keep rubbing it, or maybe this one's defective."

"Call that Dr. Bennett tomorrow. He suggested hypnotism, didn't you say?"

Hugging Randy close to him, Kyle said, "I don't want to be hypnotized. What if he makes me cluck like a chicken or do an Elvis imitation?"

"As long as it's a nonsmoking chicken, I guess it would be okay." Randy gently bit Kyle's right pectoral muscle. "Have I told you how much I love your chest? It's so fucking muscular. You have no idea what it's like to go through life with no chest. Actually, I have worse than no chest. Mine's concave. It goes in instead of out."

"Your chest is fine. So you think I should do it? The hypnotism thing?"

"You want to quit smoking. You're having trouble. How can it hurt?"

Kyle stopped twisting and kissed the top of Randy's head. "I love you," he said.

Randy tried unsuccessfully to keep his eyes from bulging. "You've never said that before."

"Well, I sort of thought it went without saying, but I figured I'd better say it, just in case. Sometimes you think the other person knows how you feel and then you find out you had totally the wrong idea. Makes you feel stupid, if you know what I mean."

"I'm glad you said it," Randy replied, "because I love you too, but I just didn't want to be the first one to say it. I kind of have a curse as far as that goes. Generally when I tell someone I love them, they head straight for the door and I never see them again."

Kyle grinned. "Well, I don't intend on heading for the door. In fact...." He shifted, moving slowly down the bed, kissing parts of Randy's body as he went. "I guess if I can't smoke, I can at least get something in my mouth. Do you mind?"

Randy returned the grin. "I'm sure I can live with it."

WHILE Kyle had mentioned Dr. Bennett to Randy on several occasions, the one thing he'd failed to clarify was that Dr. Bennett wasn't really his psychiatrist, as Randy had assumed. Carl Bennett wasn't really even a doctor—not in any legal sense of the word, at least. Years previously Bennett had worked for Ronder's Circus, billed as a world-renowned expert in mesmerism. The "world" part of his renown was, technically speaking, true, as Bennett had a distant cousin in Italy to whom he'd sent one of his handbills.

When Ronder's Circus folded in 1998, Bennett had retired to Indianapolis. He used the front room of his small house near Speedway as a workroom of sorts, not wanting to completely give up work. A sign on his front lawn proclaimed CARL BENNETT—HYPNOTIST. FORTUNES AND TAROT READINGS UPON REQUEST.

Kyle had originally gone to see Dr. Bennett on a whim. The wrestler had always been keenly interested in all matters occult, and the sign on Bennett's lawn fascinated him, especially the cartoon hand with zodiac symbols emblazoned all around it. A $20 tarot reading revealed that indeed Kyle would achieve his greatest dream, which of course he took to mean that before long he'd be climbing into the ring with Bill "Crusher" Phillips. Ever since that reading, Kyle had seen Bennett at least once a month for advice and tarot readings.

The hypnotism part of Bennett's business was something Kyle had always shied away from. He mainly worried about not being in control. Still, if it would help him stop smoking, and if Randy thought it was a good idea, Kyle was all for giving it a try. Smoking was bad for his wrestling career, and, worse, *Randy* didn't smoke. Kyle really wanted things to work out with Randy. His past romantic entanglements paled in comparison to what he felt for the thin, dark-haired owner of Outgoing Books, one of the few gay and lesbian bookstores in Indianapolis. So Kyle put aside his qualms and went to see Dr. Bennett.

He stood on the small porch of Bennett's house and rapped on the door. Immediately Pepper, Dr. Bennett's cocker spaniel, began to yelp. After a pause the porch light came on and Carl Bennett opened the door.

Bennett was tall and thin, and Kyle wasn't sure if the elderly man tried to look like Boris Karloff or if it was merely a coincidence. Bennett even had an affected British accent cultivated during his circus days that added to the effect. The old man beamed with obvious pleasure when he saw Kyle. "Mr. Temple! So good to see you again. Please come in. Pepper, get back. Let the nice young man inside."

Kyle entered and was immediately overwhelmed by the smell of incense that seemed to permeate the house. Bennett seemed addicted to the stuff. Kyle had never visited the man without finding at least three sticks of the junk burning at any given time. Kyle suspected that by now every book, every stitch of furniture, and even Pepper the dog was saturated with the thick smell. The front room was littered with incense holders, and tonight most of them held lit, sweet-smelling sticks.

Once Kyle was inside, Pepper ceased to bark, instead taking to jumping up and down to get Kyle's attention. Kyle leaned down to scratch the dog's head. "How are you doing, little guy?" Pepper was an added attraction, and one of the reasons Kyle looked forward to seeing Dr. Bennett.

In reply, Pepper licked Kyle's hand.

"He's been a bad dog today, actually," Bennett said, closing the door behind Kyle. "We got into the trash earlier, didn't we, Pepper?"

Probably trying to find something that didn't smell like incense, Kyle thought.

Bennett ushered Kyle over to what he referred to as his worktable, which consisted of a small round table covered with a dark-blue cloth. Two wooden chairs were on either side, while the top held Bennett's crystal ball and tarot cards. Generally Kyle stuck to the tarot readings. The only time he had asked Bennett to check the crystal ball for him, Kyle hadn't liked what the man had seen. Kyle wasn't interested in romance with big, muscular guys, so the one Bennett had seen in Kyle's future would just have to face disappointment. Kyle liked them tall and skinny. Like Randy.

"I suppose you're here for another tarot reading," Bennett said, sitting down in his usual place at the table.

"Actually," Kyle replied, feeling slightly embarrassed, "I was wondering if you could hypnotize me?"

Bennett's eyebrows went up, reminding Kyle of the cartoon Grinch that Karloff had done the voice for. "You've never asked me to hypnotize you before."

"You can do it, though, right?"

"Of course, it was always my specialty." Bennett's smile was obviously meant to put people at their ease, but it only made Kyle think of the scene in *Bride of Frankenstein* where the monster enjoys a smoke with the blind hermit. "Anyone can be hypnotized, providing they want to be and aren't senile or a complete imbecile. You're not a complete imbecile, are you?"

"I wouldn't ask my mom's opinion on that one," Kyle said, "or Mr. Sneed, the owner of our wrestling promotion, but no, I'm not a complete one. I don't think so, anyway."

Bennett stood back up. "Then we have no troubles. Let's get you comfortable on the couch over here."

Kyle lay down as instructed, fidgeting nervously. "I really need to quit smoking, you see. You can do that, can't you? I just don't want to end up killing people with a big old knife or anything." Seeing Bennett's puzzled expression, Kyle elaborated. "I saw this movie once where a hypnotist used a guy to commit all these murders. The guy went around with this big-ass knife and sliced people up. The movie was pretty lame, but I really don't want to become a murderer. Especially since toward the end of the flick the dude got acid tossed in his face, and that's not really a look I'm going for, if you get my drift."

Bennett chuckled. "That's Hollywood hypnotism. Believe me, when you're in the trance, you won't do anything you don't want to do. It simply isn't possible. You won't even actually be asleep. What will happen is that you'll enter into a state of hyperconsciousness."

Kyle blinked. "You mean I'll get all nervous and stuff? I'm already there, actually."

"No, no. I just mean…. Well, for you, let's just say you won't actually be asleep and leave it at that. Now, are you comfortable?"

Kyle folded his hands over his chest and took a deep breath. "Yeah, pretty much."

"What was it we're going for with this session again? Smoking, wasn't it?"

"Yeah, stopping smoking."

Bennett nodded. "Right, right. No problem. Very easy, in fact. Memory enhancement or past life regression is a bit tricky, but quitting smoking is a doddle."

"Past life what?"

Bennett sighed. "Never mind. Something I've never been able to accomplish. Now I want you to close your eyes and clear your mind."

Kyle unclasped his hands, letting his left hand dangle over the couch. Pepper scuttled over to give his fingers a lick.

"Now let's begin," Bennett said.

USUALLY Bennett could get someone in a trance state within minutes, but with Kyle it took nearly half an hour. Finally he was satisfied the young man was completely under.

"You have no desire to smoke," Bennett intoned. "Smoking has no hold over you. The thought of a cigarette makes you ill."

Bennett leaned forward, examining Kyle's face. In the trance state, the boy looked almost angelic. *The boy's an idiot*, Bennett thought. *A good-looking, amiable idiot.* Bennett knew from previous visits that Kyle was a professional wrestler, and figured the short beard and mustache were there to make him appear older and meaner than he was. It didn't work. Bennett looked closely at Kyle's skin. Not a wrinkle or blemish. Like a baby. *Just wait, kid*, he thought. *Just wait.*

"The taste of cigarettes no longer satisfies you," Bennett went on. "You no longer desire them."

Kyle's hand was still hanging off the side of the couch. Pepper returned to lick at the exposed palm. The wet tongue was making Kyle smile. Bennett didn't want the dog to disrupt the session, so he spoke firmly to the animal. "Get back. Back!"

Pepper retreated perhaps half an inch, then looked at Bennett expectantly.

"Way back!"

The dog moved another inch.

"Further back than that!"

Unseen by Bennett, Kyle's eyelids fluttered.

"Much further back!"

Pepper hesitated and then slowly slunk away.

Bennett returned his attention to Kyle. "Now, then, where were we?"

The question had been rhetorical, but to Bennett's surprise, Kyle answered. The words meant nothing to Bennett, though. Kyle seemed to rattle off a sentence in some language Bennett didn't recognize.

The hypnotist's eyes widened. Could it be? "Kyle, where are you right now?"

Again, the young man answered. He seemed to speak several sentences this time, still in the unknown tongue.

Bennett's mouth seemed unable to close. *Could I have achieved some sort of past life regression?* he asked himself. He'd actually always thought the concept rubbish, since he'd never been able to successfully bring someone to such a state before. A man who specialized in getting people to cluck like chickens didn't really have time to worry about past lives.

"Kyle, do you mind if I get a tape recorder and record the rest of this session?"

Kyle responded with a word that Bennett took to mean yes.

CHAPTER
THREE

RANDY'S cell phone rang just as he was pulling out of the parking lot of the bookstore. He answered, pausing only long enough to flip off the driver of a Volvo that had cut him off. "Hello?"

"Hey, Randy." It was Kyle.

Just hearing Kyle's voice caused Randy's heart to race a little faster. Offhand, he couldn't think of any previous boyfriend who could hold a candle to Kyle. Why couldn't Debbie see how wonderful he was instead of concentrating on the age difference or Kyle's intelligence level? "Hey, babe. What's going on?" Randy just hoped Kyle wasn't calling to cancel their date for the evening.

"Nothing much. My workout is taking longer than I expected, though. Can you pick me up at the gym?"

The "gym" was really just an old warehouse that housed the wrestling ring and some well-used workout equipment. Randy had only been there once before and had thought it smelled vaguely of dirty sweat socks and, strangely, onions. "Not a problem," he replied. "It's closer than your apartment anyway. That means I get to see you sooner."

"Aw, that's so sweet!" Kyle purred. Randy figured Kyle must not be near any of the other wrestlers. Kyle's language tended to stay on the extremely butch side when he was surrounded by his coworkers. "See you in a few, then."

Randy felt so good just from hearing Kyle's voice that he didn't even bother to flip off the woman who nearly sideswiped him at the next intersection. The euphoric feeling continued all the way to Sneed's Gym. The name Sneed conjured visions of a Simon Legree character to Randy, or at the very least a golfer from the 1940s. Instead Monty Sneed was a short, balding man who swore with every other word and smoked foul cigars. It had apparently always been Monty Sneed's dream to have a wrestling promotion of his own, and when his dad's death left him a nice little nest egg, he made the dream come true with MDW—Midwest Demolition Wrestling.

There was no sign letting the unsuspecting know that they'd found Sneed's Gym. One either knew where it was or one didn't. Randy found a place to park and rushed quickly to the door. Inside, he found the place virtually empty. The ring, set up in the center of the warehouse, contained the building's sole occupants, El Toro and Kyle.

Kyle seemed intent on wrenching Pete's head from his body. It wasn't until he'd picked Pete up and slammed him onto the canvas that Kyle even noticed Randy had entered. "Hey," he called out, pausing only to stomp his boot squarely into El Toro's midsection. "When did you get here?"

"Just now. Still practicing, I see."

"Yeah." Kyle seemed somewhat out of breath and was covered in sweat. Randy thought he looked hot as hell, but then, he thought Kyle looked hot as hell when not drenched in sweat as well. Kyle ground his heel into Pete's forehead. Pete cried out convincingly. "Hey, want to see this great finisher we've come up with?"

Randy grinned. "Sure."

Kyle helped El Toro to his feet. "Watch this," he said. "I think this will really get the fans going."

Randy watched with more than a little trepidation as Pete, with a fun-loving grin on his face, whipped Kyle across the ring into the ropes. Kyle seemed to bounce back towards El Toro, who in the meantime had quickly climbed onto the top turnbuckle. Randy blinked at the speed of the Hispanic wrestler. Once in position, Pete came flying off and wrapped his legs seemingly impossibly around Kyle's neck. The two crashed to the canvas. Somehow El Toro's legs stayed around Kyle's neck as they landed with a thundering crash. The handsome Hispanic used the momentum of the fall to flip back up to a standing position. Kyle's legs flew up, and Pete deftly caught them. The end result had Kyle hanging suspended, his legs held in El Toro's arms and his head still trapped between the boy's white boots.

Kyle grinned crookedly. His voice was slightly muffled as he asked, "How was that? Was that cool or what? What did you think, Randy?"

Randy's closed his mouth forcibly, his teeth clicking together. "Okay, be honest with me. On a scale of one to ten, how much did that hurt?"

"Oh, about a one. Honestly, it's like playing on a trampoline. That move really doesn't hurt at all. Well, I guess it might if we mistimed something and Pete kicked me in the teeth or something, but if we do it right, it's totally painless."

Pete let go of Kyle's legs. The resounding thud from Kyle hitting the canvas made Randy wince, but when Kyle stood, he bore an enormous smile on his face.

Randy shook his head. "You're crazy. That's all there is to it."

Pete and Kyle gave each other a high-five, the Latino adding a little dance for good measure. "I think we've got a winner," he said.

"Hey, you guys haven't really met, have you?" Kyle slapped an arm around El Toro and led him to the ring apron.

"Not officially, anyway," Pete said, "Although we've bumped into each other. I'm Pete. I hope you don't mind me whooping your boyfriend's ass every now and then." He reached down through the ropes to pump Randy's hand enthusiastically.

Randy's eyebrows shot up, and he looked at Kyle. "I thought you said no one here knew about you."

Kyle punched Pete's arm. "Pete knows. Hell, because of the feud between us, I wrestle him more than anyone else. Pete knows pretty much everything about me. I trust him, which is something I wouldn't say about most of the guys who wrestle with us. It's a pretty redneck crowd."

"I know too much about you," Pete agreed. He threw an arm around Kyle's waist and pulled him closer, a gesture that gave Randy a split-second pang of jealousy. It must have showed in his body language, because Pete went on quickly, "I'm straight, though, so it's not like you have anything to worry about. Even if I wasn't, though, I wouldn't waste my hot bod on this piece of trash."

"That's good to know." Randy used the ropes to pull himself up onto the apron. "I've always wondered how padded these rings were. There's quite a lot of give, isn't there?"

Pete stomped the canvas in demonstration. "There's some give, yeah, but the bumps still take a lot out of you. Don't think they don't. It's hard work sometimes. Want to give it a try?"

Randy laughed uneasily. "Oh, no. It makes me nervous just watching you and Kyle. There's no way I could do any of that stuff."

"Come on," Kyle said, making an opening in the ropes for Randy to climb through. "I promise we won't hurt you."

"I promise you won't, either, because I'm not getting in there."

Pete didn't seem to want to take no for an answer. He reached for Randy's hands and practically dragged him into the ring. "This will be good. You'll see. This way you'll know it doesn't hurt nearly as much as it looks like it does and you won't worry about Kyle as much."

Kyle seemed overjoyed at his boyfriend actually standing in the ring with them, which gave Randy an odd sense of pride. Seeing Kyle's silly grin, Randy could easily envision what Kyle must have been like on Christmas mornings as a kid.

"Pete's right," Kyle said. "Really, it's all about selling the move. Both guys have to work together or it looks like crap. Watch me and Pete. I'll dropkick him, but watch how lame it looks if he doesn't react."

Randy watched as Kyle and Pete demonstrated move after move. Finally he felt confident enough to try something himself. "Just one move, though," he warned. "And make sure it's something simple. I don't think I'm up for flipping off ropes and wrapping my legs around someone's neck."

Kyle's grin was threatening to take over his entire face. "I'll body slam you. That's pretty easy. All you really have to do is fall." He led Randy to the center of the ring. "When I go to pull you up, you'll want to kind of jump up with the momentum. As you go up, you're going to put your hand down here on my thigh. That'll help steady you. I'll sort of position you, tucking your head as you're falling. After that, it's just you taking the bump."

"That seems like a lot to remember for someone who only has to take a fall." Randy would have spoken further, but the next second Kyle had hoisted him up in the air. The next thing he knew, he was staring up at the ceiling, the air having been forced out of his lungs by the impact with the canvas. Kyle smiled down at him.

"That wasn't so bad, was it?"

One by one Randy moved all of his extremities. Everything seemed to be in working order. "Wasn't horrible," he admitted. "Knocks the wind out of you a bit."

Pete helped Randy to his feet. "It makes a hell of a lot of noise. The noise helps sell the move. Big movements are always better. Easier for the audience to catch, for one thing."

As the three of them climbed out of the ring, Randy said, "Well, I think I'll leave the professional grappling to you guys and I'll stick to retail. There are still bumps, but they don't take as much out of you physically."

"You could always be his manager or valet, something like that," Pete suggested. "That way you'd be involved with his shows but you wouldn't have to actually wrestle."

Randy frowned. "I don't know the first thing about being a wrestler's manager."

"You don't actually do any managing," Kyle told him. "You come out to the ring with me, interrupt the match, distract the ref and things like that. It's all part of the show."

"I don't know...."

"Think about it." Kyle leaned in and planted a big, sloppy kiss on Randy's cheek. "It'll be fun."

"I'll think about it," Randy promised.

CARL BENNETT pushed Rewind yet again and then hit Play. He listened for about the hundredth time to Kyle's responses. It certainly sounded like the young man was speaking in a foreign language. The inflections were all right and the tone seemed matter-of-fact. It certainly wasn't a language that Bennett recognized, though. Not that he actually spoke any language other than English. It definitely wasn't Spanish, German, French, or Italian. It didn't have an oriental flavor like Japanese, not exactly, anyway. Bennett thought it sounded vaguely Mediterranean. He wasn't familiar with any Mediterranean languages, but the words seemed to have that feel to them. They sounded like some Turkish guy threatening 007 in a James Bond film.

At Bennett's feet, Pepper was desperately trying to get his master's attention. The dog's dinnertime had been nearly an hour previous. Pepper tried a plaintive cry.

Bennett ignored the dog and ran the tape back once again.

CHAPTER
FOUR

"HE'S a Neanderthal," Debbie said.

"No, he's not," Randy insisted. "He's very sweet."

They were in line at a Starbucks behind a woman who seemed to be having trouble making up her mind. Debbie folded her arms across her chest in frustration, but whether over the woman or Randy's choice of boyfriend, Randy couldn't tell. "The very stupid have to be sweet," Debbie went on. "It's their only saving grace. Otherwise we'd have them rounded up and slaughtered like cattle."

"He's very smart in some respects."

Debbie was glaring threateningly at the woman in front of her. She tapped her foot loudly. When she got no response from the woman, she turned back to Randy. "What respects would those be? Hunting squirrels?"

Randy thought quickly. He didn't want the silence to go on too long, as there was no telling when Debbie would begin to bark at the indecisive woman. "He knows a lot about wrestling."

Debbie rolled her eyes. "Guys hit him over the head with chairs and not only is he okay with that, he's proud of it. Face it, he hasn't got a brain. I tried to talk politics with him. I asked him if he was to the right or to the left. He told me he was ambidextrous."

Randy smiled to himself. "Yeah, he is that."

"I just don't see the two of you as a long-term thing. After the newness wears off, what will the two of you have to talk about?"

Sighing, Randy asked, "Haven't you heard that sometimes opposites attract?"

The woman seemed to have finally made up her mind. "I'll have a caramel macchiato." The grateful barista at the register started to ring in her purchase, but she stopped him. "Wait. Maybe I'll have a caramel Frappuccino instead."

Debbie exploded. "For Christ's sake, lady, it's just coffee! Get something! Get it hot, iced, frapped, frothed, or whatever, but just get it! Jesus, in the time you've been standing here they've opened three new Starbucks, and that's just on this street alone."

The woman turned, eyes bulging, looking like she'd just been hit with a mallet. The kid behind the register stifled a laugh.

"I'm giving up coffee and tea. Drinks in general, actually. These places just aren't working out for me," Randy said to no one in particular.

BOTH Pepper and Bennett seemed equally excited when Kyle knocked on the door. Bennett practically pulled the wrestler into the front room. "Come in, come in, my dear boy. Please have a seat. How is the smoking situation?"

Kyle sank onto the sofa, not sure of what to make of the new, overly attentive Bennett. Pepper jumped up onto his lap, and he gave the dog a scratch behind the ears. "Pretty good, really. I've been able to keep from smoking almost entirely. It's just the first thing in the morning that's killing me. I can't seem to wake up without wanting a cigarette. It tastes awful, but I smoke it anyway. Nearly tossed my cookies this morning."

Bennett nodded so quickly that Kyle thought of a Boris Karloff bobblehead doll. "Yes, yes, yes. Excellent! We're certainly making progress. We'll need to get you back into a trance state, and I believe we can alleviate that morning craving. Why don't you go ahead and get comfortable?"

Within minutes Bennett had Kyle hypnotized. He intoned various warnings about smoking, telling Kyle how he didn't want to smoke at all anymore. He quickly tired of the smoking routine, however, and went on to what he considered the more important part of the session. He wasn't sure he could achieve the same state he'd had Kyle in previously, so he tried hard to remember exactly what he'd said the last time.

"Now I want you to go back," Bennett said. "Way back. Where are you now?"

"Peeing." Kyle's voice was small, like that of a little kid.

"Did you say peeing?"

"Yeah, peeing."

Bennett sneaked a glance down to Kyle's crotch, worried about stains on his couch. He was relieved to find everything dry down there. At least he'd managed to bring out a past memory from the boy. That was a start. "I'll need you to go further back. Back to the same place you went the last time we had a session. Do you remember that? Relax and let yourself go back. Way back."

Kyle's eyelids fluttered.

"Where are you now?"

Kyle answered in the same language, or so it seemed to Bennett, that he'd spoken the last time. Bennett recognized some of the same sounds and inflections. Smiling, he switched on his tape recorder.

"Do you understand me? Can you reply in English?"

Kyle was silent for a moment. His right hand twitched spasmodically. Bennett started to repeat the question, but Kyle interrupted by shouting loudly, still in the unknown tongue. The wrestler's body tensed up, and his face showed agonizing pain.

Pepper, watching from the floor, began to bark. Bennett leaned forward, alarmed. Kyle's distress was such that tears were suddenly streaming down the young man's cheeks. Bennett had never seen a person in their death throes, but he imagined it wouldn't be far from what he was witnessing. He placed a calming hand on Kyle's chest.

"You're safe," he said, urgency in his voice. Pepper yelped. "You are perfectly safe. I want you to leave that place. Come forward. Come back. You don't have to stay in that place any longer."

The pain seemed to drain slowly from Kyle's body. Pepper stopped barking and edged closer. Kyle's breathing came easier, and Bennett, feeling the young man's wrist, was pleased to find his pulse slowing down to a more normal rate.

Bennett snapped his fingers in front of Kyle's face. "Wake up. I want you to awaken, Kyle."

Kyle took a deep breath and then opened his eyes. He looked up at Bennett questioningly. He reached up and wiped some of the tears off his cheek, surprised to find them there. "That was weird."

"In what way?"

Kyle rose up onto his elbows. "The last time I felt great after you put me under. This time I feel like I've been running a marathon." He rubbed his hands together. "And the palms of my hands feel sore. That's really freaky."

Bennett frowned. "What do you remember of the session?"

Kyle shrugged. "Just you telling me not to smoke, really. Why? What else should I remember?"

Stroking his chin, Bennett asked, "You don't recall answering me in a foreign language?"

Kyle chuckled. "No, how could I? I don't know any foreign languages. Well, I did take a semester of French in high school. I got an F."

"You got very agitated. You don't remember that?"

Kyle sat up the rest of the way. Pepper jumped up onto the couch next to him. "No, should I?"

Bennett shook his head. "You really should remember everything that happens in our sessions unless you're instructed not to." Under his breath he added, "At least I think that's how it works."

BENNETT sat in his car, thinking. The engine was off, so the only sound was the rain splattering loudly onto the top of his dilapidated Dodge Dart. For the tenth time, he tapped his jacket pocket to feel that his mini-recorder was still there.

The rain increased in intensity. He watched the droplets rolling down the driver's side window. He noticed his reflection in the glass, and even he could see the ghost of Karloff looking back at him. A sudden flash of lightning added to the effect.

Why, he thought, *is it so difficult to remember to bring an umbrella?*

Sighing, he opened the door and turned the collar of his well-worn coat up. He got out of the car and bolted across the parking lot as quickly as his tired old legs would go.

Crannick Hall looked like the rest of the buildings on the campus—dark, brooding, and covered in ivy. The Hall wouldn't look out of place on *Dark Shadows*. The rain only added to the gothic atmosphere.

In the darkness, Bennett didn't see an upcoming pothole, and the result left him with a soaked left pant leg. He cursed and finally got to the ominous-looking main door. He threw it open, feeling soaked to the skin.

Waiting for him in the foyer was his old friend Mike Rashka. Rashka's large frame was shaking with mirth, and the man removed his glasses to wipe a tear out of his eye. "You look even more like something out of a horror movie nowadays," Rashka bleated. "Especially wet like that. An axe in your hand and the picture would be complete!"

Bennett swallowed the impulse to say just what he'd do if he did have an axe handy. Instead, he shook off as much of the water as he could and said, "I never seem to be able to predict the weather."

"They've got people on the news that do that for you," Rashka replied, pushing his glasses back onto his nose. "Or doesn't your crystal ball give you the insight into the weather? Never mind, let's go to my office and listen to his tape you're so excited about."

Rashka's office was small and overly cramped with books. They seemed to fill every available space. Bennett even had to clear a stack off a chair before he could sit down. Rashka sat across the desk from him, still obviously amused.

"I bet you're wondering why I contacted you after all these years," Bennett began.

Rashka raised an eyebrow. "It did seem odd, considering we've lived in the same city for a while now and I haven't heard a peep out of you."

"I've been terribly busy."

Rashka's lip twitched. "Reading tarot cards to gullible people, I gather."

Bennett felt his aggravation level rising. "I know you've never believed—"

Holding up a placating hand, Rashka said, "Sorry, sorry. Didn't mean to be insulting. Really, I'm glad you called. It's been much too long, and the fault is mine as well as yours. The phone works both ways, after all."

Bennett nervously fingered the recorder in his pocket, wishing they could dispense with the small talk. Rashka's mother had been the circus's bearded lady, and her son had practically been raised traveling with Ronder's. Bennett hadn't really been close with Rashka ever since the man had decided on an academic life. Most of the circus folk had washed their hands of Rashka, feeling that he had always boasted a superior attitude over them in any case.

"I have kept up with your career, honestly," Bennett said. "I was very pleased when you became a professor."

"And I've kept up with you as well," Rashka replied.

Bennett thought he detected a trace of a smirk, but he chose to ignore it. "I believe you're quite the expert on languages."

Rashka chuckled. "I'm a history professor, and I wouldn't even consider myself an expert on history. I do speak five languages and have more than a passing knowledge of several others."

"I'd like to play something for you, if I may. I'd be very interested if you can identify what's being said." Bennett pulled out the mini-recorder and set it on Rashka's desk. He pushed Play.

It was the tape from the first session with Kyle. The sound of the wrestler's voice filled the room. Bennett quickly adjusted the volume to a more reasonable level.

As Rashka listened, his faint smile vanished and a frown furrowed his brow. He sat forward in his chair. "Can you play that again?"

Bennett rewound a bit and hit Play again.

Rashka rubbed his chin and grunted. "I'm not positive, but I think that's Aramaic."

"Aramaic? I've never heard of it."

"I'm not surprised," Rashka said. "Very few people speak it nowadays. Rewind it again for me, could you?"

Bennett did so. Kyle's voice had barely started again when Rashka exclaimed, "That word there! Stop the tape!" He reached behind him and after a brief search pulled a large red volume off his bookshelf. He flipped several pages, then buried his nose in the book.

"Have you found something?" Bennett asked anxiously.

Rashka raised his head. "That word. He uses it several times."

"I'd noticed that. What's the word mean?"

"It's the Aramaic word for 'blessed'."

CHAPTER
FIVE

THE car moved slowly through the rain-drenched streets, Randy sitting rigidly upright in the driver's seat. The white knuckles clenching the steering wheel weren't entirely due to the driving conditions. He held back the impulse to sigh heavily and wished the butterflies in his stomach would stop dancing the tango.

"I hope your parents like me," Kyle said. He was slumped in the passenger seat, nervously tapping his fingers against his knee.

Randy knew that if one shook the Big Magic 8 Ball of Life and turned it over, the answer would be something like NOT LIKELY, but it wouldn't do to let Kyle know that. "I'm sure they will," he replied, hoping he sounded convincing.

"You don't sound sure."

"I'm sure." Randy turned a corner and flipped the windshield wipers to the fastest speed. "I wish you hadn't worn that T-shirt, though."

Kyle looked down at his shirt, which bore the MDW logo. "What's wrong with this? Too tight?"

"It's not that. It's just that my parents are kind of old-fashioned. For a dinner party, even something casual like this, they expect at least a button-down shirt. They're sort of like Ozzie and Harriet, only on crack. It's okay, though. They won't really care."

The drumming on Kyle's knee increased.

"Plus," Randy went on, "I haven't actually told them that you're a professional wrestler."

"Why not?" A note of near-panic crept into Kyle's voice. "What did you tell them I did for a living? I hope you kept it simple. I mean, if you told them I was an air traffic controller or something like that, I'm not sure I can pull that off. Those air traffic controller guys have to be really smart and know vectors and things like that."

"I just told them you were in entertainment. I didn't elaborate. They assumed you were in a band or something."

"Oh, cool," Kyle said, relaxing somewhat. "A band wouldn't be bad. I just hope it's a good one. I'd hate to be in one of those bands that suck."

"They'll like you, I'm sure. Don't worry about it."

"Next week we'll have to have dinner with my mom," Kyle said. "You'll love what she's done with the trailer. You know how most mobile homes look really junky inside? Well, she's got hers done up really nice. You wouldn't even know it's a trailer if it wasn't for the dinky little kitchen, the dinky little bathroom, and the fact that it's on wheels."

"What does your mom do?"

"She used to be a greeter at Walmart, but she got fired because she'd get cranky if people tried to go out the entrance doors or come in by the exits. Now she does the fries at a McDonald's."

Randy sighed, hoping the subject wouldn't come up with his parents, especially his mother. He could just see his mom, known in some circles as She Who Must Be Obeyed, looking down her nose if "fries" and "McDonald's" came up. "What about your dad? Is he still in the picture?"

Talking about his home life seemed to calm Kyle down enough that the drumming stopped entirely. "He never was, really. I certainly never knew him. My mom only knew him briefly, I believe. She raised me by herself. Whenever I asked about my father, she'd just say I never had one. I'm sure she didn't mean that literally, because that's impossible. I've always thought that maybe she was artificially done. What's that called?"

"Inseminated."

Kyle grinned. "That's the word. I'm pretty sure that's what happened, because I've noticed that she won't use the turkey baster, even at Thanksgiving."

Randy laughed and placed a hand on Kyle's leg. "It's just occurred to me that I don't care if my parents like you or not. I hope they do, but if they don't, that's their problem. I love you, and that's all that really matters."

"Ah, that's so sweet," Kyle purred, and then his face became serious. "Wait. You mean there's a chance they won't like me? Why won't they like me? Is it the T-shirt? Because if it's the T-shirt, I can just take it off and say it got torn off when we were attacked by a pack of wild dogs or something."

Shaking his head, Randy said, "I think shirtless would be worse that the T-shirt as is. Plus there's always the remote possibility that they might not buy the wild dog story. Don't worry. Everything is going to be fine."

He pulled into the drive and maneuvered into a parking spot. Kyle looked out the car's window, and his mouth fell open. "This is your parents' house? It's fucking huge! You could fit three or four of my mom's trailer in there and still have room left over for the garage!"

"It's not bad," Randy admitted, shutting off the engine. "Just remember to compliment my mom's decorating skills and her cooking if you want to get on her good side. She's a sucker for a compliment. And don't mention any sort of plastic surgery. My mom's had one too many face-lifts, and her face has started to take on a sort of ventriloquist dummy quality. You may feel the need to scream when you first see how tight her face looks, but please don't. It would be a bad thing."

Kyle rubbed his hands rapidly over his jeans to wipe off the sweat. "No problem. I'll compliment the shit out of her. Anything else I need to know?"

"There is one other thing. Mom will offer you a glass of wine before dinner. Be sure to accept. One glass before dinner and one during is permitted and even encouraged. Stop at two glasses, though. If you don't drink wine at all, Mom will think you're a philistine. And more than two glasses, though, and you're suddenly a candidate for an extended stay at Betty Ford in her eyes. It's a fine line, I know, but an important one."

Kyle bit his lip. "Maybe I shouldn't come in. You can tell them I'm sick. It won't be much of a lie."

"Oh, yeah, and whatever my dad says, just agree with it. If you can't bring yourself to agree with it, just change the subject. He's one of those guys that are always right, especially when they don't know what they're talking about. Dad's idea of an argument is whoever he's arguing with just nodding at him and saying, 'Yes, you're absolutely right.'"

They got out and walked up to the front door quickly, trying not to let the rain soak them too much. Randy looked nervous and Kyle looked petrified.

Randy's mother answered the door almost as soon as they knocked, as if she'd been hovering around the door waiting for them. She was a tall, thin, dark-haired woman with carefully applied makeup. Her red dress looked new and was adorned by two strands of pearls. Kyle sheepishly glanced down at his T-shirt and jeans.

Mrs. Stone's smile faltered for a fraction of a second as her eyes passed over Kyle. She lit up again as she pulled her son into a hug. "Randy! It's so nice to see you. You don't come to visit us often enough. And you look thinner and thinner every time I see you. I really don't think you eat enough." She took Randy by the shoulders and nearly yanked him inside. She then favored Kyle with a disdainful glance. "And this is…?" She sounded as if she hoped it was the newspaper boy coming to collect and that perhaps her son's date hadn't been able to make it.

Kyle thrust his hand out, grasping Mrs. Stone's hand. He pumped it vigorously. "I'm Kyle Temple, Randy's new beau. I'm really pleased to meet you."

One might think from the look on Mrs. Stone's face that a particularly loathsome octopus had just attached itself to her. She finally managed a small smile after extricating her hand. "Pleased to meet you as well, I'm sure," she said, sounding anything but.

Kyle bounded into the foyer after Randy, barely taking time to look around before saying, "I really like your decorating, Mrs. Stone. You should have one of those decorating shows. You know, like that one guy with the beard who says he's straight but sounds gayer than Christmas. I think he's gay, anyway, don't you? I mean, they say there's no smoke without fire, and that guy's flame could start *The Towering Inferno*. I know he's married and all that, but look at Rock Hudson. I mean, really."

As Kyle ran out of words, Randy rubbed his forehead, and his mother seemed reluctant to shut the front door behind them. She looked as if she might bolt outside for safety, rain be damned.

RASHKA pushed the Stop button on the recorder. They'd played sections of it over and over, Rashka pouring over his books in between listening. "And you're sure this guy doesn't know Aramaic?"

"I'd be really surprised," Bennett said. "He's a yokel. Your good-natured redneck type. I mean, he's a professional wrestler by trade. I doubt if he knows Pig Latin."

"And this tape is from your first session with him?"

"The first time I used hypnosis on him, yes. That's when he spoke the longest in the language. The second session was much shorter, since—"

"It's the Sermon on the Mount," Rashka broke in excitedly.

Bennett blinked. "I beg your pardon?"

"He's reciting the Sermon on the Mount," Rashka said. "In Aramaic."

Blinking again, Bennett replied, "You've got to be kidding."

"As far as I can tell. My translation isn't perfect by any means, but even not knowing the language, it's pretty obvious." He showed Bennett some notes he'd been furiously scribbling. "This bit here, from the words I've looked up, has to be 'blessed are the poor in spirit.' 'Kingdom of heaven', that bit's in there. 'Blessed are they that mourn.' 'The meek'. It's all there."

Bennett frowned, first at the tape player and then at Rashka's notes. "You're telling me that a professional wrestler with the IQ of a trained monkey, under hypnosis, recited the Sermon on the Mount in its entirety… in Aramaic?"

Rashka scratched his temple. "I guess I am. I can't explain it, but that's what it is."

"The Sermon on the Mount?"

"Yes."

"In Aramaic?"

"Yes."

Bennett sat back, his mouth hanging open. "There must be some way to make some money out of this. I don't know what's going on, but it just seems like there are big bucks to be made out of this, handled the right way."

Rashka nodded. "Yes," he said.

CHAPTER
SIX

MR. STONE felt like his arm was being jerked out of its socket as Randy's new boyfriend shook his hand with a tad too much enthusiasm. He bit into his lip slightly and said, "Pleasure to meet you."

"Oh, the pleasure's all mine," Kyle responded, grinning like an ape. "Randy's talked about you so much, I feel like I know you already. Did you see the game on Sunday? What about the Colts this year, eh?"

With some difficulty, Mr. Stone pulled his hand free. "I don't really concern myself with sports for the most part."

"Ah, well," Kyle said, his exuberance only diminished for a second. "It really was a good game. Trust me on that."

Mr. Stone flexed his fingers to get some of the feeling back. "I will. That's quite a grip you've got, by the way. Do you play football yourself?"

Kyle cast a worried glance about the room, hoping to get Randy's attention. Randy, however, was in deep conversation with his mother and wasn't going to come to the rescue, so Kyle blundered on. He tried to sound offhand as he said, "No, I play a game with friends every now and then. Touch football. That's about it. I don't really go into sports much myself. Too busy, you know."

"So what do you do for a living?"

Kyle gulped. "For a living?"

Mr. Stone chuckled. "That's what I asked. You do work, don't you?"

"Oh, yeah," Kyle said, speaking in the overly loud tone he used when he got nervous. "I work. I work all the time. I'm almost one of those workama… whatever you call 'em." His raised voice got him a furtive, dirty glance from Mrs. Stone, but no help from Randy.

"Workaholics?"

"That's the word."

"And just what are you a workaholic at?"

A nearly audible whimper escaped Kyle as he tried to think. Nothing came, so he replied in a small voice, "I'm an air traffic controller."

"Really?" Mr. Stone sounded impressed. "Not an easy job. A lot of stress goes with that territory. No wonder you like football. I imagine you've got a lot of aggravation that football allows you to vent."

Kyle nodded his head vigorously. "Oh, that's so true. Especially the violent sports, like football. Helps with that old pent-up aggravation, as you say."

Mr. Stone pointed a finger at Kyle's T-shirt. With an amused smile he said, "I see you're wearing a wrestling T-shirt. Not into that stuff, are you?"

"No," Kyle said, biting his tongue.

"I didn't figure you would be. No one of intelligence could watch professional wrestling. I mean, can you imagine? What sort of a moron would be taken in by that crap?"

As Mr. Stone guffawed, Kyle muttered under his breath, "An air traffic controller type of moron?"

MRS. STONE lit a cigarette, taking care not to blow the smoke into her son's face.

"I thought you'd given them up," Randy said.

"I did, dear. It just didn't stick."

"Kyle's quitting. He's had a hard time of it, but this new method seems to be doing the trick. He's using hypnotherapy."

Mrs. Stone shuddered slightly at the mention of Kyle's name. "Whatever happened to that one boy you were dating? Tony something. Freestone, I think his name was. He was very nice and had such a good job. I can't see why you stopped dating him."

"Tony? You mean the one with the crack habit who stole money from me all the time?"

"That's the one. He was sweet and very good-looking. I don't think you gave him enough of a chance. You're always too difficult to please when it comes to dating."

"Did I mention that he had a crack habit and that he stole money from me?"

"Or that other one. Joe. The one with the really nice body. Whatever became of him?"

"He's now Josephine, and he performs six nights a week at the Rainbow Club," Randy replied, not bothering to hide his irritation. "Mom, I take it you've already made one of your snap judgments and that you're already against my dating Kyle."

Mrs. Stone waved her cigarette through the air. "Oh, I'm sure he's a very nice boy, but don't you think he's a little young for you?"

"He's about ten years younger."

"That's what I mean."

"You're ten years younger than Dad."

"That's different."

"How?" Randy demanded, his anger rising further. "How is that different?"

"It just is. Relationships between two men are very different from relationships between a man and a woman. Besides, the boy just doesn't seem to be your type."

Randy rolled his eyes. "As if you know my type. This coming from the woman who set me up with Derek Martin."

"Derek Martin was perfect for you."

Although he tried to keep from doing it, Randy raised his voice to a slightly higher pitch, something that often happened when he was in deep discussion with his mother. "He was straight!"

Mrs. Stone blinked. "But he was a lawyer."

"That's two strikes against him!"

Exhaling smoke, Mrs. Stone asked, "Well, what does this boy do for a living?"

"It's not 'this boy'. His name is Kyle, and—"

Randy was saved from having to go further as the Stones' cook and housekeeper, Mrs. Pitcairn, entered to announce that dinner was ready.

"We'll chat later," Mrs. Stone told her son.

Randy didn't doubt it for a moment.

CARL BENNETT crossed the *New York Times* off the list. So far, he'd tried to interest the *Washington Post*, the *Boston Herald*, *USA Today*, *People Magazine*, and even the *Indianapolis Star* about the story. He'd received three outright laughs and one promise to get back to him "at some future date," and the others had shuffled him from department to department until someone finally just hung up on him. He hated to go to the next call on his list. Surely there was a better way to go than with a tabloid rag like *America's Crier*....

JEFFREY HARDESTY loved working for the *Crier*. One of the great things about working for a supermarket tabloid like the *Crier* was that, if for some reason you were having trouble coming up with a story, you could always simply invent a tale. If Cousin Zebe from Podunkville didn't come forth claiming to have played poker with Bigfoot, all you had to do was morph a photo of Hilary Clinton's head onto a cartoon alien's body and—voilà!—you had a front-page story.

Hardesty was at his computer, putting the finishing touches on his Elvis Stole My Child's Lunch Money story, when his phone rang. He answered on the second ring, muttering, "*Crier*. Hardesty here."

"Do you pay for stories?" asked the voice on the line.

"Sometimes. Depends on the story. If you're telling me your cat is possessed by Satan, I wouldn't be too interested. We did that one last year. If it's something new—"

"How about a small-time professional wrestler of limited mental abilities who, under hypnosis, quotes Jesus Christ in Aramaic?"

Hardesty paused. "Quotes Jesus?"

"Among other things, he's recited the Sermon on the Mount. In its entirety."

"In Aramaic?"

"In," the caller repeated, "Aramaic."

Hardesty suddenly forgot about Elvis and the lunch money. "Yeah. I'd be interested in a story like that. Very much so."

DINNER went off without a hitch up until the part where people actually sat down at the table and began to eat. After that it went horribly wrong.

Kyle, like a puppy eager to please, complimented everything from the table setting to the pictures on the wall, but to no avail. Mrs. Stone grunted an acknowledgment and ordered Mrs. Pitcairn to pour her an unprecedented third glass of wine.

Randy tried to keep the conversation flowing by telling anecdotes about customers at his gay and lesbian bookstore. "This lady came in the other day—stinking drunk—and she obviously had no idea where she was. She kept asking where the Ann Coulter books were. I thought some of the lesbians in there shopping were going to rip her head off."

Mr. Stone chewed his food carefully and then asked Kyle, "How do you deal with the stress of your job? Other than watching the Colts, I mean. You look like you work out a lot. That must help."

Mrs. Stone grimaced as she glanced at Kyle.

"Kyle here is an air traffic controller," Mr. Stone announced to his wife.

Randy dropped his fork and turned slightly pale.

Kyle's cheeks flushed red. "Well," he stammered, "I just do that part-time, really."

"Part-time?" Mr. Stone frowned. "I didn't know they had part-time air traffic controllers."

Kyle licked his lips. "Yeah. They just have me do the smaller planes. Since I'm still pretty young. Someday, though, I'll work my way up to 747s and—"

"Kyle's a professional wrestler," Randy blurted out.

All eyes immediately went to Randy, even those of Mrs. Pitcairn, who was pouring Mrs. Stone's wine.

The long silence was broken by Kyle, who muttered, "Well, yeah, I do that now. The air traffic control stuff didn't pay worth shit."

CHAPTER
SEVEN

HARDESTY leaned forward, watching the mini-recorder carefully. He saw in front of him not a recorder but a holy object on par with the Grail or the Ark of the Covenant. In his mind's eye he already had next week's cover of the *Crier* complete. The thought of how many issues he could sell out of this made him almost horny with greed. "This was definitely worth flying in for," he said, "even if it was two bloody hours I couldn't smoke. And you're sure of the translation?"

Hardesty, Rashka, and Bennett were crammed into Rashka's tiny office on a sunny afternoon, a fact they might have enjoyed had the office contained even a small window.

Rashka shrugged. "It's fairly straightforward. The first tape is definitely the Sermon on the Mount. The second, shorter session I'm not as sure of, but it appears to be quotes from Jesus on the cross."

In truth, Hardesty wasn't too worried about the veracity of the translation. Facts weren't something about which the *Crier* was overly concerned. "Quoting? I'm not sure we're dealing with quoting here."

Bennett chuckled, assuming Hardesty was joking. He stopped when he saw the man was serious. "What else could it be?" he asked. "Are you suggesting the young man is somehow 'channeling' Jesus Christ?"

"Channeling. I like that. That could work," Hardesty agreed, "but I like the idea of reincarnation better."

"Reincarnation?" Rashka repeated, not believing his ears. "You're suggesting the Second Coming has arrived in the form of a small-time professional wrestler with a smoking problem?"

Hardesty smiled wistfully. "This will be our best headline since Barack Obama's affair with the alien grub worm."

THE best part of making love, as far Randy was concerned, was the snuggling and cuddling afterwards. Well, perhaps not the best part, which he had to admit was that second when the fireworks exploded, but it certainly ranked high. He and Kyle were wrapped in each other's arms after a particularly athletic coupling during which Kyle had put Randy in a position he hadn't been in since... well, Randy wasn't sure he'd *ever* been in that position. He was still somewhat dizzy from hanging upside down for so long.

Exhausted, he held onto Kyle tightly, lightly stroking his lover's short blond beard. "I never was really into bearded guys before," Randy said. "They never had any attraction for me, to be honest. Yours, though, I love. It's cute."

"Cute?" Kyle raised his head a quarter of an inch off the pillow before deciding it was too much effort. He settled back and kissed Randy's hand. "It's not supposed to look cute. It's supposed to look menacing. I'm a heel in wrestling. I need to look mean. Heels aren't cute. It just doesn't work that way."

Smiling, Randy climbed on top of Kyle and kissed his mouth as sloppily as he could. "You couldn't look mean if you tried."

"Oh, really?" Kyle's eyes shone with amusement. "Want to wrestle? I'll show you how mean I can be."

Randy laughed. "Wrestle? Get hit with chairs and stuff? No thanks."

"I mean real wrestling. I bet I can get you to submit in under a minute. Want to try?"

"Um...." Randy put all of his weight against Kyle, thinking he'd need the beginning advantage. "Okay."

The bedsprings shrieked in protest as Kyle suddenly bucked, throwing Randy off of him. Laughing, Randy hit the mattress and barely had time to recover before Kyle flipped him onto his back. Quickly, Kyle's hands pulled Randy's arms back, and then he grabbed Randy's neck, getting him in a faultless full nelson. His naked body seemed to fit against Randy's as perfectly as a jigsaw puzzle. Randy struggled a bit, unable to break the hold. They were both giggling like little kids.

"You won't get out of this," Kyle warned, "so you might as well give up."

Randy gave one last token attempt to shrug Kyle off of him before surrendering. "Okay, I give up."

For a moment Kyle didn't let up. He brought his lips close to Randy's ears and whispered, "Now you've got to promise me you'll come to my show on Friday night and be my manager."

Randy's laugh became a nervous one. "Somehow I thought you were going to suggest something else as penance for losing. Let me think about it." There was an increase of pressure from Kyle. "Okay! Okay! I'll do it!"

Kyle released the hold and nibbled on Randy's earlobe before rolling off of him. "You'll have fun, I promise. I've already run the idea by Sneed, and he was all for giving it a try."

"You'll just have to tell me exactly what to do." Randy shifted so that he was closer to Kyle.

"That's easy. We just dress you up so you look like a scumbag wrestling manager. That's the sort I'd have. You lead me out to the ring, yell at the crowd, annoy the referee, and generally make yourself a nuisance. Just make sure the crowd hates me. Distract the ref so I can cheat. Maybe even smack my opponent if he gets close enough to your side of the ring."

"I couldn't do that!" Randy protested. "You can't expect me to hit someone I don't even know. I can't hit people I *do* know. Well, I might make an exception for my mother, but that's about it."

Kyle rolled his eyes. "It's not like he won't be expecting it. I mean, I'll be kicking, punching, and beating on the guy. One slap from you won't kill him. Besides, I'll introduce you before the match so you won't be strangers. You'll like him. He's cute. He's just starting out, but he's picking up the stuff really quick. Kind of a pretty boy, but we need that look in the MDW. His name's Jimmy Murdoch. The crowd loves him. The plan for the match is for me to totally wallop him right from the start. Really beat the shit out of him. Then, right at the end, I get cocky and I'll start talking with you or something like that while he's dying there in a heap. He gets up, dropkicks me, rolls me over, and pins me. The crowd cheers because the cute guy wins, but then of course I knock the ref out of the way and stomp Jimmy into the canvas. You can join me for that, if you want."

"I'd be afraid I'd hurt him."

"No way!" Kyle laughed. "You couldn't, believe me. Not with those scrawny legs of yours, anyway—"

"My legs are not scrawny!"

"Anyway, I can show you how to do a stomp that looks vicious but doesn't hurt. Come on, I'll show you." Kyle started to get up, but Randy held him firmly.

"Show me later," Randy said. "Right now, something else has come up."

Kyle grinned and nearly engulfed Randy's mouth with a kiss.

CHAPTER
EIGHT

THE Friday-night show of the MDW was at the Southside Middle School gymnasium. Jeff Hardesty entered behind a middle-aged couple who were busy arguing loudly over the parking job the man had accomplished. By the time he got to the table where a pimply-faced kid was selling tickets, Hardesty was wishing the guy had run over his wife before parking.

The kid looked at Hardesty blankly. "How many?"

The arguing couple had moved on. Hardesty looked around, but no one else was in sight. Unable to contain his penchant for a smart-ass comment, Hardesty told the kid, "Well, let me see. There's no one with me, so I'm guessing it'll just be one ticket."

"No date and no friends on a Friday night." The kid remained deadpan. "You must be really popular."

Hardesty slid his money across the table. "I'm just here to whack off while watching the sweaty guys in tights roll around with each other."

The kid didn't seem fazed. He handed Hardesty a ticket stub. "Keep this. Check your number. Later on we'll be raffling off an MDW T-shirt. If you win you can use it to wipe the jizz off your hands when you're done whacking."

Touché, kid, Hardesty thought. While part of him wanted to smack the boy on the jaw, he had to acknowledge that the kid was good with a quick retort. Hardesty tipped an imaginary hat at the kid and turned to enter the gym proper.

The ring was set up in the center and was surrounded by several rows of folding chairs. Hardesty was surprised to find that most of these seats were already occupied. The overflow of people was starting to fill up the bleachers that had been pulled out. Hardesty had expected maybe a dozen or two people in attendance, tops. He guessed that there were at least a hundred people already seated, with a few more straggling in.

It is *Indiana*, he reminded himself.

He wanted to find a chair close to the ring, since he wanted to take some fairly close-up pictures if at all possible. Luckily, he found an empty seat near one of the corners. There were four teenage boys in the adjoining chairs. They looked well beyond intoxicated to Hardesty. He hated teenagers as a general rule, and intoxicated teenagers were, to him, slightly below maggot-covered roadkill on the list of things he wanted to share his personal space with. The kid on the end, a shaggy-haired moppet with a dirty wife-beater T-shirt and a homemade tattoo of a cross on his scrawny right arm, gave Hardesty a glare as he approached.

"Is this seat taken?" Hardesty asked.

The moppet shook his head. "Knock yourself out, dude." He turned back to his friends, and the quartet cackled as if some wonderful joke had just been told.

Hardesty treated himself to a fantasy of kicking the kid's teeth in as he settled into his chair. He breathed in, enjoying the aroma of hot dogs, buttered popcorn, and nachos coming from the concession stand. These scents were mingled with the reek of whiskey coming from the kid next to him. The teenagers held cups in their hands, supposedly of cola, but Hardesty suspected they contained something more potent. He wondered briefly how the not-overly-bright band managed to smuggle in the booze.

Tinny music suddenly blared from the loudspeakers, and the announcer, seated at a table not far from Hardesty, spoke. "Welcome, ladies and gentlemen."

Hardesty scanned the crowd, deciding the titles fit no one in attendance.

"Welcome to Midwest Demolition Wrestling's Friday Night Smash!"

The crowd clapped and cheered. The inebriated kid next to Hardesty let out a wolf call.

"We've got plenty of action in store for you tonight, including matches with El Toro!"

The audience whistled and stomped their feet enthusiastically.

"Kyle Temple!"

Boos and catcalls followed the announcement.

"Mr. Indianapolis himself, Shawn Booker!"

There came more applause and whistling. Hardesty wondered if the audience was programmed to know the first wrestler announced would be a 'good guy', the second a heel, and so on, or if they really did know all the wrestlers by name.

"Now if you will all rise for the playing of our national anthem."

The tinny music, which had been muted while the announcer spoke, switched to a bad recording of "The Star-Spangled Banner." Hardesty stood with his hand on his heart, watching various people in the crowd. A large number were singing along, although few seemed to know the actual words. Hardesty wondered if he should point out to the people behind him that the song actually did not begin with the words "José, can you see?" He decided the lesson would be lost on them.

By the song's end, most of the singers had run out of words and were just mouthing along until they reached the final line. Most seemed to know America was the land of the free and the home of the brave, even if most of the rest of the song was lost in obscurity. Lukewarm applause greeted the song's last note.

The crowd resumed their seats. Hardesty expected the lights to dim, but this didn't happen. Apparently the gym's lights were either on or off, with no choices in between. The announcer started up again. "Let's get right to the action. Our first match of the evening has a fifteen-minute time limit. Let us first introduce our referee for the evening, Rusty Simms!"

Hardesty found himself hoping that Temple's match was the first one. He wasn't sure how long he could sit in his chair without hitting someone across the back of the head. The kid beside him hooted and took a long swig of his drink. A loud belch followed, and Hardesty's nose was attacked by the smell of whiskey mixed with whatever fast-food hamburger the kid had eaten for supper.

Rusty Simms, dressed in the referee garb of black pants and a black-and-white striped shirt at least a size too big for his skinny frame, pulled himself into the ring. He was greeted with a smattering of applause.

The announcer deepened his voice dramatically. "First into the ring, from Marion, Indiana, weighing in at 195 pounds, would you please welcome Jimmy 'Crash' Murdoch!"

The music changed to a popular hip-hop song, and Jimmy Murdoch made his way to the ring. Hardesty thought the kid looked too young to be wrestling. He had short, spiked hair, which was a blond shade that obviously came from a bottle. The music had led Hardesty to assume Murdoch would be black, but if the kid were any paler, he could possibly qualify as an albino. Murdoch wore baggy pants and walked with the hip-hop swagger, though, smacking outstretched hands of fans as he approached the ring. He made his way to the corner opposite Hardesty. As he climbed through the ropes, the boys next to Hardesty jumped to their feet and punched their fists in the air. "Murdoch!" they screamed in unison.

This kid is the good guy? Hardesty smiled to himself. Murdoch did have a good ol' boy, redneck quality to him, right down to the slight paunch around his middle. Hardesty could see why the crowd liked him. He was one of their kin. Murdoch strode around the ring, shaking his head to acknowledge the cheers from the audience.

"His opponent, from Indianapolis, weighing in at 210 pounds, the Circle City Killer—Kyle Temple! He's accompanied to the ring by his manager, Money-Mad Randy Rock!"

Hardesty turned and craned his neck. He held his camera ready as he spotted Temple entering the gym area. As soon as he saw Temple's face, his mouth dropped open. *Too, too perfect. Beard and mustache, neither of them too long and both kept neatly trimmed.* The guy looked like every Renaissance painting of Jesus Hardesty had even seen. *Stick him in a robe and he could preside over the Last Supper.*

At the moment Temple was clad in black trunks, black boots, and a black leather jacket. The crowd booed and hissed as he passed. The guy following Temple, presumably the manager, seemed nervous and somewhat out of place. He kept close behind the wrestler as if seeking protection. A rather rotund woman with bad teeth stood up and spat in Temple's direction. He, in return, gave her the finger. The manager seemed to pale a little watching the exchange.

The crowd obviously saw Temple as the bad guy. Hardesty grinned to himself. He saw Temple as a story. A front-page story. Hell, several front-page stories. Hardesty snapped away with his camera.

The pair entered the ring at the corner where Hardesty was sitting. *Fantastic*, he thought. *I get to study him up close.* And Hardesty liked what he saw. Despite the character of a mean badass he was attempting to put over, Temple was obviously a sweet-natured and extremely good-looking young man. There was a snarl on his face, but his eyes couldn't hide the childish joy he got from just stepping into the ring. Hardesty envisioned the all-time highest-selling issue of the *Crier*, complete with Temple's face adorning the cover.

In the ring, Temple whispered something hurriedly to his manager. Blushing, Money-Mad Randy nodded his head and then climbed back out of the ring. He stood looking uncertain for a moment. He then bit his lip and folded his arms in an attempt to look tough.

Hardesty eyed the manager carefully. The guy was probably in his early thirties and was so obviously new to the wrestling world that it was almost laughable. He was good-looking in the boy-next-door way, wearing an ill-fitting suit and Ray-Bans, which Hardesty guessed were not only part of the character but also to mask the nervousness in his eyes. Although he was supposed to be Temple's manager, he seemed to be taking his cues from the wrestler rather than the other way around.

The bell rang and Temple pulled off the leather jacket. As he handed it to the manager through the ropes, Hardesty snapped a picture he hoped would show off the wrestler's muscular physique. *Our Jesus is a stud*, Hardesty thought.

The match itself was a surprise to Hardesty as well. He'd expected some lame, amateurish production, but these guys seemed to know their stuff. Only once, when Murdoch jumped up and dropkicked Temple, did Hardesty detect air between the bottom of Murdoch's boots and the "collision" with Temple's chest. Temple, of course, still sold the move and hit the canvas.

The match was fairly one-sided, with Temple dominating most of the action. He played to the audience, shouting at them in between bashing his opponent about the face and neck. Murdoch, much to the delight of the crowd, rebounded for a moment, throwing fists and kicks into Temple's abdomen before trying the not-so-successful dropkick. He then pulled Temple up by his hair, which Hardesty had to admit looked good, and snapped the young man into a headlock. Murdoch then ran across the ring and threw himself down, driving Temple's face into the canvas (a move the announcer called a "bulldog"). It seemed Murdoch was going to pull off the victory after being thoroughly trounced until the manager, Money-Mad Randy, jumped up onto the ring apron and distracted the ref. With the referee's back turned, Temple reached up and punched Murdoch right in the crotch.

Hardesty chuckled at the over-the-top reaction Murdoch sold to the crowd. The guy clutched his groin, his mouth open in a surprised and agonized O as he walked around the ring, ensuring that everyone saw he was in excruciating pain. When the referee turned back to the action, Temple, having climbed back to his feet, sailed across the ring and kicked Murdoch in the face. Murdoch's head snapped back so fast that Hardesty was certain the blow had made contact. The crowd scrambled to their feet, screaming catcalls at Temple. Temple leaped onto Murdoch as soon as the kid hit the canvas and grinned smugly as the referee counted to three. Randy the manager entered the ring and raised his fighter's hands in victory.

Hardesty was impressed. It had been entertaining and well done, but more than that, he was thrilled with how Temple looked. With the flowing blond hair and tight muscles, he'd be a great cover photo. Hardesty was putting his camera away just as the wrestlers were leaving the ring. Randy the manager was leading Temple away, and they passed within inches of Hardesty. Hardesty waited until they'd gone a few paces, and then, on a whim, said just one word in a normal tone that would be hard to hear over the boos from the crowd. He said, "Jesus."

Temple turned and looked at Hardesty questioningly. Hardesty arched his eyebrows and looked into Temple's eyes but said nothing more. Randy pulled the wrestler away.

The smile that grew on Hardesty's face would have made the Cheshire Cat proud.

CHAPTER
NINE

RANDY sat on the bench while Kyle, still wet from his shower, began to pull clothes out of his gym bag. Kyle had just yanked up his boxer shorts and was getting his left sock on when he noticed that Randy was staring forward, hardly moving a muscle. "You okay, man?" he asked. He nearly said "baby" instead of "man" but stopped himself when he realized that Jimmy Murdoch was climbing into a pair of jeans within earshot. "You don't look so good."

"I'm fine," Randy replied in a voice devoid of emotion.

Kyle sat down beside Randy to pull on his other sock. "You did good tonight. And I'm not just saying that. For your first time, it was really good. You should have seen me my first time in the ring. I got so nervous I forgot and really punched the guy hard in the face during the match. Broke the dude's nose. We really laughed about it afterward."

Randy sighed and began to chew on a fingernail. "I guess at least I didn't permanently disfigure someone's face. I've got that going for me."

"You think you did badly, huh? You do, don't you? I can tell."

Finding enough courage to look Kyle in the eye, Randy replied, "I froze out there. I was scared shitless. I had no idea what I was doing. I felt like everyone was watching me. Laughing at me."

Kyle's smile was crooked. "To be honest, not that many people were paying attention to you. They were watching the ring. In order for anyone to pay attention to you, you've got to really get in there and make it big. Yell. Hit the other wrestler. You really didn't do much of that."

"I was too scared to do anything like that! I don't think I'm cut out for this sort of thing."

"You're not giving yourself a chance. It was only your first time. Try it again tomorrow night and see how that goes. Once you get the hang of it, you'll be great. I know you will." Kyle made sure no one was looking and then blew Randy a kiss.

Randy smiled.

"I'm going to hear it from Debbie, though," he said with a groan. "She was watching tonight. You know how critical she is."

"She's never critical with me." Kyle snapped his jeans in the air before getting into them. "Every time I see her, she's got some kind of compliment for me. Remember how the last time we were out, she told me I made ignoramuses look good? I thought that was pretty cool. A lot of people seem to think I'm pretty dumb, but she can see right through all that. She's a really good judge of a person. Obviously she is, because she's your friend."

Randy touched Kyle's elbow and shook his head slightly. "I wouldn't brag about the ignoramus crack too much if I were you."

"Why not?"

"Um… it's just not the politically correct term. I think the current jargon is 'mentally stunted person'."

Kyle frowned. "Is that what ignoramus means? We'd better not tell Debbie. She was trying to compliment me, so it wouldn't do to point out to her that she was using totally the wrong word."

Nodding, Randy said, "Yeah, let's just keep quiet about it. Don't want to embarrass her, after all. Either way, she's going to kid me mercilessly about tonight. I must have looked like such a dork."

Kyle's voice lowered to a whisper as he cast a furtive glance around to ensure no other wrestlers were nearby. "I didn't think you looked like a dork at all. I thought you looked sexy as hell."

"I didn't look…." Randy paused, as if his memory was faulty and needed jogging. "I looked sexy?"

"Yeah, especially when you were strutting outside the ring, your arms all folded and shit. You looked like a badass."

"I didn't look like… you think I looked sexy?"

Kyle nodded enthusiastically. "I thought you looked tough as hell. You wouldn't have looked out of place in the ring, beating the tar out of Jimmy." Catching sight of the wrestler in question, he raised his voice and pointed to the youngster. "Hey, Jimmy. Don't you think that Randy did a good job on his first time out?"

Murdoch shrugged. "Yeah, I thought he did okay. Of course, after you kicked me in the teeth, I wasn't really paying much attention to anything outside the ring."

"Yeah," Kyle said apologetically. "Got a little carried away there in the beginning. Sorry about that."

"No problem. Maybe the next time I can return the favor," Murdoch said with a smile.

"Anytime," Kyle replied. "You know how I like a good kick to the teeth. Hell, I might get lucky and you'll knock out that crooked one on the side that I hate so much."

"I can always try."

Randy waited until Murdoch moved off before saying in an awed tone, "Like brothers."

"What?" Kyle asked.

"You guys are kind of like brothers, or at least how I've always imagined brothers to be. It was the same way with Pete. El Toro, I should say. Just the way you guys talk with each other when you're not wrestling. It's like brothers."

Kyle shrugged. "We are, in many ways." Now that they were alone in the locker room, he slid an arm around Randy's shoulders. "Now you're part of it. Part of the MDW family."

"I don't know." Randy sighed and lowered his head. "I just don't know if I'm cut out for this. I was really self-conscious out there."

"That's because you were still Randy Stone. You've got to leave him in the locker room. When you're out there, you're Money-Mad Randy, the manager who'll do anything to keep his fighter on the winning side." Having finished dressing, Kyle threw his sweat-soaked wrestling gear into his gym bag and picked it up. "Ready to head out?"

Randy stood up slowly. "Ready as I'll ever be."

"Hey, if Debbie kids you too much about it, just turn it around on her. Suggest that tomorrow night she join us as my valet or something. We can get her in a bikini or something. Some high heels. She'd get the crowd's attention, that's for sure."

Laughing, Randy said, "Yeah, I can see that happening. Do me a favor and don't bring that up around her. I'd like to keep us both alive."

As Randy expected, Debbie was lounging in the hall outside the locker room, smoking a cigarette. When she saw Randy, a smile crept across her face and her eyes sparkled with mischief.

"May I just say—" she began.

Randy held up a hand. "I wish you wouldn't."

She feigned innocence. "I was just going to say how wonderful I thought you were. Quite the wrestling manager."

Kyle grinned and smacked Randy's shoulder. "See? I told you that you were fine." He turned from Randy and wrapped his arms around Debbie in a friendly hug. As he pulled her in, Debbie's eyes bulged in surprise. "I'd glad you could make it," he said. "How did you think I did tonight?"

Released from Kyle's grip, Debbie seemed somewhat nonplussed. Randy hid his smile by pretending to cover his mouth for a cough. Running a hand distractedly through her hair, Debbie said, "Um... I thought you did just great." She seemed to search for words. "I... I think... I mean, it really seemed to me that you really did kick that poor guy in the face at one point. It scared me the way his head snapped back. I thought he was really hurt."

"Yeah, I misjudged the whole thing and whacked him a good one. It was cool, though. Made his mouth bleed like a son of a bitch. Sneed gives us a ten-dollar bonus if we bleed. Fifteen if it's a gusher. The audience likes a bit of blood. They think it's more real with blood."

Debbie stomped her cigarette out even though it was only half-smoked, a sure sign she was thrown for a loop, uncertain of how to deal with Kyle's "now we're best friends" attitude. "So the guy wasn't mad or anything? You nearly snapped the kid's head off and he doesn't care?"

"Hey, ten bucks is ten bucks. I've had guys kick me in the face before and all I got for it was a sore face. It's better to at least get some dough for it."

Debbie frowned, looking at Kyle as if seeing him for the first time. "I guess that makes some kind of sense. I'm guessing you had it pretty rough growing up."

Kyle snorted dismissively. "I don't know how rough it was. I had three cousins around all the time, all bigger and older than me. They usually beat the crap out of me, mostly because they could, being as I was the runt of the litter. I think they were just trying to toughen me up since I didn't have a dad."

"Or maybe they were just assholes."

Kyle nodded. "That's another possibility."

Debbie smiled and took both Randy and Kyle by the arm. "Let's get out of here. I say we hit the Taco Hut and screw any diet anyone's pretending to be on. I'll buy."

"Excuse me." A smallish man with a wrinkled corduroy jacket had approached them. He smiled at Kyle and bowed slightly to the trio. "My name's Jeff Hardesty. I'm a reporter. I wonder if I could borrow Mr. Temple here for just a moment."

Randy looked at Kyle questioningly. When Kyle nodded, he said, "Sure. We can wait out in the parking lot."

As they moved toward the exit, Debbie glanced over her shoulder. "A reporter? What sort of reporter would be interested in talking to Kyle? No offense, but he's just a small-time operator."

"That's the first time you've ever referred to him by name. It's usually been The Idiot, or That Dunce You're Dating," Randy said. "And I guess it could be one of those local rags doing a story. A county newspaper or something like that. And don't underestimate a local wrestling show like this. They do a pretty good business for an independent production."

Frowning, Debbie pushed the exit door open. "I don't know. I got a weird vibe from that guy. He reminded me of a snake."

"Yeah, well, you thought Ben Kingsley was up to something odd when we watched *Gandhi*."

"No one's that nice." Debbie was pulling another cigarette out of her pack and nearly ran into a short, balding man who was furiously chomping on a fat, foul-smelling cigar. Randy recognized him as Monty Sneed, the owner of MDW and Sneed's Gym.

Sneed was prepared to snarl at whoever had jostled him until he looked up and saw Debbie. A sly grin spread slowly over his pockmarked face. "Let me light that for you, dear lady."

Debbie stepped back as if trying to get away from a loathsome rat. She cautiously held out her cigarette and allowed the man to light it. "Thank you," she said without inflection.

"Did you enjoy the show? We put on quite the fucking extravaganza, don't we?"

"Um… yeah. I was really here for Randy and Kyle Temple. They're friends of mine."

Randy's eyebrows went up when he heard Debbie refer to Kyle as her friend, but he kept quiet.

A light bulb seemed to glow above Sneed's head. "Temple, eh? You're a friend of his? I'm not fucking surprised. The babes fucking flock around that boy." He stuck out his hand for Debbie to shake. "Sneed here. Monty Sneed. I own MDW."

She gave his hand a brief touch. "Nice to meet you."

So far Sneed hadn't so much as given Randy a glance. His eyes seemed reluctant to leave Debbie's chest. Randy coughed discreetly. "I met you earlier, before the show, Mr. Sneed. Randy Stone. I'm a friend of Kyle's."

"Oh, yeah. Weren't you going to be his manager or something like that for the show tonight?"

Confused, Randy said, "Um… I did. I was. I was out there."

The short man shook his head. "Don't remember seeing you. Good match, though. Got a little blood. Always fucking good to get some blood in the first match. Makes the audience think they're really in for a great show. Which, of course, they are. Always, with my shows."

Debbie tried to move past Sneed, but the man managed to shift himself to keep right in front of her. "We're probably going out for tacos or pizza or something," she said. "We ought to get going. Don't want all the pepperonis to go stale before we get there."

Sneed laughed hard. "Don't let me keep you, little lady."

Randy could see Debbie's ire rising at the "little lady" reference, but before he could say anything, someone came up behind Sneed and inserted himself between the cigar-chomping promoter and Debbie. It was Jimmy Murdoch, who, out of view of Sneed, winked conspiratorially at Debbie before taking her hand. "Hey, Monty," he said. "You looking after my girl for me?"

Sneed choked on air. "Your girl?"

Murdoch looked at Debbie with theatrical love in his eyes. "Yeah, my girl. You weren't making a play for her, were you? You know how mad I get when someone makes a play for my girl."

"Making a play?" Sneed tried his best to act offended. "Making a fucking play? I would never... we were just... we were... talking about the match. That's what we were doing. The blood. That's it. I was saying how the blood is always a good thing in the first fucking match. Wasn't I?" He looked beseechingly at Debbie for confirmation.

"Yeah?" Jimmy Murdoch's face registered uncertainty. "From where I was, it looked like you weren't letting her pass. And we have a date to get some...."

"Tacos," Randy said.

"Pizza," Debbie said at the same time.

Murdoch nodded and squeezed Debbie's hand. "Taco pizzas."

Sneed smiled. "Good. Good. I was just heading back in to check the night's take. Have to look after the fucking money, after all." He laughed weakly. "It was nice meeting you folks." Quickly, he squeezed past them and beat a hasty retreat back into the gym.

As soon as he was gone, Debbie turned to Jimmy Murdoch, who was still holding her hand. "Nice to meet you as well."

The young wrestler smiled and said, "Sorry about that. I figured you needed some help. Monty can be a little forceful where the ladies are concerned. You might have been stuck here for hours if I hadn't rescued you."

"I can take care of myself, thank you."

Randy noticed that Debbie's voice was softer than usual, plus she kept her hand in Murdoch's. To top things off, she used her free hand to toss her hair back, a sure flirtatious sign.

"You're a friend of Kyle's?" The wrestler seemed unable to take his eyes off of Debbie's face, a malady apparently also reciprocated by her.

"Yeah. And Randy's. I was here to watch Randy's debut in the world of wrestling."

"What did you think of the show?" Murdoch shifted his feet, a movement that miraculously brought him several inches closer to Debbie.

She seemed uncertain how to answer. "Um... I guess it was pretty cool. I really got worried when Kyle kicked you in the mouth, though. That really looked like it hurt. I know it made me wince."

Murdoch shrugged, finally releasing her hand. "It was nothing. Just taking a harder bump, that's all. These things happen."

The exit door opened and Kyle, all smiles and bounce-off-the-wall energy, came bounding out to join them. "That was so cool!" he exclaimed.

Randy, out of habit, nearly put his arm around Kyle. Remembering Murdoch's presence, at the last moment he changed the gesture to a playful punch on Kyle's arm. "Your first interview, eh?"

"Yeah, although he really didn't ask that many questions. Just the basic stuff. Still, at least I'll get my name in the paper."

"Did he say what newspaper he was with?" Debbie asked.

Kyle's brow furrowed in thought. "I'm not sure. He asked me if I had his permission to print my picture, though. I just hope it's a good one."

Jimmy Murdoch shuffled his feet. "I guess you guys have plans. I'd better get going myself." To Randy, he said, "You really did pretty good for your first time. I hope you'll come to tomorrow night's show. It can really be a lot of fun." Turning to Debbie, he lowered his gaze sheepishly. "And it was a pleasure to meet you, miss."

"Technically speaking," Debbie said, giving him the double hair flip, a move designed to drive men to want to buy out the nearest flower shop and send their entire inventory to her, "you haven't met me, since I haven't even told you my name. Debbie Jacobs, by the way. And it was sweet the way you came to my rescue. My knight in shining armor."

Randy shook his head as if he wasn't hearing her properly. Surely this wasn't the same woman who had needled him mercilessly for weeks for dating a younger guy who was a professional wrestler. *I can't wait to get her alone*, Randy thought to himself. *She's going to get such an earful.*

Debbie tilted her head, showing her milky white neck (which Randy knew she considered one of her best features), and went on. "We were just going out for tacos slash pizza. I don't think we'd made our minds up yet. You could join us if you don't have any plans. That is, if you'd like."

Murdoch's smile was huge. "I'd love to."

Debbie grabbed the boy's elbow and began to lead him toward the car. "And you can tell me all about yourself. And explain to me why you do what you do, that sort of thing."

"It'd be my pleasure."

Randy and Kyle tagged along behind them. Randy's mouth refused to close as he stared at the couple before him. Every couple of feet they walked, he muttered "holy shit" under his breath.

CHAPTER
TEN

WHENEVER MDW didn't have an off-site show booked on the weekend, they filled in by having a show at Sneed's Gym. These affairs tended to be smaller in nature, mainly due to limited seating and the fact that, since the gym bore no sign, a lot of people couldn't even find the place. Therefore the shows at Sneed's Gym tended to attract only the most rabid wrestling fans, most of whom lived in the neighborhood.

This fact made Randy especially nervous.

He could hear the crowd even in the locker room. The show hadn't begun and yet the chanting and catcalls had already started. "What the hell?" he said, hovering near the door. "Are they all drunk, or what? They sound like a lynch mob. If there's a stout tree out back and I see that someone has a rope, I'm not going out there and that's that."

Kyle grinned as he laced up his boots. "Yeah, they can be pretty rambunctious. I kind of like it when they're this rowdy, though. You can really play with the audience. When we get out there, just follow my lead. I'll start yelling at someone in the crowd, and you join in. Just tell the guy to sit down and shut up and watch as your wrestler destroys the competition. That'll establish you with the audience as my evil manager."

"Who is your opponent tonight? Murdoch again?" Randy's voice lowered to a slight growl as he spoke the wrestler's name. He was still miffed over Debbie's instant attraction to Jimmy Murdoch, especially since she seemed to detect no hypocrisy on her part.

"Naw, Jimmy's not wrestling tonight. I go against Pete in tonight's match. And win, of course."

Randy began to pace up and down, going from the door to where Kyle was finishing getting his gear on. "Can you believe Debbie? After all the flack she gave me about dating you, she starts to hang all over that kid. Is he even out of high school?"

Having finished dressing, Kyle started twisting and turning, stretching out his muscles. "She gave you flack for dating me? You never told me that. And Jimmy's out of high school. He's older than he looks."

"He's what... eighteen, nineteen? And she really didn't give me flack. Just kidded me. You know the type of thing. Telling me I was robbing the cradle. She likes you. Honestly."

"Jimmy's a good kid. I think they make a good couple."

A roar sounded from the crowd. The announcer had started his spiel. Randy took in a deep breath. "Now I know how gladiators felt back in Roman times. That crowd wants blood. And while I look ravishing in red, one has to draw the line somewhere."

Kyle chuckled. "They'll probably get their blood. Derek Wilson's wrestling tonight, and he does that trick where you nick your forehead with a razor blade before the match starts. That way during the match it opens up and bleeds like hell. Just a little cut on your forehead can bleed a lot."

"You don't do that, do you?"

"Hell, no. It causes scars. You think I'd scar a forehead this pretty? Well, anyway, prepare yourself. I think we're about to be announced."

ALTHOUGH there were fewer people at this show (Randy's quick count showed somewhere between fifty and seventy-five), the sound of the boos that greeted his and Kyle's entrance nearly deafened him. He took a deep breath and decided that he'd treat the whole show like an acting exercise. He hadn't actually acted since his high school senior play (where he had famously skipped two whole pages of dialog and died fifteen minutes too soon), but he remembered how he enjoyed immersing himself in a different character. *That's all this is*, he told himself. *Acting. You're Kyle's manager. You're mean. You're greedy (presumably, otherwise why would it be Money-Mad Randy?). You'll do anything to ensure that your wrestler wins. Even if you already know he's going to win because he and Pete decided the outcome before the match even started.*

By the time they reached the crowd, Randy's walk had changed from his usual saunter to a swagger. He pursed his lips and nodded his head, inwardly thinking, *Yeah, I'm bad. My wrestler's bad. We're bad.*

A middle-aged man with a bad comb-over leaped to his feet as Kyle came near his chair. "You suck!" he screamed at Kyle. "My mother could beat the shit out of you!"

Kyle got right in the man's face, his mouth twisted into a snarl. "Shut up!" he yelled back. "I'll whoop you, your mother, and any other member of your stinking family stupid enough to get into the ring with me!"

Kyle turned his back on the guy, continuing his way towards the ring. Randy, sensing an opportunity to show his mettle, flashed the guy his best evil glare. "Your mother wears army shoes," he sneered. "And smells like day-old piss."

The man's face paled, and he rocked unsteadily on his feet. "Who the fuck are you to talk about my mother that way?"

"I'm Money-Mad Randy. Who the fuck are you?"

The guy jabbed a finger into Randy's chest. "Look, you skinny little squirt. I'll punch your lights out if you don't take back what you said." He reared his fist back to back up his claim.

Kyle's reaction was immediate. He bolted back to Randy's side, scooping the man up into his arms before Randy could even react. Kyle's face was red with fury, and Randy knew him well enough to know that he wasn't playacting. Kyle was in fierce protector mode. The guy had threatened his mate, and Kyle wasn't happy about that in the least. The man let out a strangled cry as Kyle flipped him over and threw him to the ground. The guy landed on his back, the air puffing out of his lungs. While a few people in the crowd laughed and cheered, others stared, dumbfounded at what was taking place. Monty Sneed, who'd been sitting at the announcer's table, pushed his way through the crowd in seconds, his face even redder than normal. He grabbed Kyle by the arm.

"What the hell have you done?" he demanded. "Want to get us sued?"

It was as if Kyle had suddenly woken from a dream. He looked down at the groaning man as if wondering how he got there. "I didn't mean—" he began.

"Get back to the locker room," Sneed hissed. "Now!"

Randy pulled a white-faced Kyle away. "Come on."

Sneed, kneeling beside the fallen man, took the time to glance back up at Kyle. "And clear out your locker. You're fired." Sneed, in a voice meant to show concern but that really just sounded like a softer growl, asked the man if he was all right. When the man sputtered and raised his head slightly, Sneed looked back at the announcer sitting at the desk. "Announce the next match!"

Randy led Kyle back to the locker room. The audience members they passed were no longer whistling and cheering. They looked more like a crowd watching the aftermath of a car wreck. Some whispered excitedly to each other. Some just watched Kyle's retreat in silent awe.

By the time they'd hit the locker room, a single large tear had found its way down Kyle's cheek. Other wrestlers, unaware of what had taken place, watched them questioningly. Kyle was unable to look anyone in the eye. Keeping his face down, he muttered, "I'm fired. What the fuck. I'm fired."

Saying the words brought the tears out in a flood. When Kyle's shoulders began to shake with grief, Randy couldn't help himself. He pulled Kyle close and hugged him tight. Other wrestlers stared, but Randy didn't care, and Kyle seemed oblivious to his surroundings. Kyle's closeted status was the least of their problems at the moment, Randy figured.

"It's okay," he whispered. "It'll all be okay."

A huge black wrestler, still in the process of dressing, came over to them practically naked. "What happened?"

"I'm fired, that's what happened!" Kyle shouted in between sobs.

Randy patted Kyle's back. "Some guy was going to punch me," he explained. "Kyle body slammed him."

A silence fell over the room. Randy ignored the other wrestlers. All he knew was that his boyfriend was soaking his shoulder with tears. He could feel Kyle's strong hands clutching his back. His grip was approaching an uncomfortable level, but Randy wasn't going to complain. How could he? He stroked Kyle's hair. "It's going to be okay," he repeated.

The door banged open and Sneed sailed into the locker room, his cigar mangled from nervous chewing. He glared at Kyle and Randy. Reluctantly, Randy pulled himself out of Kyle's embrace. Kyle sniffed loudly and kept his head lowered. He seemed to have shrunk. Randy thought he looked like a small child who'd lost his puppy.

Oddly, Sneed didn't look as mad as Randy thought he would. The man pulled the cigar from his teeth and asked Kyle, "Do you want to explain to me what the fuck that was all about? The last thing I need is someone suing my ass."

Kyle couldn't answer. He just shook his head.

Sneed snorted and patted Kyle's shoulder. "Don't let it fucking get to you, son. Dry your tears. I've got someone who wants to see you."

Kyle raised his face. His eyes were swollen and red. "Who?"

Sneed smiled. "The guy you slammed. Turns out he thought it was great. He's always wanted to wrestle, but somehow as an accountant it's just never come up. Anyway, he loved it. You took the wind out of him, throwing him on the hardwood floor like that, but once he could speak, he started to laugh. He's outside now, and he wants to shake your hand and thank you."

"Does this mean I'm not fired?" Kyle asked.

"Fired?" Sneed frowned. "Why the fuck would I fire one of my best attractions? All I had to do was promise an autographed picture of you for him and his kids. I'm off the fucking hook, that's all I care about."

Kyle wiped his face with his arm. "So I'm not fired?"

Sneed slapped Kyle's back. "No, for fuck's sake, you're not fired." He glared at Randy, as if noticing him for the first time. "Who the fuck are you, and what are you doing here?"

"I'm his manager," Randy said. "Remember? Money-Mad Randy?"

Nodding, Sneed said, "Oh, yeah. I remember now. Next week, I want you to get in the ring after Kyle smashes his opponent and kick the guy a time or two. Make sure he feels it too, or else you're fired."

"You're not paying me, if you'll recall. You told me I was on a trial basis."

"You'd still be fired," Sneed said. "This will be great. We'll have everyone hating the two of you. Even your own mothers will hate you."

"Too late," Randy said quietly.

Sneed turned to let the accountant in but stopped at the door. He glanced back at Kyle. "You got away with it this time, fucker," he warned, "but if you ever pull a stunt like this again, I'll fire your ass so fast you'll think it was on fire. Savvy?"

Kyle looked at Randy questioningly. "What's savvy mean?"

"Just say yes."

Kyle nodded. "Yes, sir."

Sneed ushered in the accountant, who, although he moved somewhat stiffly and slowly, had huge grin on his face. He thrust a hand toward Kyle. "That was fantastic, my friend. I always wondered what one of those body slams felt like. Now I know. I don't know how you guys do it all the time."

"I'm sorry," Kyle said sheepishly. "I didn't mean—"

"Don't apologize," the man said. "I loved it." He turned to Randy. "And I really wouldn't have hit you, son. I was just caught up in the moment. You know how it is. I figured you knew that."

Randy shook the guy's proffered hand. "Honestly, all I could see was a broken nose in my future. I'm Randy Stone, by the way."

"Phil. Phil Wilkinson. Pleasure to meet you boys." He looked around the locker room, spying wrestlers in various stages of undress. "Wow. There's Madman Mark. And Top Rope Tony. And—"

Sneed stopped the litany. "Just to show you we harbor no ill will and that we appreciate your patronage, I've got a little proposal for you. How about autographs from all the wrestlers? For you and your kids."

Wilkinson's face lit up. "Really?"

"Least we can do," Sneed said. "And of course we'll let you in free to next week's shows. Why don't you come back with me to my office? I've got publicity shots of all the guys back there, and I'll make sure we get them signed for you." He opened the door and ushered the accountant out, pausing to look back at Kyle in disgust. Sneed whispered to him, "Next time make it worth all this shit. Don't just body slam the fucker. Beat the shit out of him."

When they'd gone, the massive black wrestler looked at Kyle and Randy suspiciously. "You guys were holding each other awfully tight. Too tight, some might say. Almost looked like two faggots holding each other."

Randy glared at the man, whom Wilkinson had identified as Madman Mark. "Some might say that," he said, looking down at the man's uncovered crotch. "And some might say you've got one hell of a tiny dick for a guy weighing 250 pounds. Everything's relative, isn't it?"

Madman Mark nodded, seeming satisfied with Randy's answer. "You've got a point there, my friend." He slapped Randy across the back. The friendly blow nearly knocked Randy off-balance. "Welcome to Midwest Demolition Wrestling, kid."

HARDESTY had flown back to his office in Chicago and had spent his Saturday furiously working with the folks at *America's Crier* to ready the next weekly issue, set to hit the stands on Tuesday.

When he saw the results, his heart nearly skipped a beat. It was wonderful. It was perfect. It would piss people off.

It would sell.

CHAPTER
ELEVEN

RANDY was on his knees, his face buried in a pillow. Kyle was behind him, his sweaty hands gripping Randy's hips. Randy was sure Kyle was about to come. The thrusts were getting harder and faster, plus Kyle's fingernails were starting to dig into his flesh, always a sign that the end was near. A particularly wonderful and hard thrust shoved Randy's head further into the pillow. "Jesus!" he yelled out. "God, that feels so good!"

Kyle groaned and shifted his hands to Randy's shoulders.

"Jesus!" Randy raised his head, feeling Kyle's cock throb within him as it neared release. "Give it to me, baby!"

One final thrust brought Kyle to climax. He moaned with pleasure and fell against Randy's back. They stayed motionless for a moment, enjoying the feel of each other's flesh, and then slowly Kyle pulled away from Randy. He slipped the condom off and tossed it to the side of Randy's bed.

"Don't forget that's there," Randy said as they settled against the pillows. "I'd hate to step out of bed later and feel something squish against my toes."

Kyle held Randy's head against his chest. "I'll get it. Don't worry, babe. I know what a neat freak you are."

"I'm not a neat freak. I just like my toes to be cum-free." Randy lifted his head slightly but still couldn't see the clock on his dresser. "What time is it?"

"Eight in the morning. Too damn early. Do we have time for a little more sleep before you have to go to work?"

"Probably not. I have to shower and all that stuff. Do you want some breakfast?"

Before Kyle could answer, the telephone on the nightstand rang. Frowning, Randy answered it. "Hello?"

It was his mother's voice on the line. "Did I wake you?"

"No," he replied, knowing that it wouldn't have mattered to her if she had. "Is something wrong? You never call this early."

"Nothing is wrong. I was thinking I should invite you and that nice boy you're seeing to dinner Friday night."

Randy pulled the phone away from his ear and looked at it. He knew he wasn't asleep, so it must be some kind of joke phone that Debbie or someone planted in his room with a recorded voice of his mother saying impossible things. "You mean Kyle, right?"

"Of course I mean Kyle," his mother said. "Such a sweet boy, and the two of you are so obviously in love. I'm having some friends over Friday, and I wanted the two of you to join us. Does Kyle like fish? I was thinking of having fish."

"He likes fish." Randy spoke carefully, still wondering what the joke was. Any second now he expected his mother to explode into a cackling laugh. He put his hand over the receiver and looked at Kyle. "When is April Fool's Day?"

Kyle thought hard. "Um… April first."

"And what's today?"

"It's February fifth."

"So it's not April Fool's Day?"

Kyle shook his head. "I don't think so. Maybe it is in Africa or Asia or something, though."

Randy returned to the phone conversation. "Mom, are you feeling okay?"

"Of course I am. What's wrong with asking my son and his handsome new boyfriend over to a little dinner party?"

"Those blue pills Dr. Nelson gave you. How many have you taken this morning?"

Mrs. Stone gave a short laugh. "I haven't taken any pills. So will you come? Please say you'll be here."

"We can't Friday. Kyle's got a show that night." Randy's frown deepened. Did his mother just use the word *please*?

"Oh." Randy could hear the disappointment in his mother's voice. "How about Thursday, then?"

"You'd change the date of a dinner party to accommodate Kyle and me?"

"Of course! I want my friends to meet my son's good-looking new boyfriend. After all," she said, lowering her voice suggestively, "he might someday be my son-in-law. Shall we say seven o'clock?"

"Um," Randy said. "Sure." A click sounded on the line, indicating another call coming in. "Mom, that's my call waiting. Someone else is trying to ring in. Can I talk to you later?"

"Of course, dear. Say hello to that gorgeous hunk of yours for me."

Randy pressed the button to switch to the other call. "Hello?"

"Oh. My. God." It was Debbie.

Sitting up, Randy asked, "What the hell is going on? My mom just called me, and now you. Generally my phone doesn't ring before noon. Shouldn't you be on your way to the office?"

"I was. I am." Debbie sounded ruffled. "You mean you don't know? You haven't heard? Oh. My. God. That's all I can say. Oh. My. God."

"What are you nattering on about? What's going on?"

Debbie asked. "Where are you right now?"

"I'm here in bed with Kyle. If you'd called about a minute ago, you'd have heard the moans."

"Get dressed. The two of you. Go down to that convenience store at the corner. Just take my word for it. Look at *America's Crier*. Oh. My. God. I bought six of them, just to make sure it wasn't some weird kind of misprint."

"The *Crier*?" Randy asked. "You never read supermarket tabloids. What—"

Debbie shouted into the phone, "Just do it! You'll see why. I'll call you back in twenty minutes."

Randy was about to protest, but she'd hung up. He cocked an eyebrow at Kyle as he replaced the receiver. "Something weird is going on. First Mom acts all weird—she invited us to dinner Thursday night, by the way—and then Debbie starts acting all flipped out. Debbie's been strange ever since she hooked up with that Murdoch kid. Did I tell you they've gone out twice now since they met? I'm starting to think there's something in the water. Debbie dates lawyers and doctors. Suddenly she's dating a professional wrestler. I'm pretty sure that's one of the signs of the Apocalypse."

Kyle slid out of bed and began to slip into his jeans. "You're dating a wrestler."

"That's different. I'm dating the hottest wrestler around, and the sweetest."

"Jimmy's a nice guy."

"He's just a kid."

Kyle snorted. "Shall I bring up the age difference between us?"

"You're over twenty. That makes you officially not a kid anymore." Randy found his shirt discarded at the bottom of the bed and started to put it on. "Debbie wanted us to check out something at the convenience store. Want some breakfast before we go?"

Kyle's eyes twinkled. "Got some Cap'n Crunch with Crunchberries?"

Shaking his head, Randy said, "We can pick some up at the store." He got out of bed and immediately grimaced. "Jesus, Kyle!"

"What?"

"I told you to remind me about that condom."

KYLE was scanning the candy counter, his mouth nearly watering. "They've got NECCO Wafers. I haven't had NECCO Wafers in ages. Can we get some NECCO Wafers?"

Randy, however, couldn't take his eyes off the rack of tabloids set up near the register. He was feeling light-headed and slightly sick to his stomach. He reached over, intending to grab hold of a shelf to ensure he was steady on his feet, but he only managed to smash a bag of potato chips.

"I really feel like some chocolate, though," Kyle went on. "Maybe a chocolate bar with almonds. I like almonds, especially with chocolate. Maybe we can get both and I can save the NECCO Wafers for later. What do you think?"

Randy pointed, unable to speak.

Kyle followed his gaze. "What?"

Randy pointed again, feeling like the Ghost of Christmas Yet to Come showing Scrooge the stone with his name carved on it.

Cocking his head, Kyle read the headline on the top tabloid, a rag called *America's Crier*. "'Jesus Is Back... And He's a Professional

Wrestler!' How cool. Those papers are always good for a laugh. I saw this one once which claimed that big purple aliens ran the phone company, which they claimed was why they always seemed so strange when you have to contact them. I think it's because so many of them are from New Jersey, though. You ever notice that? Nearly everyone at the phone company has a New Jersey accent. It's kind of...." The last word died on Kyle's lips as he saw the picture of himself under the headline. "Hey, that looks like me."

With shaking hands, Randy pulled the top copy off the rack. Indeed, the photo was of Kyle. The black-and-white shot showed Kyle in the ring, handing his leather jacket to someone just out of frame. Randy knew it was his hand outstretched to take the jacket. "Holy shit," he said.

Eyes wide, Kyle yanked the newspaper from Randy's grip. "They can't do that! What the hell?"

Several people in the store, including the bored-looking woman behind the counter, suddenly looked up. Quickly, Randy shushed his boyfriend. "Keep it down. Let's not panic. We'll get a lawyer, that's what we'll do. We must be able to sue them or something." He thought back. "That reporter that came to the show. Did he have you sign anything?"

"Yeah, but it was just a release form so that they could use my picture. There wasn't anything about calling me Jesus. I may be dumb, but I'm not that dumb." Frantic, Kyle opened the magazine. Finding the article, he read a few lines. "Well, this is just stupid. It says here that I recited the Sermon on the Mount in Aramaic. Hell, I don't know Aramaic. I've never even been to South America!"

Keenly aware of eyes on them, Randy gritted his teeth. "Don't shout. We'll get one of these things and go home and then we'll figure out what we should do. We'll get a lawyer. Even if you signed something, I'm sure they can't do something like this."

Kyle gasped loudly. "It says here when I wrestled one night, a stigmata developed. What the hell! How can they say that? My eyesight is fine!"

"Stigmata. You're thinking astigmatism. Stigmata are spots of blood suddenly appearing on the palms of your hands, where they pounded the nails into Christ on the cross."

The paper fell from Kyle's hands. He sniffed back the urge to cry. "That was when I kicked Jimmy Murdoch in the teeth. I picked him up by the head right after that and got blood on my hands. He had blood on his mouth. I don't see them calling him the reincarnation of... of... some guy with a bloody mouth!"

Randy grabbed another *Crier* off the rack and shoved some money across the counter at the woman. He didn't even wait for the change, instead taking Kyle by the elbow and leading him to the door. "I'll take care of this. Don't worry. There's got to be something we can do."

"That's it for my wrestling career," Kyle said loudly. "Who's going to want to fight me after this? Hell, they'll be afraid I'll wave my hands and toads will rain all over the ring or something. Fuck. I'm fucked, that's what this means. I'll have to become a nun or something. Fuck. I can't even do that. Who's going to take a nun that's had his picture in a newspaper saying he's Jesus Christ? No one, that's who!"

Randy thought about pointing out that nuns were women and that Kyle probably meant a priest, but instead just repeated, "Don't panic. We'll take care of this."

Finally a tear found its way down Kyle's cheek. "I won't be able to leave the house. People will throw eggs at me. Hell, *I'd* throw eggs at me. I'll have to become a hermit."

As Randy propelled Kyle down the street towards his apartment, his cell phone chirped to life. He answered it gruffly. "Yes?"

Debbie's voice was shrill. "You've seen it, then?"

"Yes! Why the fuck didn't you warn me? I almost fainted when I saw it. Poor Kyle's in shock. He keeps ranting about becoming a nun."

"If I'd told you, would you have believed me? Besides, I figured Kyle must have known about it—"

"No, that asshole reporter didn't tell Kyle what he was up to. He had Kyle sign a release, too. I'll have to find out what was in that release. Do you know any good lawyers that you haven't slept with and then unceremoniously dumped?" Randy guided Kyle to the right to ensure the wrestler didn't walk into a lamppost.

"What's my mother going to say?" Kyle muttered, oblivious to his surroundings. "Jesus Christ! Her name's Mary! What if that gets out? And our last name is Temple! Like that doesn't sound suspicious! And I don't know who my father was! Fuck, I'm screwed. That's all there is to it. I'm screwed. If I could turn water into wine, I'd get drunk. But no, I can't do that because I'm not Jesus fucking Christ!" The last part he shouted heavenward.

"I'll have to call you back," Randy said into the phone. "Kyle's having a meltdown." Hanging up, he started walking Kyle at a faster pace. "Look, I know you're upset, but I'm sure you don't have that much to worry about. How many people read that shit, anyways?"

Kyle turned to glare at him. "About as many as watch Jerry Springer, I'd imagine!"

"Even so, it wasn't a clear picture. No one's going to realize it's you—"

"They printed my fucking name!"

Randy gestured wide with his arms. "Still, I think we may be overreacting. I don't think people are going to pay much attention to this. After all, the *Crier* has probably been out for days, and this is the first we've heard of it."

"It comes out Tuesday mornings! I know because my mother reads the damn thing religiously!" Kyle winced. "I really have to stop saying things like 'religiously'."

"Still, I'm sure...."

Randy stopped speaking as a boy on a skateboard skidded to a halt in front of them. He stared at Kyle. "Hey, you're the wrestler dude, aren't you? The one that's supposed to be Jesus?"

Kyle let out an inarticulate cry.

"My mom says you should get struck by lightning. She says you're evil."

The kid stepped back onto his board and wheeled away.

Pointing after the boy, Kyle said, his voice hitting a shrill pitch, "You see? People are either going to curse me or ask me to touch their boils and heal them! Randy, I don't think I can touch boils. Things with pus make me want to puke."

Randy spun Kyle around, gripping him by the collar. "Look. We've got to get back to my apartment. Then we'll decide what to do. Shouting out on the street isn't going to do anything except get us noticed, which is exactly what we don't want right now."

Kyle shook his head. "You're right. I'm sorry." They started walking again, but Kyle opened the *Crier* to read some more as they moved along. His lips moved as he read a few lines. Suddenly the color drained from his face and he stopped in his tracks and yelped.

"What is it?" Randy asked. "What else could there possibly be?"

Kyle lowered the paper. "They listed my birthday."

Shrugging, Randy asked, "So? What's so horrible about that? I mean, what could—"

His lip quivering, Kyle told him, "I was born on December 25."

CHAPTER
TWELVE

BACK at Randy's apartment, they spread the *Crier* out onto the dining room table and read the article carefully. "It was your psychiatrist," Randy said, unbelieving. "He's the one that started all this. It says here that he used hypnosis to regress you to a past life, which is when you began to speak in Aramaic. I can't believe a psychiatrist would be party to—"

"Yeah, about that," Kyle said sheepishly. "I've been meaning to tell you. Dr. Bennett isn't so much a psychiatrist. He's more a circus performer."

Randy looked up from the paper. "Pardon?"

"He used to make people cluck like chickens."

Rubbing a weary hand over his face, Randy said, "I'd better stay home today. I'll call Shelly to watch the store. Then we'll call a lawyer and see—"

Kyle's sad eyes made Randy pause as he was reaching for the phone. "Maybe we shouldn't get a lawyer just yet."

"What do you mean?" Randy asked.

"Maybe that might make things worse. You know, a great, big, drawn-out lawsuit might not be the way to go. This thing might blow over in a day or two. Besides, I don't think I could take going to court or something like that. People in suits make me nervous. They remind me of funerals."

Randy bit his lip thoughtfully. "You know, you might be right. By the time the next issue of the *Crier* comes out, this will be old news. No one will care." He slid a loving arm around Kyle's waist. "It won't be easy this week, though. I bet the phone at your apartment is ringing off the hook. Luckily, no one will think of looking for you here. This just means you'll have to spend the week with me."

"So there is one good thing to come out of this."

Randy nodded. "Yeah, there sure is. We'll just hide away in here, fucking like rabbits, and let the rest of the world go mad. Once it's all over, we'll emerge out of seclusion and go on with our lives."

Kyle kissed him tenderly. "You're really good for me, you know that? I don't know what I'd have done if I didn't have you right now."

"You're good for me too," Randy replied. "Now I'd better call Shelly. After that we can head back to bed. We'll just stay there most of the day. We'll turn off the phone, just in case, and refrain from watching the local news. Just to be safe."

Kyle held him close. "I feel safe already."

Randy found that the best way to really learn about a new boyfriend was to hole up with him in an apartment for a whole day. It was the first time Randy had sat on the couch in only his underwear and socks, cuddling with a similarly clad Kyle, watching *Blue's Clues*. He knew he should find it disturbing that Kyle sang along (off-key) with Joe and his blue cartoon dog, but instead he found it endearing. He'd rather be watching American Movie Classics or something, but as long as Kyle's head was nestled against his chest, he didn't really care. He did, however, draw the line when Kyle wanted to watch a rerun of *Gilligan's Island*. They settled instead for the Syfy Channel and Captain Kirk leading the *Enterprise* to yet another planet of strangely unrealistic-looking rocks. Just as Shatner was defeating the alien menace, the doorbell rang. Kyle shot Randy a worried look.

"Go into the bedroom," Randy whispered. "Shut the door. I'll make sure it's okay."

Once Kyle was out of sight, Randy threw a robe on and looked out the peephole. Standing out in the hall, distorted by the tiny glass, was Monty Sneed. The circus mirror effect made the man's cigar seem larger than his face as well as making his eyes cartoonishly huge. Cautiously, Randy opened the door an inch. "Yes?"

"Is Kyle here? I've been looking for him all day."

Randy shook his head. "Haven't seen him." He started to close the door.

Sneed placed a hand against the wood and kept the door from shutting all the way. "Wait! Wait! I just want to talk with him and let him know that he's still working for me. I thought he might be worried."

Randy paused. Hearing the bedroom door open behind him, he said to Sneed, "Okay, just let me make sure it's okay with—"

"It's okay," Kyle said.

Nodding, Randy took the chain off and let Sneed inside. The small man entered hurriedly, carrying a bag with the JCPenney logo on it. He did a double take when he saw Kyle standing in the living room clad in only patterned jockey shorts and white socks, but he said nothing. Instead he closed the door behind him and made straight for the dining table, where he placed the bag over the still-open *America's Crier*. He sneered when he saw the article. "That rag," he snarled. "I hope you're going to fucking sue."

"I thought maybe it'd be best to just ride it out and let the whole thing die," Kyle said. He joined Sneed at the table. "What's in the bag?"

Sneed waved his hands in the air. "Later. Later. First I want to know how you are. This must be hard for you."

Randy thought the words sounded insincere, but not knowing Sneed all that well, he reserved his judgment.

Kyle shrugged and said, "Once the shock wore off, it wasn't too bad. We've just been in here all day, watching TV. Since no one knew where I was, it hasn't been too bad."

Pointing his cigar at Kyle approvingly, Sneed said, "Good plan. We don't want people bothering you all week. Certainly not when you've got shows this weekend."

Kyle sighed with relief. "When I first saw it, I thought you might fire me."

Sneed made a face. "Please. Who the fuck do you think I am? Some nasty, vile snake only looking out for himself? I care about my wrestlers. You guys are like fucking family to me. That's why I think hiding out here is such a great idea. I mean, I wasn't even mentioned in the article, and they didn't specify Midwest Demolition Wrestling by name, either, which would have been free publicity, but that's neither here nor there. Anyway, what I'm saying is I've had the phone ringing off the hook today. Reporters have been calling trying to get an interview with you. I've had the *Indianapolis Star* call. Hell, I've had the *Chicago Tribune* call. I've even had a call from someone at that religious show on cable. You know, the Reverend Isaac show? Anyway, I've spent all day trying to track you down. Finally I figured this is where you had to be." He looked at Kyle's nearly naked body with arched eyebrows. "I did think you might have some clothes on, but what the hell."

At the mention of reporters, the color faded from Kyle's cheeks. He looked to Randy for support. Randy came over and placed an arm around him. Sneed took a deep puff off his cigar and decided to examine the frayed cuffs of his jacket, obviously uncomfortable with the display of affection.

"We'd prefer that no one find out that Kyle is here," Randy said. "We'd appreciate it if you did your best to keep reporters away. Don't give them my name or anything."

Sneed shook his head, although he kept his eyes lowered. "Fuck, I wouldn't do that. I want to keep you boys safe. What you do in… well, fuck. Anyway, there's no way I'd let reporters get to you. Like I said, you've got shows this weekend. And I think we should capitalize on this shit. Throw it right back in their face. That's why I got this." He indicated the bag.

Kyle picked it up and looked inside. He frowned and looked at Sneed. "What is this?"

"Your new entrance robe. That's what you'll wear coming into the ring."

Kyle yanked a garment from the bag. It was a white terry cloth robe, and someone, presumably Sneed, had ironed letters onto the back. Large black letters spelled out JESUS.

"I can't wear this," Kyle said, aghast. "I'd get lynched. We want to forget this whole thing, not make it worse. There's no way in hell I'd wear this. Hell, I was thinking I'd shave off the beard and mustache, just to be on the safe side, and—"

Hands waving, Sneed said quickly, "Okay, okay, you're right. The robe is a bad idea. We'll forget the robe. But don't shave off the facial hair. That would mean that they won, don't you see? You'd be giving in to them. We'll just go on like nothing has happened. You'll have your matches as normal, and fuck the *Crier* and all the other papers that have been calling."

Tossing the robe back into the bag, Kyle said, "So I get to wear my usual gear? I get to stay the heel?"

"You sure as shit do. You're fighting Murdoch on Friday night, right?"

"I was supposed to, yeah. Saturday night I go against Pete."

Sneed nodded. "I'll check with him and make sure everything is on track. We're at Richmond High School Friday, aren't we? That's good. There should be a good crowd there. I'll get some extra security in, just to be on the safe side."

"I think that would be great," Randy said. "We appreciate anything you can do to help out."

"Like I said," Sneed replied with a crooked grin, "my wrestlers are like fucking family. I don't like assholes messing around with them." As if suddenly remembering something, Sneed reached for the bag and pulled out a glossy photo that Kyle had overlooked when he'd examined the bag. "I brought this along. I though you wouldn't mind autographing it for my mom."

It was a shot of Kyle in gear, braced against the ropes of the ring. Kyle shrugged and took the photo from the promoter. "Sure. I guess I could."

"Could you sign it 'with my blessings' and then your name? I'd really appreciate it." Sneed chomped happily on his cigar.

BOREDOM, coupled with hunger, struck later in the evening. Kyle and Randy showered and dressed, planning on hitting some fast-food drive-through and eating in the car. Not having brought a change of clothes, Kyle found a T-shirt that was large on Randy and tried it on. It was a tight squeeze, but not uncomfortable. After Randy checked to make sure the coast was clear, the two quickly made their way to the street, where Randy's car was parked. They got in and both let out a breath of relief. "So far, so good," Randy said.

"Maybe you're right. Maybe this won't be such a big thing," Kyle said. "If we keep a low profile like this for a few days, I don't think it will be so bad."

"Not as bad as dinner at my parents' house on Thursday, anyway."

"Should we still do that?"

Randy started the car. "I don't see why not. No one's connected you with me as of yet, so as long as we don't go to your apartment, we should be fine. Sneed's going to have extra security in place at the shows. By the end of the week, this shouldn't even be a problem."

Settling back in his seat, Kyle said, "Just to see, why don't we drive by my apartment? See if any reporters are there."

Randy agreed. They drove by slowly, with Kyle's head ducked out of sight. At first Randy thought their worries had been for nothing, but then he saw the small camp of reporters and photographers perched at the base of the steps leading into Kyle's building. One of them craned his neck to check out the passing car, but seeing only Randy, he went back to chatting with his crew.

Randy sped up after he'd turned the corner.

"Well?" Kyle asked, getting back to a seated position. "How bad was it?"

"On a scale of 1 to 10, I'd say 10. Not good."

Kyle sighed. "Shit. All my stuff is in there. I'll have to get my gear at some point before Friday. And I'll need clothes. Let's face it, you're skinny, and if I keep on having to squeeze into your shirts, I'm going to pop some seams."

"I'll get your stuff. They aren't looking for me, just you. Just give me your key and tomorrow I'll go over and grab some things for you."

"You'd do that for me?"

Randy smiled. "Of course."

Kyle's hand rubbed Randy's thigh. "Just be careful. I mean it. You're too skinny. You can't take care of yourself. Without me there to look after you—"

"Hey, I can take care of myself. I've been around for over thirty years now without much mishap. I can certainly do this. How bad could it be?"

CHAPTER
THIRTEEN

RANDY parked around the corner, hoping to find a back entrance to Kyle's building. There was one, but it was also guarded by a contingent of reporters. He decided to use the front and walk in as if he lived there. After all, the other occupants of the building surely were free to come and go as they pleased. He avoided eye contact with the gaggle of newshounds and stepped right up the door. *Made it,* he thought. Then he heard someone shout behind him, "Wait a second, that's Money-Mad Randy!"

Oh, fuck, he thought. *How the hell did someone make that connection? Hell, I've only been Money-Mad Randy for two shows now!* He flung open the door and bolted inside, not daring to look back. He heard shouts and sounds of frantic scrambling, but he ignored them and ran up the stairs to Kyle's second-floor apartment. His hands shook as he tried unsuccessfully to get the key into the lock. Forcing himself to concentrate, he unlocked the door and made it inside. There was a flurry behind him, and as he was slamming the door he heard someone shouting, "Excuse me, Mr. Randy—"

He flipped the lock just in time. Knocks and thumps rattled the wood, and he could hear shouts and exclamations coming from the other side. "Go away!" he shouted.

"We just have a few questions for you!" a female voice shrieked.

"No comment!" he screamed back. Inwardly he cursed the *Crier,* reporters in general, and especially the ex-circus performer who started the whole mess. As more knocks sounded, he put his hands over his ears and made his way to Kyle's bedroom. Finding clothes was no problem. Kyle had them flung everywhere. The floor was littered with dirty laundry, and a pair of boxer shorts even hung over a lamp shade. One blade of the ceiling fan had one of Kyle's white socks hanging off of it.

In the closet, a jumble of clothes, boxes, and empty hangers greeted Randy. He did a quick search and came up with a suitcase. This he quickly filled. Then he sat on the bed and flipped his cell phone open.

Debbie answered on the first ring. "Where the hell have you been?" she demanded. "I've been worried sick."

"I know. I got your messages. We've had the phone switched off and have just been watching TV in my apartment, hiding out. Up until now, I think we were safe, but now someone's twigged onto the fact that I'm Money-Mad Randy, so I doubt if my apartment is safe anymore."

"Where are you now?"

"At Kyle's, getting his stuff. The place is surrounded by reporters, though. I barely made it inside."

"What's the address?" she asked. "I'm coming to get you."

RANDY hadn't heard anything from the reporters for over half an hour, so when a knock sounded at the door, his heart skipped a beat. He carefully checked the peephole. Debbie was there, as well as some other dark shapes behind her he couldn't identify. Cautiously, he asked, "Is it safe? Who's that with you?"

"Bodyguards," she replied. "Jimmy and Pete. You know, your wrestler friends."

Under other circumstances Randy would have come back with something referring to one of them being the barely-out-of-high-school kid she was currently fucking, but he was too relieved she had arrived to bother. He opened the door and let them in. Debbie immediately fell into his arms.

"You look awful," she said, holding his face for examination. "There are circles under your eyes."

"No, really?" Randy said sarcastically. "You try going through something like this and see how much sleep you get. Are they still out there?"

Pete nodded. "They're at the bottom of the steps. Didn't pay any attention to us, though."

"Yeah," Jimmy Murdoch said. "I was kind of upset by that. After all, it was my bloody lip that got the blood all over his hands, and they didn't even—"

"Do you mind if we concentrate on the problem at hand, which is namely getting me out of here in one piece?" Randy asked.

Randy wasn't sure how they accomplished the task, but they got to Debbie's car without undue mishap. Randy himself kept his head down, clutching Kyle's suitcase to his chest like a life preserver. Jimmy Murdoch took the lead, elbowing the more insistent reporters out of Randy's way. One tried to shove a microphone into Randy's face until Murdoch whirled on him, growling, "No comment means no comment. You shove that thing toward him again and I break your finger. You try to touch him and I break your hand."

Randy couldn't see the reporter's reaction, but they made it to the car fairly easily after that. His opinion of Jimmy Murdoch went up a notch.

When they pulled up to Randy's apartment building, they found that another smaller group of reporters had planted themselves by the front door. With Jimmy running interference, they made it inside without any problems. The door shut behind them and Randy breathed a sigh of relief. "This is a nightmare."

The foursome took the elevator up in silence. When Kyle opened the door for them, his face was ashen. "They've found me."

"We know," Randy said, throwing himself into Kyle's arms. "I can't believe they're putting any stock in this stupid story. Surely it'll blow over by tomorrow. I mean, don't they have bank robbers and murderers to report on?"

After he released his boyfriend, Randy was surprised to see Debbie give Kyle a quick hug. "Are you okay, baby?" she asked.

Kyle took it in stride, but then of course he hadn't heard Debbie's numerous diatribes putting down his intellect like Randy had. "I'm fine, I guess. I probably won't sleep for a least a week, though. I've been jabbering to myself the whole time I've been here alone. It was in English, at least. I haven't begun babbling in Aramaic, at least not yet."

Pete and Jimmy in turn each gave him a quick pat on the back. "Dude," Pete asked, "how did all this happen?"

Shrugging, Kyle replied, "You've got me. All I know is that I tried hypnotism to stop smoking, and the next thing I know I'm in a tabloid proclaimed as the reincarnation of Jesus Christ."

Jimmy nodded thoughtfully. "That bites," he said.

"You're telling me. I figure, though, all I have to do is wait things out until next Tuesday when the next issue of the *Crier* comes out. After all, people have short attention spans. That's why they make commercials so short. Did you know that? Otherwise people start to zone out halfway through."

Debbie started to grab a cigarette before remembering Randy's ban on smoking in his apartment. She grimaced. "I'm famished. Got any food?"

"I keep it in a place I call the kitchen. Unlike you, I use my refrigerator to store more than ice cubes," Randy said. "Anyone else hungry? I can make sandwiches."

Everyone claimed to be starving. Randy and Debbie crowded into the kitchen and began to slap together a variety of sandwiches, while the three wrestlers huddled around the television to enjoy a professional wrestling show that was on.

Alone with Randy, Debbie nearly looked contrite. "Okay," she said. "Go ahead and let me have it."

"What do you mean?"

"I gave you hell for dating Kyle, and then I turn around and start fucking Huckleberry Finn out there."

Randy laughed. "Debbie, I'm used to you fucking every straight guy you meet. Granted, usually you check out their bank balance first and make sure they drive a BMW at least, but what the hell? He seems like a nice kid."

She nodded. "He's even younger than Kyle. Did you know that?"

"Yep."

"And you're not going to razz me on that? Hell, I would."

Randy got a plate down to start stacking sandwiches. "I'm above that. Haven't you learned that about me by now? Although I could point out that you once referred to anyone under twenty-five as sexual Bic pens. Good only to use and abuse, and when they're empty you just toss them away."

Debbie bit her lip. "I did say that, didn't I?"

The threesome in the living room let out a shout as some exciting move happened on the show. Debbie smiled wistfully. "It's not like you and Kyle, though. At least not yet. With us it's mostly the sex. Kyle really loves you. You can see it in his eyes and the way he acts around you. Have you noticed he almost stands guard over you when the two of you are out in public? I'm not sure he's even aware he's doing it, but he does. He stands close by, ready to come to your rescue. It's not like that with me and Jimmy. We're just mostly into the fucking."

"Fucking can be good."

She nodded. "Oh, it's good all right. He's in his sexual prime, after all. That boy can rut like a weasel. And I guess he's good for some laughs, but it doesn't go any deeper than that."

"It hasn't even been a week yet." Randy finished another sandwich and piled it onto the plate. "Give it time."

Debbie made a face. "I'm not sure if I want it to develop into something else. How am I supposed to bring him home to meet my parents? They already think I'm loopy on paint fumes. If I bring home a young redneck who thinks getting his teeth kicked in is cool, God only knows what they're going to say. But we shouldn't be chattering on about me. What about you? How are you holding up? Did you boys decide to get a lawyer? I actually do know two or three that I haven't slept with. I'm pretty sure they're gay, which explains the whole haven't-slept-with-me thing, but—"

Randy interrupted. "Kyle thought about it and decided it would be best to let the thing die. After all, it's just the story of the hour. A day or two and it will be something else everyone is rabid over. All we have to do is ride it out."

"For such a dummy, Kyle can be pretty astute. You know, I couldn't believe it when I saw his picture. I'd stopped on the way to work to get a coffee and there he was, a portrait in black and white. I dropped my coffee. That's how shocked I was. I had on white canvas shoes too. I'll have to see if I can dye them or something now."

In the other room, Pete let out a shout and Jimmy hooted.

"I blame the hypnotist," Debbie went on. "He's the one that went to the *Crier* with the story, obviously. Kyle should beat the snot out of him."

"He's an old man. An ex-circus performer, I guess."

"Well, at the very least Kyle should ring the guy's doorbell and run."

Randy picked up the plate, now piled high. "You know, some other guys might have used this publicity for their own gain. Not Kyle. He doesn't want anything to do with it. I respect him for that."

Debbie looked into Randy's eyes. "You really love him, don't you?"

Randy bit his lip. "More than anything."

Smiling, Debbie gave him a quick peck on the cheek. "Things will work out. Just hang in there."

Randy nodded. "Well, right now I'm going out to watch wrestling with my boyfriend and try to pretend that the *Crier* doesn't even exist. What is needed right now is sustenance and dropkicks."

CHAPTER
FOURTEEN

BY WEDNESDAY afternoon things had calmed down quite a bit. Randy and Debbie both went to their respective jobs. Leaving the apartment, Randy only had to dodge one solitary film crew. During a slow period at the store, Shelly cornered Randy at the register. He knew she'd have to give her opinion at some point. A militant lesbian who wore combat boots and kept her hair shorn, Shelly had an opinion about everything and liked to share. "Saw your boyfriend on the Channel 9 news," she said.

Randy smiled. Kyle had agreed to a short interview in which he denounced the *Crier* story. "We recorded it. Kyle's probably at my apartment right now, watching it for the hundredth time. He thought he looked pretty good. And I have to admit, I think he did a good job. A few too many *um*s and *er*s maybe, but he got his point across. And he was still wearing my T-shirt, so he really showed off his muscles. I think that was the part he liked best."

Shelly snorted. "He didn't go far enough."

"What do you mean?"

"He had a perfect opportunity to denounce the straight world and its outdated belief in an all-knowing God."

"He was setting the record straight, not making a political statement. And there are plenty of gays and lesbians who are religious. It's not just a straight concept."

"I did enjoy the bit where he said he didn't want to touch boils because pus made him puke."

Randy sighed. "Yeah, I was rather hoping they'd cut that part out." A customer came up with several books, which Randy hoped would put an end to the discussion. However, as soon as the woman was gone, Shelly began again.

"You know my views on religion—"

"Everyone knows your views on religion, Shelly."

"—and the fact that I want the Pope to be eaten alive by fire ants—"

"A bit extreme, I'd say."

"…but I do believe in reincarnation."

Randy frowned. "What are you getting at?"

"Maybe," Shelly said pointedly, "your boyfriend really is the reincarnation of Jesus."

Randy let out a strangled cry and looked heavenward. "Not you as well!"

"Hear me out. I believe Jesus existed, of course. I don't think anyone disputes that. Of course, I think he was just a carpenter's son who went about the place saying a lot of nice things and people took it to an extreme. Why shouldn't your boyfriend be his reincarnation? After all, I'm the reincarnation of Sarah Goode, who—"

"Was the first witch to be hung at the Salem Witch Trials, yes, I know. You've told me on several occasions. Look, even if I believed in reincarnation, what are the odds that Kyle would be Jesus in a previous life? It's so unlikely!"

"But not impossible."

Randy sighed. "I'm sure Kyle isn't the reincarnation of Jesus, or anyone else, for that matter. Trust me on this. He's just a really sweet guy."

"Sweet? He's a professional wrestler. He hits people with chairs."

"Okay, he's a really sweet guy who hits people with chairs. But he's not Jesus in any way, shape, or form. And another point in my favor, would someone who was the reincarnation of Christ hit people with chairs? Hardly Sunday school behavior."

Shelly didn't look convinced. "Hearing him on the tape, though, I'd have to say…."

Randy looked up sharply. "What are you talking about? When did you hear a tape? What tape?"

"This morning as I was getting ready for work. That Dr. Bennett guy, the one who hypnotized Kyle, was on *Good Morning, Indianapolis* today. He played a tape of Kyle under hypnosis. I have to say, it sounded pretty convincing. They even had a language expert there who translated."

Closing his eyes, Randy muttered, "Oh, shit."

"They suggested getting Kyle on the show, where he could be hypnotized with everyone watching. Just to show there was no trickery."

Randy rubbed his hands over his face in frustration. "Well, that's never going to happen. When is everyone going to get it in their heads that we don't want anything to do with any of this? We just want to get on with our lives. We didn't ask for any of this."

Shelly shrugged. "But if he really is the reincarnation of—"

"He's not," Randy hissed through clenched teeth. "Now, don't we have work to do? Don't we have a shipment to be checked in?"

With another shrug, Shelly left him to worry about Kyle. The lunch he'd had seemed to be jostling around in his stomach, and suddenly Randy had a splitting headache.

THURSDAY night Kyle was in good spirits. He seemed to have temporarily forgotten about the *Crier*, the tapes, and everything connected with his "reincarnation" and instead concentrated on picking out just the right shirt for dinner at the Stone residence. "I don't want to look too dressed up," he said, putting yet another shirt back into Randy's closet. "You know, I don't want to be seen as trying to suck up. On the other hand, I don't want to show up in another wrestling T-shirt. This time I plan to win your mother over."

Randy smiled and nuzzled his face against Kyle's ear. "Don't strain yourself. I haven't won her over and I came out of her womb. That shirt there should be fine."

Kyle stood back and examined the closet. "You know, my clothes look really good hanging next to yours."

"It does look right, doesn't it?"

"Maybe we should make this a permanent arrangement."

Randy's head shot up from Kyle's shoulder. "Are you suggesting that you move in?"

"I think it's time," Kyle replied. "I mean, if we can get through this whole Jesus mess, we can get through anything. And I should move in here, since your apartment is bigger and nicer and I know you wouldn't live in mine in any case."

"Maybe because of the nightly drive-by shootings and the bugs."

"Besides, I'm here most nights anyways."

"This is true. What will your mom say? I have the feeling I already know how mine will react."

"Mine won't care. We can tell her this weekend. We can drive out and take her to lunch on Saturday. She needs to get out more, anyway." Kyle pulled a shirt out of the closet and held it against his bare chest, examining it critically. "This one's not bad. Do you think we should bring the tape of me on TV, or do you think your parents have already seen it?"

CHAPTER
FIFTEEN

MRS. STONE bore a huge grin as she opened the front door. "Boys! You're here! I'm so glad!"

Randy blinked and looked past her into the foyer, half expecting to see an alien pod there containing his real mother. He narrowed his eyes as she pulled him into a hug.

"Mom?"

"What, dear?"

"Why are you smiling like that? It's kind of creeping me out."

She held him at arm's length, shaking her head. The smile stayed in place as if plastered there. "I am always like this when I see my two favorite young men."

"The last time I saw you smile this broadly was when Ford pardoned Nixon. And what do you mean 'always'? This is only the second time you've seen Kyle. Are you sure you're feeling okay?"

"I'm fine, dear." She turned to beam at Kyle. "And there's our future son-in-law, the wrestler. Come here." She and Kyle embraced.

Randy had to grab hold of the doorframe to keep from falling over. He knew he was awake, but surely he had to be in some sort of parallel universe where his mother was nice and actually liked the guys he dated. He did note with more than a little satisfaction that Kyle's hug was as exuberant as always, resulting in Mrs. Stone being lifted off her feet. Randy thought he even heard her back crack a little.

He decided if his father hugged them both, they were going to leave immediately and call the men with the white coats to come and get his parents.

When she was released from Kyle's bear hug, Mrs. Stone's smile faltered just for a second. "My, you do have some muscles, don't you, Kyle?"

Kyle looked sheepish. "Sorry, I get carried away."

She punched him on the arm, the sight of which caused Randy's eyes to bulge. "Nothing to be sorry about. You're a strong boy. I'm sure you've got to be, throwing those big wrestlers all over the ring. My husband was showing me the website for your promotion. Midwest Demolition Wrestling, I think it's called? They've got some lovely pictures of you on it. Mr. Stone and I are planning on coming to your show tomorrow night."

Randy's mouth fell open. "What? No, you can't...." The thought of his parents seeing him as Money-Mad Randy was not something he even wanted to contemplate. "Don't you have... drinking to do, or something?"

Mrs. Stone chuckled. "Darling, we wouldn't miss it for the world. Do you think you'll win tomorrow night's match, Kyle?"

"I already know I will. I win most of my matches," Kyle replied, trying to look modest. "Even when I lose, I usually come back and beat up on the winner. I'm the bad guy, you see."

"Oh," Mrs. Stone purred, patting Kyle's cheek. "How could they make such a sweet boy into the bad guy? I'll have to have words with the man who runs the show."

Kyle shrugged. "I kind of like being the bad guy. It's my thing, really."

Mrs. Stone seemed not to hear. "Well, why are we standing here in the doorway chatting about it? Come inside, boys. I've got some people I'd like you to meet."

She led them to the living room, where a small cocktail party was taking place. Several middle-aged couples were standing around the room, engrossed in conversations. The men were all dressed in suits, and the women seemed to have their best dresses on. Randy noticed his father off to the side, talking animatedly to a smallish man and a horse-faced woman. They were near the small bar that the Stones rarely used, which was being manned by a young Hispanic person wearing a white coat. They hired a bartender? Randy had a sick feeling in his stomach. *What the hell is going on?*

Mrs. Stone stood between Kyle and Randy, her arms around their waists. "Everyone," she announced loudly, "I want you to meet our special guests for the evening. This is my son, Randy." She reached up and tousled his hair, then released him and threw both arms around Kyle. "And this is Mr. Kyle Temple."

The horse-faced woman gasped and looked as if she might swoon. Several other people clapped their hands.

"Mom," Randy whispered, "who are all these people?"

"They're from our church group," she told him. "Let me introduce you to Reverend Toll and his wife." She brought the couple over to the short man and Horse Face. "Reverend, Agnes, this is my son and his boyfriend, Kyle."

The couple completely ignored Randy, instead gazing rapturously at Kyle. The small man shook Kyle's hand enthusiastically. "It's such a pleasure, my boy."

A confused Kyle replied, "Um... yeah. A pleasure."

Mrs. Toll was clutching a small black book to her bosom. Randy thought she looked like a rabid Elvis fan finally meeting up with her idol. Gushing like a schoolgirl, she pushed the book into Kyle's hands. "Would you mind autographing this?"

Kyle frowned. "It's a Bible."

Mr. Toll took the volume back, smiling gently at his wife. "Now, Agnes, don't embarrass the boy."

"You're kidding me, right?" Kyle asked. "You really wanted me to sign... oh, come on."

Randy's laugh was hollow. "This is incredible. I don't know what my mother's said, but Kyle is definitely not—"

Quickly, Mrs. Stone yanked Kyle away. "We must let everyone get a chance to meet you. I'm sure the reverend will have some questions for you after dinner." She led Kyle over to another group while Randy turned to his father, who was contentedly sipping what looked to be whiskey.

"Dad, what the hell do you guys think you're doing?"

Mr. Stone smiled and took another sip. "We're having a catered do, son. I can't believe your mother suggested it, but I'm fine with it. I don't have to lift a finger, and this is Glenfidditch I'm drinking. Glenfidditch. And your mother doesn't even care. Usually she doesn't let me drink anything other than wine, feeling that hard liquor is somehow not sophisticated enough. Tonight she hired in caterers and a bartender, and I'm allowed to drink whatever I want. Life has suddenly become pretty good, and it's all because of that boy you're seeing. In my mind he's a keeper. Latch onto that one. He makes your mother happy, and God knows that's not an easy task."

Like most of the couples in the room, the Tolls had moved closer to where Mrs. Stone was showing off Kyle, so Randy had his father all to himself. He groaned in frustration. "She couldn't stand Kyle just a week ago, and suddenly he's her golden boy. It's all because of that stupid story in the *Crier*. We didn't have a thing to do with that! The whole idea is ridiculous. Kyle isn't anyone's reincarnation, least of all that of Jesus Christ."

Mr. Stone made a face. "Of course he isn't. But it makes your mom happy to parade him in front of her friends, so let people think he is. What does it hurt?"

Throwing his arms up, Randy nearly shouted, "It hurts us, that's who! All we get are calls from reporters and weirdos, and sometimes weirdo reporters."

Having finished his drink, a grinning Mr. Stone turned to the bartender. "Another one of these, please, my man." As his drink was being refreshed, his father said, "I'm sure it's been a little difficult for you, son. But this will blow over quickly, believe me. It's that whole Andy Warhol thing. This is your friend Kyle's moment in the spotlight. He should enjoy it. Capitalize on it. Use it to his advantage. Just like I'm using your mother's temporary insanity over it to my advantage to down as much scotch as I possibly can. Enjoy it while it lasts." He took his glass back from the bartender. "Thanks, my man."

"But we can't capitalize on this!"

"Why not? Get your friend a book deal or a TV movie of the week while this is still hot. Rake in the dough while you can."

A bit of the fire went out of Randy as he thought of what a book deal could mean not only to Kyle but to his bookstore as well. "But isn't it unethical to make money off of this? Especially when Kyle and I know that he's not the reincarnation of Jesus?"

Mr. Stone chuckled and put an arm around Randy. "Son, you don't have to be unethical. This is something you can be honest about and still make good. Have him tell his story. Deny everything. The people who believe that he's Jesus are still going to believe he is, and those who don't will praise him for his honesty. Hell, they'll even feel sorry for him if it's handled right. Look at Reverend Toll over there. Do you think he really believes that your boyfriend is Jesus Christ? That Jesus puts on tights and climbs into a ring to beat up people? Of course he doesn't. He's playing it cool, though. Hedging his bets. He can always laugh it off as a joke later. His wife, however, thinks the whole thing is gospel, pardon my pun. Look at her. She hasn't taken her eyes off Kyle for a second. I wouldn't be surprised if she fainted if he touched her."

Randy's shoulders slumped. "I just keep thinking this will all be over in a few days."

"That's possible. Then again, it might not be. That's why I'd suggest getting your hunky friend a book deal or something while it's still news. You fellows might as well get something out of this."

Looking at his father, Randy managed a smile. "You called him hunky. Do I detect a little admiration from an ex-military man?"

Mr. Stone grinned. "He's a nice boy. You could do worse. He makes me laugh. That whole business with him trying to pretend to be an air traffic controller! I got a good chuckle over that. The boy's dumber than a box of rocks, but he's sweet natured, and he obviously loves you." Mr. Stone sighed and then took a large gulp of his scotch. "I never wanted my only son to be… well, a homosexual. But if you've got to be one—"

"And I do."

"Then you could do worse than Kyle over there. Like I said, he's a good kid."

"Wow," Randy said, blinking. "This from a lifelong Republican and right-winger. Mom should let you have scotch more often."

Mr. Stone laughed. "There might be something to that. Maybe that's what this country needs. A little understanding, a little Glenfidditch, and a lot of unclenching."

Kyle found his way back to Randy, an embarrassed smile plastered across his face. "Those people are crazy. Not only did Mrs. Toll have me autograph her Bible, but one guy even asked me if I had trouble swimming, what with the walking on water and all. I think he had Jesus confused with The Flash, 'cause when The Flash gets running really fast, he doesn't break the water tension, so…."

Randy kissed his boyfriend. "Jesus did sort of the same thing."

"Really? I never heard he could run fast like that. Jesus was kind of like the world's first superhero, then, wasn't he?"

Mr. Stone raised his glass in a toast. "He was at that, my friend. You've hit the nail right on the head."

Randy did note that he'd just kissed Kyle in a room full of religious types, most of them probably Republicans, and there wasn't a flicker of anger or outrage. The Reverend Toll had been looking their way, and his only reaction was a smile. Mrs. Toll continued to follow Kyle's every move with rapt attention

Just then Mrs. Pitcairn entered the living room and cleared her throat loudly. "May I have your attention, please," she shouted. "Dinner is served." She turned, and Randy heard her mutter under her breath, "And for once, I didn't have to lift a finger to make it."

Mrs. Stone swooped over to take Kyle by the arm. "I'd be so happy if you'd escort me into the dining room."

"It would be my pleasure, Mrs. Stone."

They led the way into the dining room. On entering, Randy stopped suddenly in the doorway, causing the Reverend Toll to bump into him. The table leaves had been added to make the dining table as long as possible, and chairs had been placed at either end and all along one side, but the side facing the door was totally chairless.

Mrs. Stone was ushering Kyle to the central seat. "You sit here, dear."

"What the hell are you doing?" Randy demanded.

Mrs. Stone looked up at him. "What do you mean?"

"Why are there no chairs on this side?"

She looked at her son as if he were an idiot. "I just thought Kyle would be used to this sort of setup. I mean, we've all seen the picture. This is how they used to sit back then."

Randy groaned. "This is too much. You've gone completely and utterly mental."

His mother looked hurt. "Don't be mean, dear. This is all for your boyfriend, after all. To celebrate the two of you getting together. Look, I even got him a special cup for the occasion. Isn't it pretty?" She smiled at Kyle, holding the gold wine glass. "Would you care for a chardonnay, dear?"

CHAPTER
SIXTEEN

MIKE RASHKA was, at the moment, not a happy man. For one, he was already sweating like a pig, and he hadn't even walked out under the hot television studio lights yet. The makeup girl, a pretty young thing named Brittney, had offhandedly patted his face down with some sort of sponge and declared him camera ready. Rashka was sure that whatever she had applied had long since washed away with the rivulets of perspiration. Makeup was only the smallest part of his problem, however. What worried him was the beating of his heart, which seemed dangerously fast and loud to him. He glanced over at Bennett, who was sitting on a small couch, looking calm and collected. Rashka wanted to kick him. Why had be agreed to come on *Good Morning, Indianapolis* anyway? Bennett was the showman. He was used to speaking before an audience and even thrived on it. The only audience Rashka ever spoke in front of was his history students during lectures, and they usually slept through them. Rashka glared angrily at the No Smoking sign and bit his fingernails.

"My dear boy," Bennett said in his faux British accent, "do calm down. You're pacing like a child who has to potty."

Rashka paused. "I do. Did you happen to notice where the closest one is?"

Bennett chuckled. "The show has already begun. There isn't time, I'm afraid. They should be coming to get us any moment now. The whole show is only a half an hour long, and we go on after the cooking demonstration. It'll all be over before you know it."

"You go on without me. I don't think the university will like me endorsing this in any case. I really shouldn't be involved."

"You're already involved," Bennett told him. "It was your translation that got us calling the *Crier*. Relax. I'll do most of the talking. I did the show the other day, and the host was rather pleasant. Sweet girl. Very red hair. I'm sure it's not her natural color, but it was very becoming on her."

"Screw the host and her red hair!" Rashka bellowed, throwing his hands up in disgust. "What good is her hair if I shit in my pants out there, or die of a heart attack? Tell me that!"

Bennett's eyes shone. "I wouldn't mind screwing her, but I think she might object. I don't know why you're so nervous. Not that many people watch this show. I think they only have it on to fill airspace. They must have trouble getting guests to even come on, or else they wouldn't have asked me back in the same week. Granted, I have a marvelous speaking voice and can command an audience, but—"

The makeup girl, Brittney, popped her head into the green room. "It's time," she said cheerily. "You're on right after we come out of commercial break."

Rashka tottered on his feet. Slowly, Bennett got up and patted his friend on the back. "Just follow my lead. This is a piece of cake, believe me."

Gulping loudly, Rashka followed Bennett and Brittney down the short corridor to the studio. There, he was aware of lights and people moving about, but his senses couldn't focus on any one thing. It was all a blur. Someone deposited him next to Bennett on a comfortable leather couch on the familiar *Good Morning, Indianapolis* set. He blinked, focusing his gaze on the host, Emma Olsen (she of the suspect red hair). She sat a little forward, visible to the tiny studio audience but also placed to see her guests. Olsen, all smiles whenever he'd tuned in to the show, looked annoyed. Brittney was behind her, fluffing the woman's curls. "Stop pawing me," Olsen growled.

A young man standing near the cameras shouted, "Out of commercial in ten, nine...."

Brittney fluttered off the set and Olsen's face exploded into a cheery grin. When the young man signaled, she purred into the camera, "Welcome back. We have with us again Dr. Carl Bennett, the hypnotist who used past life regression on a local professional wrestler with amazing results. Today he's joined by noted historian and language expert, Professor Michael Rashka."

At the words "noted historian," Rashka suddenly perked up. He liked how the phrase sounded. Immediately the butterflies in his stomach subsided and he beamed at the camera. "I'm hardly a language expert, Emma," he said smugly. "I'd classify myself as a language enthusiast."

Olsen leaned forward intently. "And when did you become involved in this controversy?"

Rashka steepled his fingers together and crossed his legs theatrically. "Knowing my interest in languages, my old friend Carl Bennett here contacted me right after his second session with the Temple lad. It didn't take me long to recognize the language as Aramaic. The rest was fairly simple."

"And what is your professional opinion? Do you really believe that this young wrestler is, as some are saying, the reincarnation of Jesus himself?"

Rashka gave an exaggerated shrug. "I leave the hypothesizing to others. I can only state categorically that the tapes played to me were biblical quotes in Aramaic. I can certainly see where someone could draw the reincarnation conclusion."

Bennett cleared his throat. "As the only person to witness the sessions, I must also point out that the boy seemed to go through a physical change as well. The second session I had with him in fact worried me. I was afraid for him. He seemed to be in his death throes. I didn't know at the time that what he was speaking were the words and phrases generally associated with Christ on the cross. Which is why"—here Bennett looked seriously into the camera—"I again challenge this young man, Kyle Temple, to come forward and be put under hypnosis on this show. We can even arrange to have a translator with us. Let's find out once and for all just what is going on with Mr. Temple."

RANDY'S lunch of a hamburger and fries was going largely untouched. Debbie looked at him from across the tiny table in the crowded fast-food joint. She pointed to his fries. "Are you going to eat those?"

Her words broke Randy out of his reverie.

"Huh? No, I guess not."

"You're gathering enough wool to make a sweater. What's wrong? Well, besides the obvious."

Sighing, Randy said, "My father thinks we should capitalize on Kyle's sudden fame before it all dies out. My mother had us over for dinner last night to meet chums of hers from church. Kyle even had to autograph a Bible for the minister's wife."

Despite Randy's dour look, Debbie chuckled. "You've got to admit, that's pretty crazy. How's Kyle taking it?"

"You know Kyle. As long as he gets to wrestle, he really doesn't care. He's at the gym working out today. Sneed says he'll have extra security at the match tonight, but I'm not sure that it's going to be enough. After all, you saw how caught up in the whole spectacle those crowds can be. A mild-mannered accountant suddenly became a fist-wielding maniac. What are they going to make out of this? It could get ugly, but there's no way I could ask Kyle to give up wrestling. He loves it too much."

"Maybe things won't be as bad as you envision," Debbie said, munching one of Randy's fries. Her own food had long since vanished. "What does Sneed mean by extra security?"

Randy shrugged. "Who knows? I didn't even know he had security to begin with. There's that smart-assed kid who takes the tickets. Other than Sneed himself, the announcers, the refs, and the wrestlers, he seems to be the only other employee of MDW. If that's Sneed's idea of security, we're in big trouble."

"The other wrestlers will be there. Jimmy and the others. They'll look after Kyle."

"That's true. I can't help but worry, though. And I still can't get over my mother. I should have known something was brewing when she was being so nice about Kyle. One minute he's not good enough for me, and the next he's her golden boy and she's welcoming him as he future son-in-law. And then there's my dad's suggestion of making money off this. The weird thing is, he sort of made sense. I'm just not sure about it, though. It seems wrong to capitalize on something that we not only want no part of but also didn't ask for. On the other hand, this could be a jump start for Kyle's career. What do you think?"

Debbie took another fry. "Your father could be right. Your mother's insane, I've always said that, but your father is one smart cookie. Other people are raking in dough over this, I guess. The *Crier*'s sold out all over town. I did a Google search on my computer last night, and you wouldn't believe how many Kyle Temple websites have sprung up. People are selling pictures of him from his matches. There's even a Kyle Temple fan club now, apparently."

"Websites?" Randy asked, aghast. "I hadn't even thought of checking that out. Were they all positive?"

Debbie made a face. "I didn't check them all out, but I did see one blog that suggested that Kyle should be stoned to death on Monument Circle."

Randy rolled his eyes. "Just what I want to hear. I'm already seeing weirdoes on every street corner and enraged religious freaks in every shadow. Maybe we should have gotten a lawyer in the first place."

"Might have made the situation worse."

"True. It's not like we've got much to compare this to, though. To my knowledge, Kyle is the first pro wrestler to be accused of being the reincarnation of Jesus Christ."

Debbie nodded sagely. "I think we can safely assume that."

Randy took a slurp of his soda. There wasn't much left, so he ended up sucking in mostly air. "So what's new with your new beau?"

"He's fine," she answered, looking like she was somewhat disappointed in her reply. "I mean, the sex is marvelous still, but now we're getting to that what-do-we-talk-about stage."

"It's been a week. You're already at that stage? Christ, and I thought fags moved quickly."

"You of all people shouldn't use Christ as an epithet any longer. Anyway, about me and Jimmy. We were talking about going to a movie tomorrow afternoon, and he won't see anything unless someone gets brutally murdered in the first ten minutes. I want to see the new Cameron Diaz flick."

"I don't suppose she brutally murders someone in the first ten minutes, does she?"

"It's unlikely."

"You could always compromise and just stay home and have sex."

Debbie nodded. "Probably the most sensible solution."

Randy picked up the barely eaten burger, examined it carefully, and then set it back down. "What gets me about this whole mess is how unfair it is. I mean, it's sort of malicious. After all, the *Crier* is making money out of it, and I guess now people are selling pictures and God knows what else of Kyle on the Internet, but is anyone really making enough dough off of this to make it even remotely worth it?"

CARL BENNETT smiled as Pepper jumped up and down excitedly at his feet. Bennett held out a doggie treat and the dog dutifully barked. Bennett released the goodie, and Pepper easily caught it in his teeth.

Bennett lit yet another stick of incense and spoke to the dog, who was busy chomping on the treat. "I'm thinking we should get a new couch. And some better curtains over those windows. Something nice and heavy. I think that would give the room a classier look, don't you?"

Pepper didn't answer, being much too occupied.

Gazing into the small mirror by the front door, Bennett took a moment to slick back his hair. He didn't mind what he saw. True, he was old now, but at least he'd grown into that "distinguished" old instead of that "decrepit" old. He still had a lot of years ahead of him, the good Lord willing, and now he could indulge himself a little. He could enjoy his remaining years in style.

Bennett cleared his throat. "Should we let in the first guest, Pepper?"

The dog paused a moment to look at his master and then went back to chewing. Bennett opened the front door. Immediately the crowd in front of his house burst into a noisy frenzy. Bennett smiled, noting that the line of patrons stretched all the way down his walk and nearly to the corner of the street. The middle-aged lady who was first in line burst into tears as Bennett ushered her into the house. As he began to close the door behind her, a collective groan came from the crowd. Bennett paused and beamed at them. "Don't worry. I'll make sure everyone gets a chance for a visit tonight. Just be patient."

Inside, he rubbed his hands together and looked at the woman. "Now, then, what shall it be tonight?"

The woman sniffed and looked up at Bennett with red-rimmed eyes. "I have to be hypnotized. My husband flatly refuses to believe that I'm the reincarnation of Cleopatra."

Bennett patted the woman's shoulder sympathetically. "Some people just don't understand, do they?"

Pepper, his treat finished, decided to hide under the coffee table.

CHAPTER
SEVENTEEN

KYLE was worried.

He wasn't worried about the wrestling match. He never worried about those. In fact, Kyle felt happier and more confident while wrestling than nearly any other time. Before meeting Randy, he'd have said nothing made him happier. Lately—*Crier* stories notwithstanding—he felt the same when he was with Randy as he did in the ring. The tall, skinny (and Kyle never thought he'd be attracted to a skinny guy until he met Randy) bookstore manager made Kyle feel that maybe, just maybe, there was a chance for him outside the world of wrestling.

And looking at Randy as he shuffled into the oversize suit to become Money-Mad Randy, Kyle felt his worry grow. Randy's face was pale, and the guy seemed to jump at every sound. When Jimmy Murdoch banged his gym bag down onto the bench, Randy nearly leaped out of his skin. Kyle asked him if anything was wrong, but of course Randy replied that there wasn't.

Kyle placed his foot up on the wooden bench to finish lacing his boot. Randy, having finished dressing, sat staring at a locker. Kyle wished he knew what to say. After all, didn't Randy know he was there to look after him? There was no way in hell Kyle would let any harm come to his boyfriend. Didn't Randy understand that?

Just as Kyle finished lacing his other boot, the locker room door opened and Monty Sneed entered. A large unlit cigar was firmly grasped between the man's teeth. Seeing Kyle, the promoter beamed. "Full house tonight," he announced. "Fuck, we've got 'em stuffed into the top of the bleachers. Biggest crowd we've ever had, and they're here to see you, my boy." He slapped Kyle's shoulder. The resulting smack of skin on skin made Randy jump.

Kyle wished Randy were in a more communicative mood. He really needed Randy to help him sort out just how he felt about this. Kyle was undecided. Part of him (and he had to admit it was a pretty big part) was thrilled that not only would he be wrestling in front of the biggest audience of his career, but he'd also have the coveted main bout to do it in. He and Jimmy had never wrestled in the main bout. Another part of him, though, was saddened that it took a bogus story in *America's Crier* to bring the whole thing about. Was it wrong to enjoy something brought about by happenstance? Kyle honestly didn't know.

Randy finally seemed to come to life as Sneed, standing right under a No Smoking sign, brought a match up to his cigar. "What about the extra security you promised?" he asked.

Sneed grinned. "Already in place. I got the school's football team to be security. Didn't even have to pay them. Just let them in for free."

"That's your security?" Randy sounded doubtful. "A bunch of football players who have no training that you let in free? That's the worst security arrangement since the Hell's Angels at Altamont."

He got blank looks from both Sneed and Kyle. He looked down at Jimmy Murdoch, who was pulling on his socks. Jimmy shrugged.

"It's a cultural reference, guys," Randy explained. "A rock festival back in the sixties where the Rolling Stones hired… never mind. What I'm trying to say is that a bunch of football players aren't going to know what to do if anything goes wrong. They could do more harm than good."

Sneed waved his cigar in the air. "Not a fucking thing is going to go wrong. And those are big, corn-fed Hoosier lads. Just the sight of them is going to keep anyone from doing anything wrong. You've got to learn to relax, boy."

"I'm sure they're big guys, but they have no training in security scenarios. They won't know how to handle anything out of the ordinary. They won't dissuade any crazies. Hell, I'm not sure they'd dissuade me."

Jimmy said matter-of-factly, "They'd dissuade you. Come on, you were almost decked by a middle-aged accountant."

"A fairly big middle-aged accountant, thank you very much," Randy said. "And that's just my point. If a regular joe like that can get out of control at one of these shows, what's to stop some borderline psychopath from totally wigging out? He could take out half the audience before your football team does anything about it. I wouldn't doubt that, after the *Crier* story, there really *is* some freak nut job out there tonight, either."

"Son," Sneed said, placing an arm around Randy's shoulders, "you just worry too much. Have you ever considered Prozac?"

"It'll be okay," Kyle said. He tried to will some of his confidence into Randy. "You'll see. Besides, we go on last. By then we'll be able to gauge the mood of the crowd."

Randy sighed heavily. He didn't seem entirely convinced, but he did say quietly, "Okay."

Surprised, Kyle shook his head. Maybe he did instill some of his confidence into his boyfriend. Not that he thought for a second it had anything to do with the Jesus angle. He knew he didn't have any preternatural powers. He just had an overflow of self-assurance when it came to wrestling, and he was able to project that feeling into Randy. Yeah, that had to be it.

Sneed bit into his cigar happily. "Good boy. Glad we put your fears to rest. Now I'd best be getting back out there and check on the T-shirt sales. There were going like hot cakes the last time I checked."

Jimmy Murdoch ran a hand through his hair as if to put it in place. As the blond-colored strands were thick with product in order to get them to stand straight up, it was a futile gesture. "We got the T-shirts back in? Hell, yeah. We've been out of stock on those for ages."

Sneed's cheeks colored to a deep crimson. "Well, these are some new shirts. Just an idea I had. Seems to be working great, if I do say so myself."

Kyle noticed that Sneed was avoiding both his and Randy's glances. "New shirts? You mean they're different from the ones we've always had."

"That would be the definition of new, yes," Sneed said.

"Do I get one?" Randy asked.

Sneed took the cigar out of his mouth and seemed to examine it carefully. "These are different" was all he said.

Jimmy's voice showed excitement. "Did you have a new logo designed? Do we get to see it?"

"It's not exactly a new logo," Sneed replied. "Well, you're going to see them soon anyway." He opened his jacket to reveal the white T-shirt he wore underneath. It was emblazoned with the same photo of Kyle that had been on the *Crier*'s cover. "Temple" was written under the picture in large black letters.

Randy's mouth dropped open. Kyle and Jimmy merely stared.

"Well," Jimmy said after a short silence, "at least it's a good picture. You always have been photogenic, Kyle. You take a good picture; I'll say that for you."

"Were you going to tell us about these at some point?" Randy asked.

Sneed closed his jacket back up. "Yeah, I was, but then you seemed so put out about the football team I didn't want to add to your mood. I thought I'd give you some time to cool off before telling you."

"Don't you have to ask Kyle's permission to do something like this? After all, that's his picture—"

"As long as Kyle wrestles for Midwest Demolition, we can use his likeness for any sort of advertising or promotion." Sneed started for the door, pausing only to tell Randy, "Don't worry. I plan on giving him a bonus for all the extra stuff we're selling. The eight by tens we're selling off the website alone are worth a bonus. This boy's become our cash cow."

MRS. STONE, looking overdressed in her midlength red dress adorned with a rope of pearls, stood behind her husband as he paid for their tickets. Behind the Stones in line was a young couple, probably not even out of their teens. The boy wore a somewhat grimy white T-shirt and jeans. The girl had on a maternity top and sweatpants. She looked due at any moment. In her arms was a squirming toddler who kept reaching up to yank at Mrs. Stone's hair.

"Two, please," Mr. Stone said to the ticket seller.

The sullen kid took Mr. Stone's money and slid across the tickets. He indicated Mr. Stone's immaculate dark-blue suit. "Enjoy the show. You just came from a funeral, I take it?"

Mr. Stone frowned. "No, why would you think that?"

"The monkey suit." The kid nodded as if suddenly understanding. "Oh, you're with the Mob, then. That's cool. I figured it was only time before the Mob decided to get their fingers into this racket."

Mr. Stone brushed a hand down the front of his dark jacket, suddenly feeling very noticeable. "No, we're here for our son. Do you know when Kyle Temple is wrestling?"

Mrs. Stone tried pretending to straighten her hair and gently smacked the toddler's hand away. The mother was oblivious.

"That's the main event," the kid said, sounding bored. "He's your son?"

"No," Mr. Stone explained. "Our son is his manager, I guess."

"Well, you can get some T-shirts at the concession stand. I don't recommend getting the popcorn. It's usually pretty stale. The nachos are fresh, though."

Mr. Stone nodded grimly. "I'll bear that in mind. Thank you." He looked at the tickets. "Does someone show us to our seats?"

The kid gave him a deadpan look. "Sorry, milord. The butlers have all gone on strike. The seats are mostly full and there are no reserved seats, so you'll have to rough it at the top of the bleachers. That's okay, though. The blood rarely splashes that far up, and you wouldn't want to ruin the Brooks Brothers special."

Mrs. Stone led her husband into the gym area, mostly to get away from the hair-tugging brat. "It doesn't matter, Neil. I'm sure anywhere we sit will be fine."

Scanning the crowd, Mr. Stone spied an area that looked likely. He sighed, not relishing the climb to the top of the bleachers. As he started to move, however, his wife tugged at his sleeve.

"Before you find us some seats," she said, "do you think you could get me one of those T-shirts?" She indicated a Temple shirt on a rotund woman nearly.

Mr. Stone sighed again and reached for his wallet.

DEBBIE had arrived early, having come in with Jimmy Murdoch, so she had a folding chair right in front of the ring. A young family was seated next to her. She assumed the husband was a farmer. He was either a farmer or he'd bathed himself in Eau de Pig. His wife was doing her best to make sure their three kids behaved. The youngest, a boy of about four, fidgeted in his chair and loudly demanded popcorn. His lips bore the remains of the chocolate bar he'd just consumed.

"You don't need no damn popcorn," his mother chastised. When she spoke, she revealed the absence of a front tooth. "Tell him he don't need no popcorn, Henry."

The man snorted loudly. "You don't need no goddamn popcorn."

"Eat your other candy," the mother said.

"Don't like it," the youngster whined. "It's licorice. I don't like licorice." He pronounced it lick-rish.

"Then give it to your brother. Maybe he'll trade you some of his malted milk balls."

The boy stuffing his mouth with malted milk balls just shook his head violently.

Debbie settled back in the uncomfortable folding chair and sighed. Under her breath, she said, "You date lawyers and you go to the opera. You date pro wrestlers and you spend your evenings with the cast from *Hee Haw*."

JEFF HARDESTY had also arrived early. He'd found a chair on the opposite side of the ring from Debbie and was once again in the midst of a group of drunk teenagers. He wasn't sure if they were the same teens from the previous show, but either way they annoyed Hardesty. He did notice with a smile that two of them wore white T-shirts with Kyle Temple's picture on them.

The one seated next to him was on the edge of his seat. Hardesty noticed that his underwear was showing, which was probably not by accident. With young kids, Hardesty knew, showing your underwear was a fashion statement. But surely it should be clean underwear that didn't show brown stains? The kid spoke overly loud to his friends. "This is going to kick ass!"

The others hooted in agreement. One raised his cup into the air and screamed, "Start the fucking show!"

As if in response, the tinny music began to play over the loudspeakers. The crowd went wild. The sounds of chanting and yelling nearly deafened Hardesty. He winced as the announcer began to speak.

"Welcome, ladies and gentlemen, to the Brownstown High School gymnasium for Midwest Demolition Wrestling!"

Making sure his camera was ready for more shots of Kyle Temple, Hardesty settled back and did his best to ignore the throng around him.

MRS. STONE didn't know if she was going to last to the end of the show. For one thing, the hard wood of the bleachers was beginning to make her butt go numb. The two young girls seated next to her were maybe thirteen or fourteen and had kept up a running dialog about how dreamy Kyle Temple was and how much they'd like to meet him.

Mr. Stone was taking everything in stride. He decided to view the whole adventure as a cultural study, so he was watching the crowd and their reactions to the antics in the ring. He had counted over twenty Temple T-shirts in their vicinity alone.

Mrs. Stone leaned closer to him and muttered, "What's going on in the ring now?"

Mr. Stone looked down. "It appears to be two scantily clad women busy pulling each other's hair."

"Surely that's not legal. They must have rules for these matches! Why doesn't the referee stop them?"

"Well, the women are both bigger than him, for one thing," Mr. Stone replied. "They do have rules, of course. The main rule is to entertain the crowd. And I'd say they're doing a good job of that. See that guy down there? He's nearly spilling his popcorn, that's how excited he is. I never realized that these wrestling shows are a group phenomena. You've got to see one of these shows live to really appreciate them. The crowd is half the show."

"But they're all yelling and screaming and just generally acting poorly."

Mr. Stone smiled. "It's the Coliseum. The modern day equivalent, in any case. Better in many ways, since at least here no one gets fed to a lion, but the audience gets the same thrill. I'm beginning to have more respect for Randy's boyfriend."

Mrs. Stone grimaced. "But they had midgets, Neil. How degrading."

"For whom? Those two midgets beat the snot out of that other guy."

Mrs. Stone tried shifting from one butt cheek to the other to see if that felt better. It didn't. "I just hope Kyle and Randy come out soon. I don't think I can sit here much longer."

Glancing quickly at his watch, Mr. Stone told her, "I'd bet they're up next."

"There seem to be people with large pieces of cardboard in the crowd. What are those?"

"I've spotted them too," Mr. Stone said, nodding. "I think they're signs, but I haven't seen anyone hold one up yet, so I don't know what they say."

Mrs. Stone shifted again in her attempt to keep her ass from going totally numb. Next to her, one of the girls was gushing. "What if he kissed you? What would you do?"

Her friend squealed. "Oh, God, I'd just die. Could you imagine? I bet he's a good kisser too. You can tell. He's got kissable lips."

"And those muscles," the first girl said, sighing deeply. "Not too big and not too small. Just right. I think I'm going to marry him."

"Nuh-uh," the other girl said, clearly offended. "He's mine if he's anybody's."

Mrs. Stone thought about telling them that the object of their affection was actually more likely to marry her son, but she didn't want to start an argument with girls still in braces. She instead tuned the girls out, concentrating instead on thinking of the words she'd use to invite Randy and Kyle to church services of Sunday. Sitting there with Kyle, she'd be the envy of every person in the church. Thinking of that brought a smile to Mrs. Stone's face, and she temporarily forgot about the numbness of her posterior.

THE match between the two women wrestlers ended with one of them being carried out of the ring by her boyfriend/manager. The crowd cheered as he lugged her seemingly lifeless form through the ropes and off to the changing rooms. An expectant hush fell over the audience as the announcer began to speak.

"And now for the main event of the evening."

A collective roar came from the crowd. It was an ear-splitting boom of sound that threatened to shake loose the foundations of the gymnasium.

It was time for Kyle Temple to make his appearance, and the crowd knew it.

CHAPTER
EIGHTEEN

KYLE was stunned as he stepped out of the locker room with Randy close behind him. The sound of the crowd was like a tidal wave: beautiful yet dangerous. He couldn't believe the noise was for him, but he knew it was. There was a short hallway leading from the locker room to the gym, and Kyle could see people jumping up and down with excitement, awaiting his arrival.

"Dear God," Randy muttered under his breath.

Kyle gave him an encouraging grin. "Don't worry. This is just the usual thing, only bigger. If I'm ever going to wrestle for the big time like the UWE, I've got to get used to this kind of thing." He took a deep breath and changed his walk to the confident swagger of the wrestling heel he portrayed every weekend. Behind him, he knew, Randy was trying desperately to copy Kyle's bluster.

When he hit the gym, the screams of the crowd increased, something Kyle wouldn't have thought possible. He put a scowl across his features and walked purposefully toward the ring, trying his best to block out the shouts and cries of the crowd. People were stretching out their hands, trying to get just a touch of his skin. Kyle nearly faltered when he saw the first T-shirt with his picture on it, but he thought of his hero, the unstoppable Bob "Crusher" Phillips. The vision of that muscular giant enabled him to move forward.

Kyle blinked when he saw a sign being held up by a young fan. The kid was shaking with excitement, making the sign a little hard to read, but Kyle finally managed to make out the words GIVE 'EM HELL, JESUS! As the words sunk in, Kyle slowed his pace. He felt Randy's hand on his back and then heard his boyfriend murmur into his ear, "Ignore it."

That was even better than thinking of "Crusher" Phillips. Just the touch of Randy's hand was all he needed. He increased his pace, feeling the adrenaline kick in. He imagined soaking in the energy from the crowd like a sponge and using it to fuel his performance. Suddenly he was no longer Kyle Temple but a professional wrestler who was on top of the world. Kyle was glad he was going against Jimmy Murdoch, since he knew Jimmy could take whatever was dished out to him. Jimmy was a brick. The kid lived to be thrown around the ring. And tonight Kyle was going to throw him about like a rag doll. Tonight was going to be Kyle's best performance ever.

Climbing into the ring, Kyle noticed several other signs dotted about the crowd. He couldn't read them all, but he did see KILL THE FUCKER, JESUS inscribed across one. Kyle wondered briefly if the person holding the sign had quite grasped the message of the New Testament. Several signs, mostly held by scantily clad girls, simply read WE LOVE YOU, JESUS. Kyle frowned even harder in an attempt to send a message to the audience. He was the heel, dammit. They weren't supposed to love him.

Ignore them, he told himself, *like Randy said. Just do what you do best. You can't control the crowd, but you can control what you do in the ring. Just give them the best show they've ever seen. That's what you're here to do.*

Randy took his leather jacket from him and said something. Kyle couldn't hear him over the noise around them, so he shook his head. Randy tried again, louder this time. "You're the best. Remember that. Don't let this other stuff distract you."

Kyle nearly forgot the scowl and almost smiled. He remembered his character in time and simply nodded to Money-Mad Randy. He did allow himself a small wink at his boyfriend.

The bell sounded.

Kyle took a second to take in his surroundings. Across the ring from him, dressed in his usual ghetto garb of baggy shorts and scuffed boots, was Jimmy Murdoch, looking somewhat bewildered at all the attention they were getting. Placed around the ring at several spots were the high school football players Sneed had promised, easy to recognize since they wore their jerseys. Their attention was not on the crowd but on the ring, however. Kyle allowed himself a brief glance at the audience, which seemed a blur of sound and motion. He then focused solely on Jimmy and forgot everything else.

The two met in the center of the ring. Jimmy raised his hands, signaling that he wanted to start with a "test of strength." This consisted of both wrestlers linking hands. Then, after a lot of back and forth tussling, one of them would force the other to his knees. There were tons of variations, one of which would have Jimmy starting to gain control of the test of strength only to have Kyle suddenly kick him in the stomach. The main component of the move was to firmly establish the heel as the bad guy and the jobber as the wrestler for whom the audience was supposed to be rooting.

Kyle and Jimmy had done tests of strength hundreds of times, each knowing just how the other would react. Kyle planted his feet solidly and threw his head back, looking for all the world like someone putting every last ounce of muscle into trying to drive Jimmy to his knees. The blond-spiked wrestler did the same, but after a few moments he allowed his face to show strain. Slowly, Kyle forced Jimmy's hands down. Jimmy even managed to shake a little as if the pressure was too much for him. Kyle got Jimmy's hands all the way down to the canvas, and then he jumped forward, stomping loudly. It appeared to the crowd that he smashed Jimmy's fingers, but of course Kyle made sure his weight was on his heels so that the pressure on the other wrestler's hands was minimal. Jimmy howled in pain, throwing himself back onto the canvas and clutching the damaged digits.

Kyle loved that about Jimmy. He knew how to sell a move to the audience.

Expecting the usual boos and derisive calls from the crowd, Kyle was surprised to hear someone scream out, "Way to go!" The throng was enjoying Jimmy's discomfort.

That's not right, Kyle thought. *They're supposed to hate me for that.*

Shrugging off the crowd's reaction, Kyle strode over to Jimmy and pulled him up by his hair. Cockily, he waited too long before locking Jimmy into the next move. Instead, he held Jimmy by the hair, scanning the crowd with a smirk on his face. Jimmy, realizing this was a signal to retaliate, rammed an elbow into Kyle's midsection.

Kyle doubled over as if in pain. He heard someone boo. When Jimmy rammed both fists into Kyle's back, the boos increased and were now mixed with gasps of astonishment.

"You goddamn fucker!" some guy screamed. "You can't do that!"

An empty cup sailed into the ring and hit Jimmy in the forehead. He blinked, not sure of what to do.

Kyle thought fiercely. There was a lull as Jimmy stood there, incapable of making a move. Kyle knew he had to do something, so he smashed a fist into Jimmy's groin.

The crowd went wild. Most of them were on their feet, screaming encouragement. The referee, who should have admonished Kyle for the low blow, merely stared out of the ring in awe.

True to form, Jimmy clutched his balls and cried out. Quickly, Kyle grabbed Jimmy and put him in a reverse headlock. He figured the safest thing was to make the match short and get everyone out safely. He whispered "DDT" in Jimmy's ear to let his friend know the move ahead of time. Then he threw himself back, still keeping Jimmy's head tucked under his arm. He made sure it looked like Jimmy's head hit the canvas hard. Then he flipped the boy over and covered him for the pin. The referee suddenly realized what was going on and quickly counted Jimmy out. He raised Kyle's arm in victory.

Pandemonium broke out. Popcorn flew everywhere. Drinks were thrown up into the air. People stomped and whistled their approval. Several people, not all of them women, had tears of joy streaming down their faces.

The announcer brushed some stray popcorn off of his desk and spoke into the mike. "Your winner, Kyle Temple!"

Randy crawled into the ring and nearly ran to Kyle's side. "Let's get the fuck out of here," he said. "As fast as possible."

Already several patrons were leaving their seats and climbing into the ring. Kyle started to follow Randy out only to find a woman behind him who was stretched out on the canvas, clutching onto his right boot. He shook her off and trailed after Randy back to the locker room, trying to ignore the mayhem around him.

MRS. STONE sat staring ahead. The remains of someone's soda were dripping down her face. A few drops settled briefly on her chin before falling to stain her prized Dior dress. Mr. Stone brushed a few kernels of popcorn off his shoulder and turned to his wife. "Well, that was fun, wasn't it?"

Mrs. Stone didn't reply. The exuberant kid in front of her continued to jump up and down, spilling more of his drink. An ice cube flew out of his cup and landed in Mrs. Stone's cleavage. She bit her lip.

As long as Kyle agreed to go to their church service on Sunday, she could put up with a little chilled boob.

CHAPTER
NINETEEN

KYLE'S Beetle was making some odd sounds. Randy didn't know much about cars (his personal philosophy concerning them consisted of turning the key in the ignition and, if that didn't work, calling for help), but he didn't think engines were supposed to emit high-pitched whines. Whenever Kyle stepped on the brakes, a grinding sound came from under their feet. In the passenger seat, Randy tried not to let his apprehension show. He looked out his window at the fields of cows passing by.

"We're still in Indiana, aren't we?" he asked. It seemed they'd been on the road long enough to get them to Kansas.

"Of course we are," Kyle replied, turning onto a gravel road. "This is the real Indiana. Indianapolis is the city. This is the real thing. Smell the country air!"

"Is that what that is? I thought the motor was on fire."

Kyle sniffed appreciatively. "No, that's a definite cow smell. They have a different odor than pigs. Wait until we pass a pig farm and you'll see the difference."

"Can I take your word for it? Are we anywhere near your mom's yet? We haven't passed a town in ages. I don't even think I've seen a sign for one. I'm beginning to think we're in a *Twilight Zone* episode." Randy's brow furrowed as they drove past a cornfield. Although corn had yet to be planted in the field, he shivered theatrically. "I think that's where they filmed *Children of the Corn*. Did you see that one? If we run into any creepy kids out here, we're heading right back to town, let me tell you."

"We'll be fine."

"We should have brought water. And blankets. Water and blankets. In case the car breaks down."

Kyle sighed. "We can huddle together for warmth. Would you relax? The car is fine and we'll be there soon."

"We should have brought my car. If we did have a breakdown out here, I'd be afraid to ask for assistance. God, I think I just saw Ned Beatty back there, and he was doing his *Deliverance* squeal."

The reference was lost on Kyle. "See? You do know people out here in the sticks."

That brought a laugh out of Randy. "I don't get out of the city much. I guess you could tell that. I mean, I consider those schools in the suburbs where you have your shows the sticks. This is… country. Overalls and hayseed sticking out of the mouth type of country. Pig-smell country."

"That's still the cows." The car lurched as Kyle hit a deep pothole. "They've been meaning to fix this damn road for years now. Clark's Hill is just a mile away from this point."

Before long Kyle was turning again, this time into a trailer park. They made their way to the back, where Kyle stopped next to a sky-blue mobile home with large yellow daisies painted all over it. An overhang served as a porch area. Half a dozen wind chimes hung off the overhang. A cinder block served as the step to the trailer's door.

Grinning, Kyle shut off the engine. "See? I told you she had it all decked out."

Randy nodded. "I'm going to climb out on a limb here and guess that your mom was a child of the sixties."

As they got out of the car, a woman came squealing out of the trailer. She was dressed in patched jeans and had on a loose blouse, the tails of which were tied at her navel. Randy could only register short brown hair and the scent of cut grass as she flew past him and threw herself into Kyle's arms.

"My baby boy!" she gushed, pulling his head down to kiss his forehead. "I haven't seen you in monkey's ages."

Randy had no idea what monkey's ages meant, but apparently it was a long time. Kyle blushed and muttered, "Hello, Mom."

Finally releasing her son, Mrs. Temple gave Randy a critical eye. "And who is this?"

It occurred to Randy that although he thought of Kyle's mom as Mrs. Temple, he really didn't know that she'd ever been married. After all, Kyle had never been told who his father was. Randy couldn't remember

Kyle saying if his mom had ever married. Was Temple her last name, or had Kyle taken his father's last name?

Kyle took Randy by the hand. "This is the guy I've been telling you about. This is Randy."

Kyle's mother nodded. "He's kind of cute, if you like them as thin as a rail. Me, I like a bit of flesh to grab hold of. Still, if you make Kyle happy...." She swooped forward and kissed Randy on the lips, much to his discomfort. "You can call me Mary. Welcome to the family."

She led the couple inside the trailer, where Randy was assailed by bright colors. The couch was a dismal gray, but the two armchairs in the living area were a bright orange. The walls were a dazzling blue, and knickknacks and figurines seemed to fill every available space. Over the couch was, as Randy had silently predicted, a velvet Elvis painting.

"Excuse the mess," Mary said. "I've been working extra shifts up at the McDonald's. Cassie Mae took sick, so I've taken up some of the slack." She slid a friendly arm around Randy. "So what is it you do, sugar?"

"I run a gay and lesbian bookstore in Indianapolis," he told her. "That is, when I'm not being Money-Mad Randy, Kyle's manager."

Mary snorted with laughter. "My boy's always been into wrestling. He used to have a trampoline set up out back, and he dropkicked all the neighbor kids right off of it. He broke Petey Miles's arm one time. Lawd, his mama came by and raised a fit. I told her, 'If'n your boy can't take a simple dropkick, maybe you'd best leave him in the nursery.' That's what I told her. She threatened to sic the sheriff on us, but nothing ever came of it. I reckon they knew that boy had no sense in the first place."

"Kyle must have been a handful growing up," Randy said.

Pinching her son's cheek, Mary replied, "He was as good as gold. As long as he had someone to beat up on, he was fine. Mind you, I always knew he'd turn out to be queer, because he'd kiss the boys after he'd whoop on 'em. He said it was to help them feel better. Of course, he never really hurt them. I'm not sure which he liked more, stomping on the boys or kissing them."

"Mom!" Kyle protested.

"Then there was Mark Sherman. Kyle liked to kiss him even if they hadn't been fighting. That's when I knew for sure. Mind you, Mark was a pretty one. Kyle always did have good taste in boys." She ruffled her son's hair. "Still does, apparently."

"Um," Kyle sputtered, unsure of what to say. "Aren't we supposed to be having lunch or something?"

"Oh, I'm embarrassing my boy. Okay, we can go ahead and get going. Randy and I will have plenty of time to jaw, and I can tell him about the time I found you cornholing Mark Sherman when you were only fifteen."

"Mom!"

Mary looked at Randy conspiratorially. "He tried to tell me they were just wrestling around. It's a funny kind of wrestling, I'd say, when your shorts are off and your dick is stuck up another boy's ass."

Kyle strode purposefully to the door and opened it. "We need to be heading to lunch," he said emphatically. "I've got a show tonight, so Randy and I don't have a lot of time."

"Yeah, that's true," Randy said. "We might not even have time to cornhole before the show."

Mary guffawed.

THE Fish House, where Mary chose to have lunch, was really more of a tavern. Randy was surprised to find that the catfish was perfectly cooked and was actually quite good. In between bites, Mary regaled Randy with more stories of Kyle's dubious childhood. Finally she laid her fork down and pressed a napkin to her lips.

"I always knew he'd end up famous. I just never in all my born days thought I'd see his face on the *Crier*. Alma Johnson came screaming over to my trailer, waving a copy of it. You'd have thought it was the Second Coming, which a lot of people seem to think it is."

Randy smiled apologetically. "Sorry if you've been bothered at all by that nonsense. Have you had any reporters around?"

"First day or two the phone kept on a-ringing, mostly, though, it was neighbor folk wanting to jaw about it. One guy did come around, though. Hardesty, his name was. Nice fellow. He said he was doing a follow-up story and wanted some inside information."

"Hardesty?" The color drained from Randy's face. "Jeff Hardesty? He's the one from the *Crier*. He's the guy who started this whole mess."

Kyle's eyes were wide. "Please tell me you didn't tell him about finding me fucking Mark Sherman when I was fifteen."

Mary snorted. "What do you take me for? Do you think I was born yesterday? I didn't tell him nothing. He just asked me about your daddy and whether or not you'd ever learned a foreign language. I told him you had a hard enough time learning English, getting Cs and Ds like you did. And as far as your daddy went, I told him the same thing I've always told you. I told him that you didn't have no daddy."

Randy bit his lip. "That might not have been the best thing to tell him. If he's doing another story, they might use that to fuel their fire. Maybe it would have been best to tell him the truth."

"I couldn't tell a stranger and let Kyle read in the paper who his daddy was," Mary said, frowning. "Not that I really knew myself."

"What do you mean by that?" Kyle asked, nearly choking on fish.

"Well, it was at a Stephen King party. That was the theme, anyway. My mates at that time used to have these theme parties. One was Stars of the Forties, and everyone came dolled up as Clark Gable or Katharine Hepburn. Really we just wanted to dress up every now and then. Anyway, this was a Stephen King theme, so everyone came dressed up as vampires and whatnot. I think one of his books had just come out, or one of the movies, I don't really remember. It was over twenty years ago, after all. March, it was. I remember thinking it was like Halloween, only at the wrong time of the year. The Yarnell twins went as those two little girls from *The Shining*. Very creepy, they were. Actually, the Yarnell twins were kind of creepy on their own. I went as a witch. I don't think Stephen King had actually written anything about a witch, but I didn't figure it really mattered."

"What does all this have to do with my father?" Kyle asked.

"I'm getting to that. Anyway, there was a lot of booze. I got a little tipsy. There was some guy there dressed as a ghost. He had a white sheet over his head and holes cut out for the eyes. He must have had a hell of a time getting it ready, or maybe he started drinking early, because there were holes cut all over that sheet. It was the funniest thing. It reminded me of that Charlie Brown cartoon. Anyway, he and I went out to the school playground and got to messing around on the slide, and—"

"Did you even know the guy's name?" Kyle asked.

Mary shook her head. "I really was rather drunk by that time. And I didn't know he was going to knock me up. Hell, to be honest, I never even saw his face. He just hiked up his sheet and we went at it. All I ever saw were his eyes peeking out of his JCPenney Summer Collection sheet."

"You never saw his face?" Kyle asked, unbelieving. "You mean my dad could have been ugly?"

"That was part of the excitement, not knowing what he looked like. I just imagined it was Burt Reynolds. It was more fun that way."

Randy dropped his fork. "You're telling us that you were impregnated by a guy in a ghost outfit? One with holes all over it? A holey ghost?"

"That's about the size of it."

Nodding, Randy said, "Okay, I stand corrected. Maybe it was best that you didn't tell Hardesty the truth."

Chapter
TWENTY

SATURDAY night's show at the MDW gym went a little better than the previous night's extravaganza. There were, to be sure, vastly more white T-shirts sporting Kyle's face and more signs bearing slogans such as KISS ME JESUS and KYLE'S THE TEMPLE I WORSHIP AT, but no one got beaned with a soda cup. Pete and Kyle had decided beforehand to have a one-sided squash match, so El Toro ended up totally beaten, not even having the chance to raise a fist to his opponent. The crowd loved it. They screamed as Kyle stood triumphant over his crushed opposition.

Early Sunday morning, Randy and Kyle were sleeping peacefully, snuggled against each other, when the phone jangled them awake. It was Mrs. Stone, practically begging the duo to join her for church services. Randy lied and begged off with the excuse of having a splitting headache.

"Well, Kyle could join us by himself if you're feeling poorly" was her reply.

Kyle, too, it seemed, had a headache.

In deference to their lie, the two did spend most of the day in bed, although they got little rest.

Sunday night's television fare boasted a pay-per-view of UWE featuring a main event with Bill "Crusher" Phillips, so Kyle convinced Randy to have some of their friends over to watch it. Jimmy Murdoch and Debbie arrived together. They barely moved two inches away from each other, causing Randy to wonder if they'd accidentally put on the same single article of underwear. After them, the wiry wrestler known as Top Rope Tony arrived (his real name, Randy learned, was Tony Spotts), followed shortly after that by Pete, sporting his new girlfriend. She was a small teenager with long black hair. She introduced herself to Randy. "Nice to meet you. My name's Liza. It's with a Z."

"Honey, I'm gay," Randy replied. "You don't have to explain it to me."

She looked at him blankly.

"It's Liza with a Z, not Lisa with an S, 'cause Lisa with an S goes *sss* not *zzz*," Randy elaborated.

Liza looked at Pete, as if hoping he could explain what Randy was saying. Pete just looked confused. "Huh?"

"Liza Minnelli!" Randy shouted. "'Liza with a Z!'" The young couple didn't look any wiser. "Okay," Randy went on, throwing his hands up in defeat. "That's the last fag cultural reference I make with this group tonight."

As the show began, everyone settled in front of the TV set. Kyle explained some of what they were watching to Randy, letting him know the who's who and the what's what of Universal Wrestling Extravaganza.

"That lady there," he said, pointing, "is Tamalita Edwards. She owns the UWE, and she's a huge bitch."

"But a foxy bitch," Pete chimed in.

"Well, yeah… I guess," Kyle admitted grudgingly. "Anyway, she's trying to get Crusher banned from wrestling in the UWE. That's why she's made him agree to this match tonight. Crusher has to take on two opponents at once tonight. They're supposed to act as a tag team, with only one of them against Crusher at any one time, but of course they'll cheat and find a way to double-team him."

"There's also the Mid-Continental championship match tonight," Pete said, holding Liza close to him on the couch. "I'm hoping Carlos Navarrio wins, since he's Mexican."

Liza rubbed her boyfriend's chest. "I'm crazy about Mexicans."

Pete preened. "We are pretty hot, aren't we?"

Randy thought there was a bit more soap opera than wrestling to the show and said so.

Tony agreed. "That's the one thing I hate about most of the wrestling on television today. I wish they'd just shut up and start clobbering each other."

"You've got to have the storyline to hook the viewers, though," Kyle said. "That's why to make it big nowadays you've got to be able to act as well as wrestle. Luckily I excel at both. It'd be worth putting up with the silly stories and shit to get to be on a pay-per-view with Crusher Phillips. I'd give anything to be one of the lucky bastards that gets to wrestle him tonight."

"Sometimes they go too far, though," Jimmy said. "I mean, last week they had a match where the winner got to slap the loser's mother. And who lost? 'The Natural' Brian Morman, and he's got to be fifty-five if he's a day. Hell, he was wrestling when I was a little kid. His mother's got to be over seventy. She reminded me of my grandmother."

"I saw that match," Pete said. "You're right, it was pretty silly. Mind you, that old bag could take a smack, couldn't she?"

"Oh, hell yeah."

During a lull in the show, Randy went to the kitchen to refresh everyone's drinks. Debbie went to help him. As he was pulling the required number of beers out of the refrigerator, he said, "I can't help but notice every time I see you and Murdoch together—"

"Why do you always use his last name? I call Kyle by his first name. I don't say 'you and that Temple kid'. I know at first you called him Murdoch because you didn't approve of me seeing him, but now I think it's just habit."

"Okay, Jimmy, then. I notice that every time I see you with Jimmy you seem to be even closer than the last time, both physically and emotionally."

Debbie pulled the top off of her beer and took a long swig. "I think I'm falling in love with the mug. What can I say?"

"Really? What happened to the fast cars and fancy restaurants that boyfriends had to provide?"

Debbie made a face. "I don't honestly know. I was never in love with any of the doctors or lawyers I dated. I knew that. And somehow I always thought the cars and stuff were important. Now that I've met someone I really like, I'm finding that they really aren't important at all."

"Now you see how I fell for Kyle."

"We went to the movies this afternoon," she said, leaning back against the kitchen counter. "We went to a chick flick. It was an unabashed chick flick. And he held my hand the whole time. He never complained once about the movie. Not even afterwards. When I asked him if he liked it, he said he did. I know he was lying, but at least he said he liked it."

"Sounds like this might be serious," Randy said.

"It is," Debbie replied, taking another drink. "Damn it."

RANDY couldn't help but notice that on nights when Kyle watched wrestling on television or actually had a match, the sex was just a little rougher, just a little hotter. Not that he would complain. In fact, he was starting to wish wrestling was on every night of the week.

He had his legs up on Kyle's shoulders. They'd started out gentle and loving, but soon the sex had turned animalistic. Kyle was thrusting into Randy forcefully, causing groans from both of them. Sweat was starting to drip down Kyle's beard. The droplets hung for a moment, shaking violently before falling off and splashing onto Randy's chest. Kyle's fingers gripped his boyfriend's shoulders hard enough that Randy wondered if he'd be bruised afterwards. Not that he cared.

A particularly powerful plunge by Kyle sent shivers throughout Randy's body. He convulsed, shouting, "Holy shit!"

Kyle began banging harder, managing to mutter in a gasping voice, "You shouldn't use words like *holy* or *Jesus* when we're fucking. Might make me... lose my.... Fuck! Shit! I'm going to cum!"

The thrusts increased in speed and force. Randy clutched the side of the bed. "Jes—" he started to scream, but stopped himself in time by grabbing a pillow and biting into a corner of it.

Kyle grunted several times in rapid succession. Randy felt his lover release his load into him. They stayed frozen for a minute, still connected, until Kyle shifted and Randy lowered his legs. Kyle carefully pulled the condom free and placed it on the nightstand.

Cuddling next to Randy, he said, "I put it there so you wouldn't step on it."

"I sort of figured that out."

Kyle kissed Randy tenderly. "I'm sorry I yelled at you."

"When did you yell at me? Was I around at the time?"

Kyle gave him his were-you-not-paying-attention look. "When we were fucking."

"The only yells I heard were along the lines of 'your ass feels so good'. Are you mad because I came first? If that's the case, I'm sorry, but it couldn't be helped. It just felt too good. Other than that, I don't recall any yelling other than dirty talk." Randy kissed Kyle's chest. It was still wet with sweat. "Which I love, by the way."

"Just before I came," Kyle told him, "I yelled at you. I didn't mean to, baby, and I'm sorry."

"Are you talking about that bit about not using *Jesus* or *holy* and words of that sort? That wasn't yelling. You were barely grunting at that point. Besides, you have a good point. I'll try to watch what I scream out when we're in the throes of passion." Randy kissed Kyle's left nipple, tasting the salt of his perspiration. He looked up to see Kyle's eyes beginning to water with tears.

"You shouldn't have to watch what you say," Kyle said, his voice gruff with trying to hold back emotion. "It wasn't fair of me, and I'm sorry. Hell, I made you bite a pillow."

Randy chuckled and threw himself on top of Kyle, kissing his mouth hard and long. When they broke away, he said, "You've made me bite into pillows several times. You've made me bite my own fingers. You've even made me bite into the damn mattress before. You just haven't noticed. It's a good thing. There are times when we're making love that it gets so intense that if I vocalize what I'm feeling, the neighbors are going to think that the tornado warning siren has gone off."

"I just don't want to inhabitate you during sex."

"Inhibit, I think you mean. There's no such word as inhabitate, although you've inhabited me for the last forty-five minutes. And as soon as I get the feeling back into my legs, I'm going to get us a little late night snack. How does that sound?"

Kyle held him close, running his hands through Randy's hair. "You're awfully good to me." A single tear made its way down Kyle's cheek.

"And you're good to me. We complement each other. You make me feel whole."

Kyle looked mildly surprised. "Really?"

"Of course."

A quick hand wiped the tear off Kyle's cheek. "I love you," he said.

Randy smiled. "I love you too."

CHAPTER
TWENTY-ONE

THE Tuesday edition of *America's Crier* was dubbed by Debbie as the "All-Kyle Issue." While this wasn't technically true, since there were a few scattered articles involving alien turtles bent on destroying the Earth and a Sasquatch running for Congress, the *Crier* certainly had devoted many of its pages to the Kyle phenomenon. Interviews abounded, including bits with Carl Bennett, Monty Sneed (who managed to mention that his promotion was called Midwest Demolition Wrestling in nearly every sentence), and even Kyle's mother, Mary.

Debbie and Randy poured over the tabloid on the counter of Outgoing Books, near the cash register. Tuesday afternoons were often slow, so they had few interruptions. A thin blond twink was perusing the gay mysteries, but other than that the shop was empty.

"It figures that Sneed would get his two cents in," Randy said. "He's been trying to find some way to get some extra bucks out of this since day one. You'd think he'd be satisfied that suddenly his shows are selling out, but now he's selling T-shirts and eight by tens of Kyle as well."

"He's a snake," Debbie agreed, "but at least he's an honest snake. You know where you stand with him. He doesn't make any pretense of being a kind or even a decent person."

"True."

"What I don't get is this Bennett guy. Kyle went to him for help, and he's used the poor boy for his benefit ever since. Has Kyle been back to see him?"

Randy shook his head. "Not since all this began. He doesn't trust that he'll be able to keep his temper. And since Kyle regularly bruises and bashes guys when he's in a good mood, you can imagine what he'd be like if he was mad."

"Might be a good thing, though. Get out some aggression."

Randy rubbed a kink out of his shoulder. "I think he's found a way to do that."

"Look here. Bennett's got an ad. The bastard's started a psychic hotline."

"It doesn't surprise me."

Debbie made a face. "Maybe Kyle should start up his own hotline. You know, get the daily words of wisdom from Jesus Part Two. It could be quite a cash cow."

Randy laughed mirthlessly. "I'm still not sure we want to make any money off of this. It's bad enough dealing with the reporters camped out in front of our apartment."

"Our apartment?" Debbie's look was sly.

Blushing, Randy said, "It's not official as of yet, since he still has his apartment, but he's pretty much moved in. Besides, I couldn't let him go on living in that dump of his. Shit, the rats there have started to complain to the landlord."

Debbie leaned in and rubbed Randy's shoulder for him, not noticing the wince it brought to his face. "I'm glad for you. You guys are good for each other."

"Thanks." Randy flipped over a page of the *Crier*. "Christ... I mean, heck... they've even got a picture of Kyle's mother's trailer here, in all its *Partridge Family* glory."

"It does have that seventies look to it."

"You should see the inside. It looks like Peter Max threw up in it."

"Who?"

Randy rolled his eyes. "How do you ever win a game of Trivial Pursuit? Peter Max was a counterculture artist in the sixties and seventies. He did a lot of album covers and... oh, never mind."

Debbie patted his cheek. "It's okay, honey. You just keep on throwing out those little jokes of yours that no one gets. It's part of your charm."

"Thanks for the condescending vote of confidence."

"Anytime, doll."

Flipping another page, Randy found an article about a renowned psychic who claimed she was in contact with the spirit of Mary Magdalene, who had a special message for Kyle. The psychic refrained from revealing the message, saying it was personal and private and would only be revealed to Kyle. Disgusted, Randy closed the *Crier*. "The only saving grace is that this is so ridiculous that most sane people aren't buying into it. I think otherwise we'd be overrun with reporters and weirdoes."

Debbie shrugged. "How do you know it's ridiculous, though? I mean, apparently Kyle does spout whole conversations in Aramaic while under hypnosis. Who's to say there isn't something to it?"

"I've never heard him speak in anything other than English," Randy said. Then he thought a moment and clamped his mouth shut.

"What?" Debbie asked, sensing her friend was hiding something. "You clammed up. You've remembered something."

"Nothing," Randy insisted. After getting a look from Debbie that told him she wasn't about to give up, he added, "Well, almost nothing. Last night, after he fell asleep...."

"Yes?"

"He did sort of mumble some words. It could possibly have been a foreign language, but more likely it was just garbled chattering. I'm sure it was nothing."

Debbie let out a long breath. "See? There may be something to the craziness after all. He was born on Christmas Day—"

"But Jesus wasn't. Most historians believe he was born in the spring."

"Most people, however, think he was born in December, and that's what's important. Of course, most people also believe he was a lily-white guy with silky blond hair, which, considering where he was born, is damn unlikely. Also, Kyle's mother's name is Mary—"

"Which is a very common name."

"And he had an unknown father. Who was, you told me, dressed as a ghost at the time."

"All coincidental. Except for the speaking in Aramaic. That I don't have an explanation for."

Debbie raised her eyebrows. "That's a pretty big conundrum to solve, you've got to admit."

"I'm sure that there is a logical explanation for it." Although he said it emphatically, Randy himself didn't feel convinced. Luckily, the twink had found some mysteries to buy, so Randy busied himself with ringing up the purchase.

TONY and Pete arrived at Randy's apartment toting their gym bags, ready to whisk Kyle off for a workout session. When Kyle opened the door, Pete made a beeline for the bathroom. "I've got to take a leak in the worst way," he said, hurriedly closing the door behind him.

Tony grinned. "We nearly didn't get away from the reporters downstairs. Man, they asked us everything about you. Like I'm supposed to know what toothpaste you use."

"You talked to them?"

"Sure, why not? We didn't tell them what they wanted to hear, though. I just said you were a so-so wrestler whose ass I'm going to whoop this weekend."

Kyle laughed. "You've never won a match yet. You love getting the shit stomped out of you. Hell, sometimes I even worry that I've actually hurt you."

"They don't have to know I'm the biggest jobber in the Midwest. Anyway, we should have another sold-out crowd Friday night."

The bathroom door opened and Pete came out, still zipping up his jeans. "Man," he said, "I thought I was going to have to pee down my leg. My back teeth were swimming."

Picking up his own gym bag, Kyle asked, "So are we ready to head out now?"

Tony nodded enthusiastically. "Hell yeah. I haven't been thrown around in days. My bruises are even starting to heal. We can't have that."

Pete stopped at the door and eyed Kyle carefully. "Are you sure you're ready to walk through that crowd down there? It's the worst I've ever seen it. There must have been seven camera crews."

"And you talked to each of them," Kyle said.

"At the same time," Pete protested. "As soon as we stopped to talk, every camera in the vicinity was pointed at us. Hey, we just wanted to see if we could get on the news tonight. Besides, we really didn't say much. Granted, I had to pee badly, so that helped speed things along."

Kyle shrugged. "I'll just shove my way through them like I normally do, saying *no comment* every 4.5 seconds. It seems to work."

The throng outside was indeed much larger, Kyle found. Pete wasn't exaggerating. As soon as he walked out of the apartment building, cameras turned and lights began flashing. Kyle put on his best don't-bother-me look and pushed his way through toward the sidewalk, where Tony's car was waiting. Not surprisingly, the camera crews followed them the entire length of the sidewalk, shouting questions as they moved along. Kyle noticed that Pete was smiling sweetly into the cameras and even paused to kiss one young and pretty blonde reporter on the cheek.

At the car, Tony climbed into the driver's seat. Pete opened the passenger side door, stopping to wave goodbye to the reporters before piling in. Kyle started to get in beside him but stopped when something small and furry was shoved in his face. A woman whom he'd thought he'd seen in the building on several occasions was holding a cat up to his nose.

"Please," she begged, her eyes red from crying, "it's Mr. Rodgers. He's very ill."

Kyle looked at her sympathetically. "I'm a wrestler, not a vet."

Inside the car, Pete chuckled and said in his best DeForest Kelley voice, "Damn it, Jim! I'm a wrestler, not a damn cat doctor!"

"He's been to the vet," the woman went on. "They've done all they can. If you could just... touch him. What could it hurt?"

Kyle felt like his guts had suddenly become leaden. "It wouldn't do any good, lady," he said sadly. "I honestly don't have any healing powers. I don't have any powers at all."

The woman closed her eyes. "Mr. Rodgers is dying. What could it hurt? I'm desperate. If nothing happens, I'm not out anything. But if there's even the tiniest chance...."

Sighing, Kyle petted the cat on the head. The animal opened its rheumy eyes and blinked at him. His own eyes filling with tears, Kyle stroked Mr. Rodgers's back. He detected a small purr coming from the animal. He looked at the woman. "I hope he gets better. I really do."

The woman met his gaze. "Thank you," she said softly. "You're a good person. Whether you are who they say you are or not, you're a good person, and that's what counts." She held her cat close to her heart. "Thank you," she repeated.

Kyle got inside the car quickly. "Drive," he told Tony, keeping his head lowered. The boys were silent the entire trip to the gym.

PARKING the car, Tony wore a frown as he looked around at his surroundings. "Something is different," he said.

Pete's eyes were wide. "We've got a sign," he said reverentially. "Sneed actually forked out the dough for a sign."

Kyle climbed out of the back of the car and looked above the door of the gym. Sure enough, a large white sign bore the promotion's logo, and block red letters informed anyone looking that they had found Sneed's Gym, Home of Midwest Demolition Wrestling, Featuring Kyle Temple.

"Whoa," Tony said, his mouth hanging open. "Dude, you definitely should be getting more money now."

Kyle couldn't take his eyes off the letters spelling out his name. It wasn't quite his dream of getting to wrestle in the UWE with Crusher Phillips, but this was damn close. His name was on a sign. Hell, it could be seen from the street. How many people drove down that street on any given day? It had to be hundreds, Kyle figured, possibly even thousands. All of them would see his name in red. They'd know he was special. He was the featured wrestler of Midwest Demolition Wrestling.

Oh sure, he'd had his name in *America's Crier*, but that wasn't about wrestling. This was his career, and his name was now in lights. It would burn into the night. Suddenly Kyle wished that he had brought his camera. He instinctively reached for his cell phone before realizing he'd left it at the apartment. He needed to call Randy at the store and tell him the good news. He'd have to use the phone in Sneed's office. Sneed wouldn't mind. Hell, Kyle was his featured wrestler now.

"A robe," Kyle muttered. "I want a black robe to wear for my ring entrance. It should be jet-black with my name in white across the back. Fuck, I'm going to look so hot."

After several minutes, Pete and Tony were finally able to drag Kyle inside to start their workout.

THE Channel 9 Nightly News with Belinda Peterson closed that night with a story about a cat. On the spot, reporter Ryan Collins spoke briefly with the ecstatic owner, a woman who simply cried and kept repeating over and over, "It's a miracle." Collins then announced that earlier in the day the news team had caught local celebrity Kyle Temple's encounter with the ailing cat on film. A short bit of footage, shot showing Kyle's back, did reveal him petting the sick animal. The segment cut back to Collins in the woman's living room. The cat in question, Mr. Rodgers, was running around playing with a ball. Collins had a wry smile on his face as he closed his story. "Earlier today, Mr. Rodgers here was at death's door. Now he's playing as if nothing had ever been wrong with him. It's hardly the resurrection of Lazarus, but I'm guessing that doesn't matter to Mr. Rodgers. He's one cat who's thankful to be given a new lease on life. Mr. Rodgers's owner doesn't care if it's all just a coincidence. She claims her neighbor has performed a miracle, and who are we to argue with her?"

The segment ended, and viewers saw Belinda Peterson sitting at her news desk with just the right amount of skepticism of her face as she said, "And that's all the time we have for tonight. Join us again tomorrow. Good night."

CHAPTER
TWENTY-TWO

RANDY STONE awoke on Thursday morning and immediately knew something wasn't right. He sat up in bed and felt next to him as he used the other hand to wipe the sleep from his eyes. Kyle's side of the bed was empty.

Confused, he shook the final cobwebs from his mind and looked around. A folded piece of paper bearing his name was propped up against the bedside lamp. He hurriedly opened it.

Randy, it read, *I got up early and didn't want to disturb you. I'm going for a run and then I have some other things to attend to. I'll see you tonight. I'll be thinking of you all day. Please know that I love you more than anything. I'll be here when you get off work. Love, Kyle.* There was a PS that Randy didn't understand at all, not having caught the newscast. *Oh, and about the cat. I really didn't do anything. It must have been a coincidence.* Randy noticed with a smile that Kyle had tried to write "serendipity" and had crossed that word out and substituted "coincidence."

Frowning, Randy said aloud, "But we don't have a cat." Tossing the missive aside, he got out of bed and headed for the shower.

SHELLY was waiting for Randy as he came in the door. He'd barely had time to take off his jacket before she pounced in front of him. "That was pretty amazing," she said.

Hanging up his jacket, Randy sighed. "I know you'll tell me whether I ask or not, so I might as well give you the pleasure. What was pretty amazing?"

"The cat story. I know people are saying that it was just chance, but I thought it was freaking fantastic."

Randy threw his arms up. "What is this about a cat? Kyle mentioned a cat this morning. I'm not even acquainted with any cats. Certainly none that I can go up to, shake its paw, and say hi to."

"What about Mr. Rodgers?"

"The cat from down the hall? Mrs. Trammell's cat? What about it?"

Shelly's eyes got big. "Oh my God, you really don't know! It was on the eleven o'clock news. The cat was dying, Kyle touched it, and now it's put off going to kitty heaven for an indefinite period. When last seen, Mr. Rodgers was making a ball of yarn wish that it had never been born."

Randy groaned. "No, I fell asleep watching TV. I didn't make it to the news. I got up around two and climbed into bed. Kyle was already asleep, so I didn't wake him. He must have watched the news and didn't wake me."

"The news guys treated the whole thing as a joke, but I'm sure a lot of people are taking it seriously."

"No wonder Kyle's note this morning was so apologetic. He probably thought I'd be mad or something."

"And you're not?"

Randy sighed. "I just want our lives back. I want the whole thing to be over. I'm certainly not mad at him. How could I be? It's not like he asked for any of this."

KYLE breathed deeply. He knew he shouldn't be nervous. It wasn't like he'd never performed before a crowd before. But it was different in the ring. There he was a character, a mean wrestler who wanted to beat up his opponent. He wasn't sure how to be himself in front of a television audience.

Brittney, the makeup girl, smiled at him as she put the finishing touches to his nose. "Nervous?" she asked.

"A little, yeah. I don't know why."

"It's pretty common. Most people we get on *Good Morning, Indianapolis* haven't been on TV before. It's really not bad. Emma Olsen can be a little scary and I admit she's hard to work for, but she's great with guests. She'll put you right at ease."

Kyle feigned nonchalance. "Oh, I've been on camera before. Every now and then we'll tape our shows and sell them over the Internet. I'm a wrestler. Did you know that?"

Brittney laughed. "I think everyone knows who you are by now. Did you know there's even an Internet site that's selling Kyle Temple crucifixes? I've got one over here." She opened a drawer and took out a small wooden cross. A figure wearing black wrestling trunks and boots was glued to the wood.

Kyle looked at it and gasped. "This is horrible."

"I don't know. I thought it was pretty funny."

"No, I mean the figure itself. I'm much better-looking than that. They've got my nose all wrong! It looks like a beak."

She took the cross back with a shrug. "They never get the details right. Of course, since it's unauthorized, they only had pictures of you to go by. Maybe if you had posed for it they'd have gotten your nose right. We ordered one thinking we'd use it on the show, but I guess they changed their minds." Brittney looked at him critically. "You're on first, so we'd better make sure you're ready. Your makeup is flawless, if I do say so myself."

"Thanks. So what do I do now?"

Brittney pulled him out of his chair. "Come on. We can stand in the wings until Emma announces you. It should be in just a few minutes. Don't worry. I'm sure you'll do fine."

Kyle watched as the show began, the butterflies growing in his stomach. He counted along silently with the floor director as he showed by his fingers how many seconds were left before show time. When he pointed to her on the set, Emma Olsen burst into a smile.

"Good morning, Indianapolis," she said, "and welcome to our show. We were scheduled to have Molly Ferguson and her Amazing Cloggers perform for us today, but unfortunately Molly fell off her clogs yesterday and sprained her ankle. Luckily, we received a call last night from a young man who we've been trying to get on the show for over a week now. He's the professional wrestler who has been turned into a controversial figure after a hypnosis session had him speaking in Aramaic. We're happy to have with us here today, Mr. Kyle Temple."

The small studio audience hooted as Kyle made his way out. He shyly waved his fingers at them as he sat down next to Emma Olsen.

Olsen leaned forward and touched his arm lightly. "It's so good to have you on the show," she said.

Kyle chuckled uneasily. "I've got to be honest. I'm nervous as hell."

Olsen smiled reassuringly. "You needn't be. Kyle, can you tell us what effect this controversy has had on your life?"

Kyle swallowed as he thought hard. "Well, for one, I never had reporters sticking cameras in my face before. That's been pretty different. But on the plus side, I did get my name on the sign for Midwest Demolition Wrestling, and that kicks ass!" He blanched. "Can you say 'kick ass' on television?"

Olsen's smile faltered only a fraction. "We're live, but I don't think 'kick ass' will cause any problems. Tell me, what is your personal opinion of all the stories about you? Is there any validity to what people, especially *America's Crier*, are saying?"

"I'm just me," Kyle said. "I'm just a regular guy. I like to wrestle. I drink beer. I want to settle down with the person I love and get a dog. That's really about it. I just want to be happy. I'm not anybody's reincarnation. I just think the whole thing is silly."

Olsen put on her serious look. "But how do you explain speaking in Aramaic? Knowing the Sermon on the Mount in a language you claim you don't know?"

Fidgeting in his seat, Kyle replied, "It's some sort of mistake. I didn't even know there was such a language as Aramaic until that story in the *Crier*. I certainly don't speak it. And that cat just got better on its own. I swear I had nothing to do with that."

Tilting her head in interest, Olsen went on. "Would you be willing to go along with a little demonstration, then? Just to prove that it's all, as you say, some sort of mistake?"

"What sort of demonstration?" Kyle asked worriedly.

Olsen spoke now directly to the camera. "We have waiting backstage noted psychologist Petra Newman, an expert on past life regression. With her is renowned linguist Vassar Ellinovitch, who has specialized in the Aramaic language."

Kyle sank in his seat. "Huh?"

Olsen stood. "Ladies and gentlemen, let us meet Petra Newman and Vassar Ellinovitch."

"The cat probably had hairballs," Kyle said, desperation showing in his voice. "Those can be a real bitch and cause problems with cats. People don't realize just how important hairball treatments can be to a cat's well-being."

HAVING the day off, Debbie huddled in front of the portable television she kept on her small kitchen table. A bowl of Special K in hand, she flipped the channels, having seen that rerun of *The Andy Griffith Show* hundreds of times. Oprah was on the next channel.

"No, I don't think so," Debbie muttered, pressing the remote for the next station. "I don't need to be reaffirmed today, thank you."

The next channel was *I Love Lucy*. Debbie flipped again. "Ricky's not going to let you be in the show. Get over it."

The familiar set of *Good Morning, Indianapolis* showed on her television. Debbie paused, wondering why the figure reclining on the couch seemed so familiar. She took a large spoonful of cereal into her mouth. As the camera zoomed in closer to the seemingly sleeping form, Debbie spit the Special K out in a spray, splattering both her table and television. "Oh. My. God," she said as Kyle began to babble phrases that certainly sounded like a foreign language to her.

CARL BENNETT watched the show while lying on his new couch. He smiled as he saw Kyle's face on his new flat-screen Panasonic television. "Way to go, boy," he said aloud. "That should keep the crowds coming for months yet. I'll have to raise my rates again."

SHELLY saw the show on the television they kept in Outgoing Books's back room while on her break. She said, although there was no one to hear her, "I'm not telling him about this one. He'll just yell. Randy says he never yells, but he'll yell over this. I'm not telling him."

MRS. PITCAIRN entered the Stones's living room armed with a feather duster and sporting a knowing look. She made a few feeble swipes over the mantel, all the while keeping her gaze fixed on Mrs. Stone, who was seated in an armchair with the latest Jackie Collins.

"You look like you've got something on your mind," Mrs. Stone said, a little impatient. She was just at a good point in the book, and she was a woman who disliked having her reading interrupted. "What's going on?"

Pursing her lips, Mrs. Pitcairn said, "I just thought you'd like to know that the hunky boy who's rutting your son is on the telly. Talking all foreign again, he is."

Jackie Collins went flying as Mrs. Stone leaped from the chair. She bolted for the nearest television.

JIMMY MURDOCH was watching television at that moment as well. He angrily banged the side of the set, nearly hurting his hand. "What the fuck? Let her be in the goddamn show, Ricky! She's your fucking wife, for Christ's sake!"

CHAPTER
TWENTY-THREE

"MAYBE you shouldn't wrestle tonight," Randy said.

Kyle did a double take. "What?" he asked, not believing his ears.

They were in the hall at Brownstown High School, just outside the gym area. To say that the show was sold out would be an understatement. Every possible place where a person could be crammed was filled, and still people had to be turned away, much to the delight of the kid who took the tickets. As the show went on, the crowd became louder and louder in anticipation of seeing Kyle enter the ring. Now, standing just out of sight of the rowdy throng, Randy thought the sound of the audience was like the ocean on a stormy day.

He sighed. "I've just got a bad feeling. I think maybe you should call this off. Things are starting to get out of control."

"They started off out of control. You're just mad over me doing that TV show without telling you first."

"Well, now things are *really* out of control. It's actually getting dangerous."

Standing with them was Tony, who would be announced first for the match. "You worry too much, dude," he said, jumping up and down to get his adrenaline flowing. "Kyle and I worked it out already. We know the crowd's going to be all for him whatever we do, so he's going to switch from being the heel to being the fan favorite." He grinned. "For the first time, I get to be the bad guy."

Randy looked at Kyle seriously. "Please tell me you're still going to win. They'll stampede if you don't win."

"Of course I'm going to win," Kyle said, rolling his eyes. "Stop worrying. This is what I do." Sternness crept into his voice. It was a tone he'd never used with Randy before. "You know, you just don't get it. I'm a professional wrestler. I think you hope that it's just a phase I'm going through or that it's some temper thing, but this is me. It's what I am. Maybe you should just wait back here and not come out with us tonight."

Stung, Randy said softly, "No, I want to be out there with you."

"Then quit your griping." Realizing by Randy's hurt look that he'd gone too far, Kyle cupped his boyfriend's face in his hands and kissed him tenderly. "I'm sorry. It'll be okay. I promise."

Tony stopped leaping up and down to examine his boots carefully. He shuffled his feet and tried to hide the blush that had come to his cheeks.

Kyle smiled at him. "Sorry about that. I figured that by now you'd have worked out that we're a couple. It's not really that much of a secret anymore. Not really."

Tony chuckled uneasily. "Hell, I worked that out when he sat on your lap when we watched wrestling the other night. I'm okay with queers. Really, I am. I've got a cousin that's a queer. I just didn't expect to see you guys kissing, that's all."

"Yeah," Kyle said, "I think even Sneed has figured it out, and you know how dense he is. He won't talk about it, but he knows."

"Oh, he talks about it," Tony replied. "He makes jokes behind your backs. He calls Randy here your butt monkey."

"Nice," Randy said. "Very nice."

"And ass pirate."

"I get the picture."

"And a jizz joneser."

Randy spoke through gritted teeth. "I get it." To Kyle, he said, "Remind me to kick Sneed in the ass when I see him."

"You'll have to wait your turn. I'm not having anyone talk about my baby that way." Kyle's head jerked up as a huge roar sounded. "The announcer's ready for us."

Hearing his name called, Tony grinned and high-fived Randy and Kyle. "Let's give them a great show," he said as he trotted out to the gym.

Randy thought an earthquake hit, but it was only the reaction to the announcer saying Kyle's name. Kyle twisted and stretched one last time and then went through the archway into the gym, followed by Randy.

Randy's ears hurt. It seemed people were screaming right in his ear. Hands were outstretched, hoping to touch Kyle as he went by. Randy noticed several new styles of Kyle Temple T-shirts, and it seemed the majority of the crowd now sported them. Signs were everywhere. One that caught Randy's eye read BEAT THE SNOT OUT OF HIM, KYLE! The KYLE was crossed out and replaced with the word JESUS. There were dozens of signs dotted around the gym, but Randy forced himself not to read any more of them.

Reaching his corner, Kyle bowed to the audience. They went into even more of a frenzy, which Randy wouldn't have thought possible. Slowly, Kyle took off his leather jacket and handed it to Randy.

The referee went through the motions of checking for hidden weapons, and then the bell rang.

Tony charged across the ring, only to be tossed aside by Kyle. As the lighter wrestler hit the canvas, the audience roared their approval. Kyle kicked Tony in the back, sending the wrestler sprawling out of the ring. Kyle paced back and forth, nodding to the crowd with a smirk on his face. Finally Tony climbed back into the ring. Kyle, still basking in the adoration of the masses, seemed not to notice the wrestler coming up behind him.

Tony leaped up and drove his boots into the small of Kyle's back. The dropkick threw Kyle into the ropes. The crowd gasped as one, only to shout their disapproval as Tony doubled up his fists and slammed Kyle's back. Kyle convulsed and hung over the ropes, seemingly dazed. Tony took advantage and lifted Kyle up into his arms, holding him aloft for just a second before slamming him to the canvas. He went to stomp his boot onto the fallen fighter, but Kyle "recovered" enough to kick out, slamming Tony in the midsection. Tony doubled over as the crowd went wild.

Getting to his feet, Kyle slapped a headlock on Tony. It looked like he was grinding the boy's head into his side. Then he threw Tony into the ropes. As the other wrestler bounced back towards him, Kyle ran forward with an outstretched arm, clotheslining Tony. As Tony writhed in agony, Kyle looked outside the ring, arms up as if basking in the glory.

Randy watched with his mouth open. Despite his misgivings, Kyle and Tony seemed to be reading the crowd just right. They were hitting a perfect balance, keeping Kyle mostly in control of the bout but allowing Tony a few moments to shine. Whenever Tony hit, kicked, or in any way attacked Kyle, the audience hissed and booed. The two wrestlers were careful not to let these bits last too long, however. Kyle always regained the upper hand, to the delight of the masses.

After Kyle rammed Tony's head into the canvas using a pile driver, Randy assumed the match was over. Tony twitched convincingly. Kyle stroked his beard as if he'd just completed a job well done and then strode cockily over to where Randy waited on the ring apron.

"Aren't you supposed to pin him?" Randy asked.

Kyle allowed himself a brief, out-of-character smile. "We've still got a bit more to go. We figured we'd make it look like Tony was going to win the match at the last moment, just when everyone thinks he's done for. Then I come back against impossible odds and pin his ass."

As they were talking, Tony was slowly getting to his feet.

"Don't press your luck," Randy replied, certain that no one could hear what they were saying over the din. "I still think this crowd could turn ugly."

Kyle looked over Randy's shoulders and saw some of the reddened faces calling out for him. "They've had one hell of a start," he agreed.

Tony slid out of the ring and pulled a folding chair out from under the ring skirt, where he'd apparently hidden it previously. He got back into the ring, his face set for vengeance. The crowd screamed warnings, but Kyle kept his conversation with Randy going, allowing Tony time to creep up on him.

Randy saw a huge behemoth of a guy leap out of the front row. The guy climbed quickly into the ring, shouting, "You fucker! You can't do that!"

Randy shouted to Tony, but he wasn't in time. The man plowed into Tony. Tony went flying. The chair went flying. Tony tumbled out of the ring not far from where Randy stood. Randy heard a crack as the wrestler hit the gym floor. Real pain flooded the boy's face as he clutched the shoulder he'd fallen on.

Kyle turned and grabbed the behemoth. "It's over!" he shouted. "Get back to your seat!"

Randy rushed to Tony's side. The wrestler was rocking back and forth, holding his right shoulder. Tears were in his eyes. "Are you okay?" Randy asked, immediately wishing he hadn't. The boy's face made it obvious he wasn't. "Let's get you to the locker room." Kyle joined him, and the two of them hoisted Tony up and led the way through the crowd.

There was a hush as the announcer declared Kyle the winner by default.

"IT'S my fault," Kyle repeated for the dozenth time.

Randy rested a hand gently on Kyle's knee as they sat in one of the waiting rooms at Orion Community South Hospital. Randy had just gotten off his cell phone with Debbie. She and Jimmy Murdoch were on their way.

"Oh," Randy said softly, "so now you've got control over the 250 pounds of gorilla that came out of the audience? You didn't do anything wrong. Where was Sneed's wonderful security force, that's what I want to know."

Kyle refused to raise his head. "You said something was going to go wrong, and I snapped at you. You were right. I should have listened. God, I'm so stupid."

Randy looked hard at his boyfriend. "Look at me."

Reluctantly, Kyle met his eye.

With his face set to a fierce seriousness, Randy said, "I'm going to ask you something I've never asked you, not in the whole time this farce has been going on. And I want you to answer from your heart."

Kyle looked a little wary. "Okay," he said.

"Are you," Randy asked, "the reincarnation of Jesus Christ?"

The question seemed to sting Kyle. "Of course not!" he answered.

"Are you in some way channeling his spirit or in any way connected with him?"

"No! You know that! I'm just me!"

Randy nodded. "So you can't control events. You can't control what other people do. You can't control the Earth, the stars, or the sun. You can't control what an overzealous fan does. You never could. You certainly can't now. I'm sure this isn't the first time a wrestling fan has gotten out of control and actually caused damage."

"But—"

"But nothing. You didn't hurt Tony, and you didn't cause him to get hurt. You couldn't have prevented it."

"Yeah," Kyle said, his mouth set into a pout, "but if I'd only—"

Randy gripped Kyle's arm tightly. "I can do the same thing, you know. I can find ways to blame myself. I saw the guy getting into the ring.

Do you think I don't wonder if I'd been quicker that I might have prevented this? I saw it happening and I called out, but I wasn't in time. I was too shocked at first to speak. Even if I'd managed to warn Tony, who's to say he could have reacted in time? You can examine bad events like this all you want and place blame, but the important thing is that Tony's okay."

Kyle responded by squeezing Randy's hand.

After a few minutes, Debbie and Jimmy bustled into the waiting room. Randy jumped up and enveloped Debbie in a hug. She asked breathlessly, "How is he? Have you heard?"

"He's fine," Randy told her. "He broke his collarbone. They're setting it right now. He hit his head going out of the ring and has a slight concussion, so they're keeping him overnight for observation, but the doctor told us it's just a precaution. He said Tony was even cracking jokes."

Jimmy Murdoch plopped into the chair next to Kyle. "How are you holding up, man?" he asked.

Kyle shrugged. "Okay, I guess. At least this should put an end to all the talk about me being Jesus."

"How do you figure that?" Debbie asked.

Kyle's smile was weak. "Don't you think that if I had healing powers I would have just touched his shoulder and healed him? I mean, if I can save a cat from terminal hairballs, healing a broken collarbone should be a cinch. So it ends up I'm just a simple professional wrestler who's sort of dumb."

"You're not dumb," Randy responded automatically.

Kyle rolled his eyes. "Whatever. I did flunk geometry in school, and that should have been a clue right there."

Debbie blinked. "What do you mean? A clue to what?"

"Jesus was a carpenter, right? Carpenters have got to know shit like that. Angles and stuff. It stands to reason, then, that I can't be him."

AROUND the corner from them, Jeff Hardesty chuckled to himself. He didn't know what had possessed him to follow the boys to the hospital, but now he was glad he had. Listening to Temple talk, Hardesty found himself really liking the boy. He seemed nice. He made sense.

Unfortunately, sense wasn't something in which *America's Crier* was interested. What sense was there to stories of giant intelligent hedgehogs living in Yosemite National Park or sea serpents being sighted in Cape Cod?

Hardesty figured he'd keep tabs on Temple. Maybe he could get him away from the Randy character long enough to interview him. That was what the next issue of the *Crier* needed: actual words spoken by Temple himself. It didn't matter what the boy actually said. Hardesty was an old hand a twisting words to fit the story he wanted to write.

Just ten minutes with the boy. That was all he needed.

CHAPTER
TWENTY-FOUR

SEEING Tony in good spirits and even practicing speeches he'd be making at the wrestling shows during the next several weeks while he was incapacitated helped to buoy Kyle's mood. The two plotted out a feud between them, and Tony planned on entering the ring wearing his cast and issuing challenges to Kyle. It would keep the wrestler in the spotlight while he was unable to wrestle. Kyle insisted on returning the following day, when Tony was discharged, to drive him home.

Pulling out of Tony's drive, Randy kept one hand on the wheel so that the other was free to hold Kyle's fingers tightly. "I wasn't going to ask," he said, taking a right turn awkwardly due to only using the one hand, "but my curiosity is getting the better of me. I heard you on the phone with Sneed earlier. Want to fill me in on what you said? I mean, technically speaking, I should know. After all, I'm your manager, Money-Mad Randy."

Kyle chuckled. "I think we'd better retire Money-Mad, don't you? He's really not all that effective a manager, and I think he's only doing it because his boyfriend asked him to do it. And then there's the fact that Sneed still has him on a trial basis, so he's still not getting paid. And also I think I'm going to have enough things on my mind when I'm in the ring that I don't want to have to worry about you. You understand, don't you?"

With a soft smile, Randy asked, "Am I being fired? I didn't realize I was doing such a bad job."

"You sucked," Kyle replied with a laugh. "Just go back to watching from the stands. It's okay, honestly."

"Agreed. Now, what were you talking with Sneed about?"

"I just told him I wasn't going to wrestle tonight. I wanted some time to think about how to handle the whole mess. He agreed. We're going to have a meeting on Monday with all the wrestlers to decide on how we'll proceed."

"Weren't you supposed to wrestle Pete tonight?"

"Jimmy will do it."

Randy frowned, confused. "But Jimmy was wrestling some other guy, wasn't he? What's happening with that match?"

Sighing in mock exasperation, as if Randy was a feeble-minded child one had to endure, Kyle replied, "That's easy. Jimmy has his match first. Then he changes into a different outfit and puts on a mask for his lockup with Pete. They give him a different name and pretend it's someone totally new. They do it all the time. I can't tell you how many times I've been the Masked Avenger or something similar."

"Forgive my ignorance."

"Forgiven."

"So we have a Saturday night free together," Randy said in awe. "That's a rarity. What do you want to do?"

Kyle thought for a moment. "I want to go dancing."

Randy took his eyes off the road long enough to glance at Kyle questioningly. "Like where?"

His chin defiantly up, Kyle said, "Some gay club. What's the best one for dancing? My knowledge of dance clubs is… well, I don't have any knowledge of dance clubs. The only ones I've ever seen were on TV or in movies."

"Well, don't be expecting Babylon from *Queer As Folk*. The closest we have to that is Club Meridian. That's probably the best dance club in Indianapolis."

Kyle nodded. "That's where we're going, then."

"Really?"

"Really. What time do most people go out?"

Randy eyed some fast-food places ahead, aware of his stomach gurgling. "Should we get something to eat? I'm famished."

"Sure."

"That's an excellent question about the time to go out, by the way. It's really important to hit the time just right. You don't want to go too early, when the club is just getting started. Then you look like a loser. You also don't want to wait too long or else you've got a long line getting in to contend with. Also, if you wait too long, everyone in the place is already on their way to being drunk and you're just getting started. Not good. I find that in Indy the best time is between ten thirty and eleven thirty. I try to time it so I'm there right at eleven, usually. Well, I did when I was going out to clubs, anyway."

"Hey, if it's not until eleven, the show will be over by then. Maybe we can ask Jimmy and Debbie to come with us."

Randy smiled. "Do you think Jimmy Murdoch will feel comfortable at a gay club? And does he have a fake ID that will hold up? They check them pretty good, you know."

"He's got an older brother. I know he just borrows his license to go to bars. I don't think that'll be a problem. And I can't see Jimmy uncomfortable anywhere, not as long as they serve beer."

"I'll give Debbie a call and see if they're up for it. In the meantime, shall we pass under the Golden Arches for some burgers?"

"Yeah. I'm hungry for some filet-o-clown."

RANDY had always though he was obsessive when preparing for a night out on the town. The hair had to be just right, the outfit perfect, and the cologne expertly sprayed.

Seeing Kyle get ready, he felt like abdicating his throne. The boy tried on nearly every shirt of his in the closet, stood in front of the mirror, preened, and then promptly rejected the choice. Finally, after exhausting almost every one of his shirts and a large majority of Randy's, most of which were way too tight in any case, he decided to wear one of his first selections, a shiny, solid dark-blue button-down shirt. Then he started the same procedure with jeans.

Wearing the third pair, Kyle tried to position himself in the bathroom so he could see his rear in the mirror. He craned his head around but couldn't decide if the 501s he had donned showed his bubble butt to its best effect. "What do you think about these?" he asked.

Randy checked his hair one last time, just in case he didn't get another chance at the mirror. "If I say they're great, will that mean anything? I told Debbie we'd meet them outside the club at eleven, and if they were going to be much later than that we'd go ahead inside and they could find us. At this rate, they'll be waiting for us to arrive when the bar's announced last call."

Kyle rubbed his face nervously. "It's my first time in a gay club. I want to make sure I get noticed. How horrible would it be to be new meat in a club and no one pays any attention to you? I want to make sure I get some glances while we're out there tripping the light fantastic."

"For one thing," Randy admonished him, "no one says tripping the light fantastic anymore. You might as well say twenty-three skidoo or call someone a hep cat. And secondly, you look great. And thirdly, don't you get enough people watching you when you wrestle? Isn't your ego stroked enough by that?"

Kyle playfully slapped his boyfriend. "This is different from wrestling. There I don't have to look good. I just have to look like I'm ready to pound the shit out of someone. You wouldn't want to be embarrassed to be seen with me, would you?"

Randy laughed and hugged Kyle tightly. "That could never happen."

Kyle turned and straightened his shirt, giving one last look at his reflection. "I guess this will have to do. It'll be good to be out in a crowd that won't recognize me as the guy from the *Crier*. At least, I assume they won't."

"I doubt they will," Randy replied. "I'd guess they're not the *Crier*'s clientele. That and they'll be too busy dancing their asses off to care. So are we ready?"

Kyle started to leave the bathroom. "We're ready," he said before stopping suddenly. He looked worriedly at Randy. "Should I leave my hair down, or tie it back into a ponytail?"

AS THEY pulled away in Randy's car, they failed to notice Jeff Hardesty following them a few car lengths away.

RANDY noticed as they entered the large main room of Club Meridian that Jimmy Murdoch kept Debbie firmly in hand. Randy wondered if it was an unconscious signal to all the fairies sipping drinks and dancing that This Is a Straight Boy—Hands Off or if it was just that Jimmy enjoyed holding on to Debbie. Watching Jimmy's body language, he assumed it was the latter. There didn't seem to be a tense muscle in the boy's body. Besides, he didn't need Debbie by his side. No gay boy would wear baggy hip-hop clothes to Club Meridian. Randy was surprised Jimmy even got in the door, his brother's driver's license notwithstanding.

Debbie put her head on Jimmy's shoulder. "Buy me a drink, big boy?" she asked.

"Sure thing."

Debbie winked at Randy. "We'll catch up with you boys later."

Kyle was staring out into the huge dance floor, his mouth open. "I had no idea there were this many homos in the state. Are you sure they don't bus them in from Kentucky?"

"No, I'm pretty sure most of these are home-grown fags. Did you want to get a drink or hit the dance floor?"

Kyle's face lit up. "Let's hit the dance floor, but only on the condition that you don't laugh at my dancing. I dance kind of weird."

Randy laughed. "As long as you don't flail your arms about like Kermit the Frog and hurt someone, I'm sure we'll be fine. The only rule they have around here is that you can't damage the other dancers." He thought a moment and then asked, "How weird?"

"I sort of jump up and down in rhythm. And not always to the rhythm that's playing."

Randy took Kyle by the hand and pulled him into the sweating, pulsating throng. He had to nearly yell over the din of the music. "Don't worry. We'll start off slowly and you can work your way up. Just follow my lead."

Kyle watched Randy carefully, trying to mimic his movements. Aside from a horrible sense of timing, he didn't do too badly.

"Try punching your hands out in time to the music," Randy told him. "Sort of like you're shadowboxing. Just don't throw the full punch. Yeah, that's it. It helps you keep the rhythm."

Once he got the hang of the dancing, Kyle didn't seem to want to leave their spot. The couple danced to song after song, going from Madonna to Cher to a techno song Randy wasn't familiar with. For the first time in what seemed like ages, Randy felt relaxed and free from worry.

Then he spotted the twink with the blue streak through his hair giving Kyle the eye. It wasn't a wow-you're-one-hot-fucker look. It was more a hey-don't-I-recognize-you-from-somewhere look. The twink stopped dancing with his partner and tapped Kyle on the shoulder.

"Hey," he said, struggling to be heard over the thump of the music. "Aren't you that guy? That wrestler guy who's supposed to be Jesus or something like that?"

Randy could see Kyle trying to decide whether to tell the truth or a convenient lie. "Well," he said after a short pause, "I'm a wrestler, but—"

"Whoa!" the guy screamed. He tugged on his partner's sleeve. "Hey, Marty! This is the wrestler dude! This is the Jesus reincarnation guy!"

Marty seemed suitably impressed. He stared at Kyle. "You're fucking kidding me! You're him?"

"I'm him, but—" Kyle tried to shout.

"Can I have your autograph?" the twink asked. He pointed to his shirtless and somewhat bony chest. "You can sign it right here, just above my right tit."

"I don't have a pen," Kyle yelled, attempting to keep up with the techno beat. "And besides—"

"Hey, do you go by Jesus," Marty asked, "or by your other name?"

"Kyle's my name. I'm not—"

"Hey," the twink said, gushing like he was in the presence of Jennifer Lopez, "I've always wanted to know something. Are you a top or a bottom? I think it would be so hot to be fucked by Jesus. It'd be a sort of religious experience."

Randy burst in with, "You're not listening. He's trying to tell you he's not—"

A good-looking guy on the other side of Kyle decided to join in. "You're that guy? The Jesus guy?"

"No!" Kyle shouted. "I'm just—"

"Hey!" the newcomer to the conversation screamed out to anyone who could hear him over the music, "this is the wrestler guy! Jesus himself has come to party!" He pointed excitedly at Kyle.

Randy had been in tight crowds on the dance floor before when it seemed that you could only move a fraction of an inch without bumping into a stranger. Suddenly he yearned for that much personal space. The entire dance floor seemed to convulse, and without warning, every club kid, every twink, every tweaker, every drunk, and every party boy descended on Randy and Kyle like a tidal wave. Hands were outstretched as dancers desperately tried to get a little touch of Kyle's clothing or, better yet, a touch of his skin. Randy tried to grab hold of him, but it seemed like a half a dozen gay boys popped up out of nowhere in between the two of them. Kyle raised his head, trying to keep Randy in sight. Randy heard someone shout out, "Dance with me, Jesus!" It seemed a sea of hands was threatening to engulf Kyle.

"Leave me alone!" Kyle screamed. Randy could see a flurry of motion, and then he caught sight of Kyle escaping the horde, rushing towards the exit. Kyle passed a surprised-looking Jimmy and Debbie, who were sipping cosmopolitans at the bar, before bursting past the bouncer at the door.

Randy, his shirt torn (he wasn't sure just when that had happened), tried to follow, but the dance crowd had the same idea. The dance floor was quickly abandoned as the mob followed Kyle's path of retreat. The bouncer stared in disbelief as the majority of the bar attempted to exit at the same time.

Out of breath, Randy finally made it to where Debbie and Jimmy were sitting, concerned looks on their faces.

"He wasn't that bad of a dancer, was he?" Jimmy asked.

ONE man remained on the dance floor. A very satisfied Jeff Hardesty checked to ensure that his camera hadn't been damaged by the near-riot. He felt pummeled and bruised, but happy. The *Crier* would have one hell of a cover story come Tuesday.

CHAPTER
TWENTY-FIVE

MONDAY night Kyle and Randy enjoyed a creative but exhausting lovemaking session involving a pair of handcuffs and some interestingly placed mounds of whipped cream. Therefore Randy was groggy and sluggish as he started the drive to work on Tuesday morning. A large cup of coffee beckoned in his mind, but he didn't want to wait in line at Starbucks. Therefore, he decided to pop into the corner convenience store.

He waited to pay for his large java behind an elderly man purchasing a magazine and some microwave popcorn. The man was having trouble counting out his pennies. Randy, exasperated, bit his lip and turned his attention to the candy counter, thinking maybe some chocolate would go well with the coffee. As he turned, his eyes passed over the newspaper stand. Some words burned into his retinas. His eyes popped open. Randy no longer felt fatigue, and the steaming coffee in his hands had nothing to do with his wakefulness.

In big, bold letters, *America's Crier* announced JESUS IS GAY!

Randy blinked, thinking surely he'd read wrong. No, the words were still there, just above a grainy photo of Kyle dancing at Club Meridian. A smaller headline under the picture read "Pro Wrestling Phenomenon Caught at Notorious Gay Hangout With New Lover."

The coffee slipped from Randy's fingers. The lid miraculously stayed on, causing only a minute amount of the burning liquid to seep out of the tiny sipping hole, but Randy failed to notice that his trouser legs had escaped getting soaked. Vaguely he was aware of the elderly man moving past him and the guy behind the register asking him, "Sir, was there anything I can get for you?"

Realizing someone was speaking to him, Randy said, "Huh?"

"Can I help you?"

Randy looked at the *Crier* and then back to the clerk. He quickly went back to the tabloid. It still said the same thing. "Huh?" he repeated.

The clerk was starting to get worried. "Should I call someone? Are you having some sort of attack?"

Moving like an automaton, Randy stepped carefully over the dropped coffee cup and walked out of the convenience store. He could vaguely hear the clerk shouting after him, asking if an ambulance was required, but the voice sounded like it was very far away. It certainly wasn't in Randy's world. It was a ghost voice. They were words creeping through a crack in the dimensions, spoken sentences from another reality making their tentative way into our realm. Somehow Randy made his way back to the car. He got in and sat in the driver's seat, staring straight ahead.

In order to drive the car, he told himself, *you have first got to put the key in the ignition and turn it. Otherwise, the car won't go.*

"JESUS" IS GAY. Pro Wrestling Phenomenon Caught at Notorious Gay Hangout With New Lover.

The car still isn't moving. Why isn't the car moving? Oh, yeah, the whole key thing.

Randy shook his head. Notorious? The Club Meridian wasn't notorious. It didn't even qualify as decadent, and God knows it tried to be.

What's this in my hands? Oh, yeah, these are my car keys. They start cars. Give them a try.

JESUS IS GAY.

Randy wondered if his mother would still want Kyle and him to sit in their pew on Sunday morning.

And the rabid wrestling fans at Kyle's shows? They weren't exactly the most gay-friendly group in existence. How would they react?

And how would the Tea Party Republicans react?

That thought made Randy laugh. The spell broken, he started his car. He headed for his apartment, however, and not toward work. Shelly would have to cope for a few hours on her own.

KYLE had to go out and purchase an issue to see with his own eyes. He returned to the apartment ashen-faced but fairly calm. He kicked the door closed behind him with the *Crier* open in his hands. "Have you read the article?" he asked.

Randy was sipping some tea at the breakfast table. He shook his head. "I haven't yet, no. Why? How much worse could it get?"

Wincing, Kyle read aloud. "Temple's new companion, whom insiders confirm is the wrestler's new lover, is a retail store manager, aged...."

"What?"

"Thirty-nine."

Randy exploded, leaping from his chair and grabbing the *Crier* from Kyle's fingers. "Those bastards! I'll sue them for everything they're worth!"

"They don't mention you by name," Kyle said, hoping to defuse the situation.

"They may not give my last name, but they talk about Money-Mad Randy! Everyone is going to know."

"It's not as bad as being outed," Kyle said, protesting. "Can we get some perspective here?"

Sighing, Randy tossed the *Crier* onto the floor. "You're right. This isn't about me. You realize there's no way you'll be able to wrestle for a while."

Kyle's lip quivered. "That's if Sneed even lets me wrestle ever again. Pro wrestling is pretty homophobic, especially in the independent circuits. Maybe I can talk him into letting me stay as another character. I can wear a mask. I'll shave my beard and moustache and maybe even color my hair. That'll work, won't it?"

Randy nodded. "I think that's a good idea. And if Sneed won't let you wrestle, we'll just find you another promotion. There are several in the area. We won't let this stop us."

"Let's do it today," Kyle said enthusiastically. "Would you mind running out and getting me some hair color while I shave? Hell, in an hour or so I'll look totally different. No more Jesus, no more controversy. Right?"

"Right!" Randy started for the door, but stopped when the security buzzer sounded, indicating that someone wanted to get into the building. Randy stepped over to the speaker grill and pressed a button. "Who is it?"

A plummy female voice came out of the grill. "My name is Tamalita Edwards. I'm with Universal Wrestling Extravaganza. I wanted to speak with Kyle Temple, if I may."

Kyle's eyes widened. "Tamalita Edwards? Did she say Tamalita Edwards?"

Randy nodded. "That's what she said." Into the grill, he said, "I'll buzz you in. Take the stairs to 219."

Kyle swayed a little. He gripped the top of the couch to steady himself. "How does my hair look?"

Randy opened the door upon hearing the knock. Tamalita Edwards was a tall, thin woman with raven hair, wearing an expensive blue suit. On her feet were heels most drag queens would die for. She shook off her blue jacket, handing it to Randy as if he were a servant. Her focus was entirely on Kyle.

Smiling, she extended a well-manicured hand toward him. "I'm Tamalita Edwards. I don't have to ask who you are. You're getting to be quite famous, young man."

Randy looked at the jacket in his arms, wondering if he should just drop it to the floor. Instead, he draped it over a chair, and then he looked carefully at Tamalita. She was obviously trying to look younger than her years. The carefully applied makeup couldn't hide the crow's feet around her eyes, and her chin had that stretched-out look that came from one too many plastic surgeries. *She's as much a bitch in real life as she is on television*, he thought.

Kyle was grinning shyly at her as he shook her hand. "The pleasure is all mine, Ms. Edwards."

"Please call me Tammy. All my friends do."

"Okay. Tammy. I'm Kyle, and this is Randy."

Still, she didn't acknowledge Randy's presence. "May we sit? I won't take up much of your time, but I wanted to run a proposition past you."

Kyle swallowed hard, trying to hide his embarrassment. "Of course. Please have a seat. Is there anything I can get for you? A beer, or… maybe a cola?"

Sitting down on one end of the couch, Tammy threw a half glance Randy's way. "I'll have a club soda or a ginger ale if you've got one."

Kyle sat on the other end of the couch, his fingers dancing nervously. Ignoring Tammy's request, Randy sat in a chair opposite them. Tammy didn't seem to notice.

"I suppose you're wondering what I'm doing here," she said to Kyle.

Kyle's grin was reaching manic proportions. "I can't imagine, but it's just so great to meet you. I've watched you every week on television, and I must say you're even lovelier in person."

Tammy chuckled and pretended to blush, even putting a hand against her non-flushed cheek. Randy had the idea that it was a practiced reaction to whenever she was complimented. It wasn't genuine. He felt she expected accolades on her looks and would have been disappointed if she hadn't received one. "That's so sweet of you to say," she murmured.

"What's Crusher Phillips really like?" Kyle asked, gushing. "He just seems like such a cool guy."

Smiling slyly, Tammy replied, "Well, you might be able to find out on your own. How would you feel about wrestling Crusher Phillips?"

Kyle's resemblance to an excited puppy increased. "You're kidding, right?"

"Not at all. We're always looking for new storylines at UWE, and we've got Wrestlepalooza 15 coming up in a few months. Crusher was supposed to go up against Stone Face Griswold, but dear old Grizzy broke his leg in three places taking a fall off his motorcycle."

"I heard about that," Kyle said. "I thought it was just part of the story, though. I figured he'd show up to the match in a cast or something and then he'd rip it off and wallop Crusher with it."

Tammy nodded. "We've done that sort of thing before, of course, but this time it's the real thing. The ass actually won't be able to wrestle. I thought you could take his place."

Sound tried to make its way out of Kyle's throat, but it wouldn't come.

Smiling, Tammy said, "I take it that you might be interested. We'd have to work quickly, of course, getting you established as one of our wrestlers. You'd have to come to our training camp down in Tampa for a few days, and then we could introduce you on Monday night's show. We'll get you some pathetic jobber to wrestle, and you'll totally trounce him. In just a few weeks we can get you recognized as a force to be reckoned with. We'll build you up week by week right up until Wrestlepalooza. What do you think?"

Kyle spoke, but only a few consonants escaped.

"You might want to change your mind," Randy said. Tammy looked at him as if he'd suddenly appeared out of thin air. He got up and picked the *Crier* off the floor. "Look at the front page. I'm assuming you haven't seen the new issue."

Tammy Edwards took the tabloid from him and scanned it critically. Finally she tossed it aside. "That doesn't matter. Our PR department can work with that. Our audiences believe whatever we want them to believe. If we want them to love Kyle, they'll love him. If we want them to hate him, they will."

"And which will it be?" Randy asked.

"Oh, they'll love him," Tammy replied. "They'll have to. Crusher is our nastiest heel right now. He used to be a good guy, of course, but then that fire extinguisher fell on his head and turned him evil. Kyle will be our new hero."

Kyle seemed to be having trouble breathing. "You mean I'm really going to wrestle Crusher Phillips? At Wrestlepalooza, even?"

"And you'll win the match, making you our new heavyweight champion."

Kyle nearly fell off the couch. "I win? You're kidding! I'm going to have the championship belt?"

"Naturally. If you're in agreement, we'll have to set up a meeting with your manager. I can have contracts ready by tomorrow, if you think this is something you'd be interested in."

Laughing giddily, Kyle said, "Are you kidding? I don't have a manager, though. I mean, not a real one. I guess Mr. Sneed, the owner of our promotion, is the closest thing—"

"It doesn't matter," Tammy said, cutting him off. "Managers just get in the way, don't they? The contract is pretty straightforward. I'm staying downtown at the Westin. Do you think you could come by about one o'clock tomorrow? We can have everything ready by then, and I can answer any questions you may have."

Kyle shook his head in disbelief. "And here I was just about to shave off my beard and color my hair. I still could, of course, if you—"

Shocked, Tammy interrupted him. "Absolutely not! In fact, that will be in your contract. We'll be playing up the Jesus angle." She eyed the discarded *Crier* with distaste. "And playing down the gay angle, of course.

The Jesus thing will be our whole focus. I'm envisioning having twelve disciples leading you out to the ring. A later storyline can have one of them betraying you, causing you to lose the belt back to Crusher. Oh yes, there's quite a lot we can do with this, but the hair can't be cut and the beard and mustache definitely have to stay. We've got to capitalize on the look."

Randy eyed her suspiciously. "How are you going to downplay the gay angle?"

Tammy turned to him, again seeming to be surprised that he was sitting there. "We'll bury that. It will just be an unsubstantiated rumor. Every actor in Hollywood gets called gay at one time or another. We'll just deny the whole thing. We'll give him a girlfriend to accompany him to his shows. That'll be all it will take to convince most viewers. We'll call her Mary, of course, and we'll make her look like a whore."

"If you're referring to Mary Magdalene, she wasn't really a whore. Scholars now think—"

Tammy shrugged. "It doesn't matter. Everyone thinks she was a whore, so our Mary will be one." She thought for a moment. "My daughter is about your age, Kyle. She's flunking out of college anyway. Maybe I'll bring her in to be your Mary." Tammy jutted her jaw forward, which made her look, to Randy's eyes, anyway, like a sick lizard. "This could be big. It's your shot at the big time, and believe me, I know a lot of wrestlers who'd give their right arms just to be considered for this. What do you think? Are you interested?"

Kyle shook his head in wonder. "This is unbelievable. I don't know what to say."

"I do," Randy said archly.

Neither Kyle nor Tammy paid him any attention.

CHAPTER
TWENTY-SIX

SILENCE fell for several minutes after the grand exit of Tamalita Edwards. Randy stayed in his chair, afraid to look Kyle in the eye. He could tell Kyle was beside himself with excitement, but Randy didn't want to talk about Tammy's visit or even think about it. It was, Randy foresaw, an argument in the making. Kyle was bound to ask Randy's opinion, and if Randy actually gave it, a fight would ensue. If he were honest, Randy would have to say he thought the whole idea was incredibly bad. Kyle would only see his chance of wrestling in the big time with his idol. Nothing else would matter.

Maybe I can sneak off to the bathroom for a while, and then when he's on the phone telling all his buddies the good news, I can slip off to bed and be asleep (or pretend to be) and avoid the fight until tomorrow, Randy thought to himself. He shifted in his chair, but that only broke Kyle out of his reverie.

Kyle began to pace. His grin hadn't left his face since Ms. Edwards had made her announcement. "Can you believe it? I mean, this is fucking amazing. Here we were thinking that the *Crier* was a bad thing, but now I get to join the UWE and wrestle Crusher Phillips! At Wrestlepalooza even! I mean, how great is that? What I thought was a curse has turned into a godsend!"

You didn't move fast enough, Randy told himself. Aloud, he sighed and said, "What about Tony?"

Kyle frowned. "What about him?"

"Have you forgotten that because of all this he's broken his collarbone? That he got a concussion?"

"A mild one," Kyle said dismissively. "The doctor even said—"

"This time it was a mild one, but it easily could have been much worse." Randy shook his head. "You and I have been trying to downplay this whole Jesus reincarnation thing, and yet still people are acting crazy. Tony could have been hurt much worse. That crowd could easily have turned into a riotous mob. The idea of someone—anyone—being in any way related to, channeling, or reincarnated from Jesus Christ is just too volatile. People just have too strongly held beliefs about that sort of thing. It's only been a few weeks, and already someone has gotten hurt over it. What's going to happen if you play the Jesus card for real? Shove it in people's face? Things will get much worse."

"Tony gets hurt all the time," Kyle replied in a placating tone. "He's, like, accident prone or something. You saw him in the hospital, though. He was joking. He's fine with it."

Randy bit his lip in thought. "That woman wants to play up the Jesus angle. It's no skin off her teeth. It gives her a controversial storyline, and that's the sort of thing they like. But she's not the one that could get hurt. Some religious zealot could show up at one of your shows with a gun, or the crowd could riot—"

"They have real security at UWE shows," Kyle pointed out. "Not just high school football jocks. Real big guys. Nothing will happen. You're just being overly protective."

Looking down at his lap to avoid Kyle's hurt gaze, Randy went on. "It's not just the safety issue, although I think that's pretty huge. It just seems... wrong to me, capitalizing on this. You know you're not Christ's reincarnation or anything of the sort. We both know it. To use that to further your career just seems unscrupulous in some way."

"Would it be different if I quoted Shakespeare while under hypnosis, or Pluto?"

Randy buried his face in his hands. "I don't know. I honestly don't. I've never considered myself to be religious. Not in any conventional sense, to be sure. But it does seem wrong to even suggest...." He stopped and looked up. "Pluto?"

Kyle rolled his eyes. "The philosopher guy? Knew Socrates? I thought you were supposed to be smart."

"Plato. Pluto is Mickey Mouse's dog."

"I said Plato," Kyle replied, a little too quickly. "You're just upset. It's probably the idea of me going off to the UWE training camp and the fact that I'll be awfully busy over the next couple of months. It's understandable. Hey, maybe you could come down with me. Shelly can watch the store just fine. You can hire another part-time person to help out if you want. That way you don't have—"

Randy sat up straight and blew out a lungful of air. "I don't want you to go."

Kyle's eyes blazed. "Excuse me? What did you say?"

"I said I don't want you to go. I just think this is a bad idea. I think something horrible will happen if you do this. I don't know what. I think you should do what we were going to do before that woman came in. Shave off the beard and moustache. Cut the hair. Wrestle for Sneed or somebody else in a mask until this Jesus thing is long forgotten."

As Kyle advanced on Randy, his face flushed with agitation. "I don't think you understand how important this is to me. I get to wrestle with Crusher Phillips. At Wrestlepalooza. And win. I win the fucking UWE championship belt. This is a dream come true. Hell, it's what I've wanted ever since I was a small kid. And you want me to walk away from this?"

Randy fought back the tears that were threatening to burst forward. "I've got to be honest with you. I know you want this, but I just say this isn't the way. This isn't the time. Stay with the independents for now and work your way up, just like you would have if none of this had happened."

Kyle shook his head. "Fuck you," he said vehemently.

Randy jerked as if he'd been physically hit. "What?"

"I said fuck you." Tears were now showing in Kyle's eyes as well. Angrily, he went on. "You're fucking pathetic. You just can't stand to see me get what I want because you're afraid once I'm successful I'll find somebody else." He stared hard at Randy. "Someone younger."

Looking down, Randy allowed his own tears to fall freely. "I can't believe you just said that."

Kyle's voice shook with emotion. "I can't believe you don't want me to have my dream. I thought you were my soul mate, my other half. Now I find out you just want me to do whatever Randy Stone wants to do. I've got to do this. It's my life."

"I just don't want anyone to take advantage of you."

"You think I'm stupid, is that it?" Kyle yelled. "You always told me I wasn't dumb, but when it comes right down to it, you treat me like everyone else does. Well, this stupid person is a wrestler, and this stupid wrestler has the chance to wrestle in the big time. If that takes capitalizing on some stupid recordings done during a bogus hypnosis session, so be it."

Randy shook his head. "I don't want to fight. Why don't we go out and get something to eat and talk about this later?"

Kyle's nose had begun running. He sniffed loudly. "You do what you want. I'm going out. On my own."

Randy looked up. "I just want what's right for you. Honestly. I love you."

"Yeah," Kyle replied, nearly choking on his tears. "I always thought you did too." He pulled his jacket off of a chair and stormed out of the apartment, making sure to slam the door behind him.

Randy sat unmoving for a long time. Just when he thought he was all cried out, more tears would come. He let them fall. When he finally cried all he had in him, he put on his own jacket and left the apartment as well.

"WHAT is this one called again?" Randy asked the bartender. He slurred his words slightly.

"It's an appletini." The bartender was cute in that college frat boy way. Big, but not muscular in the way Kyle was. He was strong, Randy could tell, but there was a lot of softness there as well. *Probably straight, though*, Randy thought. *He exudes straightness. He'd probably punch me out if I put the moves on him.* Not that Randy wanted to make out with the bartender or any other guy on God's green Earth. Nope, he was done with guys. He planned on buying a dog. He'd spend all his evenings in the park throwing a Frisbee. Dogs were better than boyfriends in any case.

Randy downed half of the appletini in a gulp. He winced. "It tastes like apples," he said, "mixed liberally with paint thinner." He mangled the pronunciation of liberally, but he knew the bartender got the idea.

"Want to go back to the chocolatini?" the bartender asked. He rested his beefy arms on the bar in front of Randy. Randy admired the hair covering the guy's forearms. Kyle didn't really have much body hair, and what he did have was so pale as to be nearly translucent.

Why are you thinking of Kyle's arm hair? he asked himself. *Forget Kyle. He's gone. He's off to find wrestling glory.*

Randy had finally decided to eat some food just as the sun was going down. He had returned to the apartment with a fast-food sack only to find most of Kyle's stuff missing from the closet. There was no note. There was no Kyle. There was only a decidedly empty-feeling apartment, which broke Randy's heart more than he ever thought could be possible.

He threw back the rest of the appletini. "What other kinds of martinis do you have?"

"There's a peachtini."

"Sounds vile," Randy said. "Give me two of them."

The bartender nodded and began to fix the drink.

While he waited, Randy took a look around the sports bar he'd stumbled into. It was still fairly early in the evening, so there were only a few people scattered about the place. A young couple sat at a nearby table, gazing rapturously into each other's eyes. Randy decided that if he drank enough to be sick, he'd make sure he vomited in their direction. The two peachtinis should do it.

The bartender handed Randy the first peachtini. "Girl trouble?" he asked.

Taking a big sip, Randy made a face. "If you consider trouble with a six foot, 180 pound wrestler with a seven-inch cut dick girl trouble, then yes."

The bartender chuckled. "I kind of figured you were gay."

"What gave it away?"

"Well, for one thing, no straight guy drinks peachtinis. And no straight guy would wear that shirt. No offense. It looks good. It just looks gay."

"No offense taken. I was just thinking to myself that you looked terminally straight."

"Guilty as charged."

"Good." Randy drank more of the peachtini. "It doesn't improve on repeated sips, does it?"

"Not really, no. So you had a fight with your boyfriend?"

Finishing the peachtini, Randy could feel the tears threatening to return. He forced them back. There was no way he was going to cry in front of Joe College. "I think we broke up. He took all of his stuff out of my apartment."

"Bummer."

"You bet your ass it's a bummer. He could fuck like a tiger. Best I've ever had." Randy sniffed miserably. "Or ever will have."

The bartender smiled weakly, obviously at a loss for words. "Well," he said after a long pause, "maybe he'll come back to his senses. And if he doesn't... well, there are a lot of other fish in the sea, eh?"

Randy frowned. "Are you new at this commiserating thing? Because you suck at it."

"I know. I'm better at pouring drinks."

"Well, give me my second peachtini. Only less gasoline in this one."

Halfway through his drink, Randy felt his brain start to muddle. The pain in his heart refused to subside, however, so he continued to sip. He became aware of someone fluttering onto the stool next to him, but he refused to look over to see who it was. He didn't want anyone in his world except Joe Bartender and the hypothetical dog he was going to get. The last thing he needed tonight was to strike up a conversation with some stranger. When whoever it was put their head on his shoulder, though, he thought he ought to check the person out.

It was Debbie. "I got your text message. How are you doing?"

"Fine. I text messaged you? I don't remember doing that."

"It wasn't exactly coherent, but I got the gist of what you were trying to say."

"How did you find me?"

"The message said you were getting drunk in a bar. I figured you wouldn't go far from your apartment, seeing as you wouldn't be in any condition to drive and I know how conscientious you are. I just started looking in every bar downtown. I had no idea there were that many bars in the area. It took me forever to find you. What in the world are you drinking?"

"Hemlock with a strychnine chaser. Care to join me?"

Debbie shook her head. "Want to talk about it?"

Randy sniffed. "What's to talk about? I opened my big mouth and ruined everything. He accused me of being too controlling, and in a way he's right. I just am so worried he's going to get hurt over this. And I... wait a minute. The bartender's back, and I want to try the strawberrytini. It's as fun to drink as it is to say."

"I find that hard to believe."

"Sure you don't want one? One strawberrytini, then."

The bartender looked dubious. "Haven't you had enough?"

"Nope. My brain is still working. Until that stops function...." He slurred the Ns terribly, so he tried again. "Function... working... then I've had enough. Now, if you'll excuse me, I need to take a piss."

Randy spun around on the barstool and stood up. He swayed for a moment before falling into a heap on the floor. Debbie looked from his unmoving form to the bartender.

"I think he's had enough now," she said.

CHAPTER
TWENTY-SEVEN

AT EIGHT FIFTEEN the next morning, the universe exploded.

It could also just have been Randy's alarm clock going off. Whichever it was, an amazingly loud sound crashed into his ears, forcing him to sit up in bed. As soon as he did so, his body informed him that quick movements were a bad idea, and in fact moving at all was questionable. He threw the pillow Kyle would have been using across the room, neatly knocking the alarm clock off his dresser. It stayed ringing, but at least now it was somewhat muffled by the pillow that had landed on top of it.

He rubbed his eyes and groaned. His first thought was *Kyle's not here.* His second was *What the holy fuck is a peachtini and why would any sane person drink one?*

He collapsed back onto the bed. His stomach gurgled dangerously. It hurt to open his eyes, so he refrained from doing so. His tongue felt odd, like a groundhog had just pulled its foot out of his mouth. Randy wasn't sure why a groundhog would feel compelled to perform such an act, but that was what it felt like in there. He tried to swallow but couldn't come up with enough spit.

He attempted to sit up again. The room lurched. "Stop that," he said aloud. The room refused to listen. Slowly, he swung his legs over the side of the bed and touched the carpet. Anchoring himself to the floor seemed to help. The walls stopped moving and the bed ceased to behave like a flying carpet from the *Arabian Nights.* Moaning, Randy stood.

And fell back onto the bed.

It took five minutes to repeat the process, but he got to his feet again. He shuffled to the bathroom, taking care not to look at his reflection in the mirrored medicine cabinet.

He slid the panel aside and yanked out a bottle of aspirin. He swallowed three.

It seemed like bees were attacking. Muted bees. Bees with muzzles. He could hear them, but they sounded like they were calling in their performance over a bad cell phone line.

He realized he'd left the alarm clock ringing. It was still under the pillow.

He took another aspirin and went to turn it off. The bees went silent.

Randy stood with the alarm clock in his hand and wondered what he should do with his day. He needed something to keep his mind occupied, otherwise he'd think about Kyle every second.

Nothing came to mind. It was his day off from work, and for that he was grateful. He didn't think he could stand to see any happy gay couples coming into the store to shop. He'd have to stifle the impulse to tell them that romance was merely a fleeting thing. It never lasted.

Randy stood and thought. Maybe he'd go to the zoo and spend the day watching the animals. He could always take in a museum. Anything that would engage his mind and didn't require interaction with humans would suffice.

His phone rang. His heart began to beat faster. Maybe it was Kyle. Grabbing his cell phone off his dresser, he answered to hear Debbie's voice.

"I just wanted to make sure you were still alive," she said.

"I'm fine," Randy lied, "but do you have to scream?"

"Hangover, eh?"

"Just a slight one. And by slight, I mean major. I'll call you later, okay? I really can't talk right now because my brain is threatening to ooze out of my ears."

He could hear Debbie hesitate. "Okay," she said reluctantly, "but I expect you to check back with me. If you don't, I'll come looking for you."

"I promise," he said, hanging up. He placed the alarm clock back onto the dresser and adjusted it slightly. He looked at the framed photo of himself and Kyle next to it. Kyle was dressed in his black wrestling gear and was grinning like an idiot, sweat dripping from his body. Randy was hugging him fiercely and kissing his cheek. Pete had taken the picture after one of their workout sessions. Randy usually didn't like pictures of himself, but this one was really good. Pete had captured a perfect moment of a young couple in love.

Suddenly Randy felt a hankering for a peachtini.

KYLE TEMPLE thought he'd died and gone to heaven.

The last several days had gone by in a blur. The signing of the contract—an honest to goodness contract, much more intense than the only other contract he'd ever signed (a service contract to cover his iPod)—had gone fairly well. He hadn't understood a word of it, of course, but Tammy explained everything to him in fairly general terms. Shortly after that, he'd boarded a plane, and before he knew it he was at the UWE training camp in Tampa.

There he'd met his trainer, Max Johnson. Max had put him through a workout almost immediately. There were several other "newbies" training as well, and a few of the veteran wrestlers of UWE were there to help out and give tips. Kyle felt like he was at Disneyland.

Max had asked him to stop by his office after his shower. Kyle wanted to look serious, so before he knocked on Max's door, he forced the smile off his lips. It wasn't easy. Still, he didn't want to appear goofy to Max. This was, after all, the next step of his career. Hell, it would probably be the height of his career. Kyle wanted to enjoy every second.

Max yelled, "Come in." Kyle slid in almost apologetically.

"Sit down," Max said, indicating the comfortable-looking chair across the desk from him. As Kyle sat, the big, beefy trainer continued. "I have to say, I was impressed with your workout today. A lot of kids from smaller independent promotions think they know how to wrestle, but really they just know how to fall through a table. You've got some good moves. You know your stuff, I'll give you that."

Kyle allowed himself a grin. "Thanks. That was one hell of a workout. I've got bruises in places I didn't even know could bruise. It was cool, though. I loved every second. Don't get me wrong. I could wrestle all day."

Max smiled thinly. "I'm glad you enjoyed it. I understand that because of your notoriety Tammy has got big plans for you."

Kyle's euphoria received a slight dent when he heard an underlying tone when Max used the word *notoriety*. It was almost as if the trainer was saying Kyle really didn't belong with the UWE and that his new position was due to a fluke. Not knowing what to say, Kyle merely muttered, "Yeah, Tammy's great, isn't she?"

The trainer sighed. "You weighed in at 183 today."

Again, Kyle heard a note of disapproval. "Yeah, I've been bulking up, though. I'm sure I can get to 200 pounds by Wrestlepalooza."

"Do you take any supplements?" Max asked.

"Oh, yeah. Tons. Vita-Power 4000 and other stuff like that."

"No steroids?"

Kyle snorted. "I'd never do anything like that. Those things can mess up your body in the long run. Plus, they're illegal." Kyle leaned in and lowered his voice, even though no one else was present to overhear them. "I've even heard that they can make your dick smaller. I mean, I don't have to worry about that, since mine's pretty large as it is, but still... you know?"

Max shook his head. "Steroids get some bad press, it's true. Still, there's a lot of good that can come from them, especially for someone your size. In the independents, you don't look out of place at your size. Here at the UWE, you're going to look small. Our wrestlers are going to look like giants getting into the ring with you. I'm not recommending that you take steroids, mind you," the trainer said, folding his hands over his chest, "but if you wanted to try some out, I can arrange to get you some. I'm just saying."

Again, Kyle was at a loss for words. "Um," he said, "okay." He hoped the subject wouldn't come up again.

Max gazed down at his desk, where Kyle was surprised to see the latest issue of *America's Crier*. "And you're a fag, I see."

"Um," Kyle said. "Yeah."

"Not anymore. I understand Tammy is going to whitewash that as an untrue rumor. Still, you might have some trouble with some of the wrestlers. They'll rag you. They can be a little homophobic."

The trainer paused. It seemed to Kyle that he was supposed to reply, so he said, "Um, okay."

"Do you have a boyfriend at home?"

Kyle thought of Randy back in Indianapolis. He wanted to say yes, but he didn't know how Randy felt about their fight. Were they still together? Kyle wanted to think that Randy knew that what was said had been in the heat of the moment. Then Kyle remembered how forcefully he'd told Randy to fuck off. Kyle bit his lip. "I guess I don't," he said.

"Good."

"Well, there is a guy, but we had this huge fight. I probably should call him and patch things up."

Max sat unmoving for a whole minute before saying, "I'm not sure that would be such a good idea. With Tammy doing her best to bury the gay angle, it would be in your best interests to have nothing to do with anything even remotely homosexual right now. If I were you, I wouldn't call any gay friends. I wouldn't go out to any gay clubs. I wouldn't glance at *The Advocate* on the newsstand. From this moment on, I'd be the straightest guy that ever lived."

"Um... okay."

Max nodded. "Smart boy."

Kyle didn't feel smart. In fact, he'd never felt dumber in his life.

"ARE you sure you're up for this?" Debbie asked. She was entwined with Jimmy Murdoch on Randy's couch. The television was blaring a commercial in front of them.

"I'm sure," Randy replied from his easy chair. He avoided looking at Debbie directly to make sure she couldn't read the indecision on his face.

"He's got to see it," Jimmy said, hugging Debbie tightly in his arms. "It's Kyle's debut on UWE. This is a big deal."

Debbie sighed. "He hasn't seen Kyle since their fight, though. This could be tough."

"Have you tried to call him? Phones work both ways, you know," Jimmy pointed out. "This might be one of those times when you've got to make the first move."

"I've tried. His cell phone's always off."

"Have you left any messages?"

"No, I haven't," Randy had to admit. "I just can't find the words. I've got to talk to him, but it has to be in person, or at least live on the phone. A message just won't cut it." Randy glued his eyes to the television set. "I'm just worried about how these bozos are going to treat him. For his sake, I hope this ends up as good as he's always dreamed it would be."

Jimmy scoffed. "How could it not be? It's everything he's ever wanted. Hell, it's everything I've always wanted. Any of the guys would kill to be where Kyle is right now."

The *Monday Night's Clobbering Night* edition of UWE was coming back after the commercial. The images of Tamalita Edwards and announcer Ted Parnell filled the screen.

"Tammy, up next we've got something special," Parnell said, looking like he was ready to introduce the President of the United States. "We have the first nationally televised match of young Kyle Temple, the young man who's been the subject of much controversy."

Tammy nearly winked at the camera. "That's right. Temple is the young man who, when put under hypnosis, spoke in Aramaic, quoting Jesus of Nazareth, leading many people to believe that he was either channeling Christ or was, indeed, the reincarnation of Jesus."

"And this is an especially important match for this youngster, isn't it?"

"That's correct. The winner of this match will go on to fight Ollie Marshall on next week's Clobbering Night telecast. The winner of that match will be in line to go up against Crusher Phillips at Wrestlepalooza, being held this year at the Indiana Dome in Indianapolis." Tammy's grin widened. "That show will, of course, be available on pay-per-view."

"Isn't it somewhat dangerous, putting a fairly green wrestler such as Kyle Temple in matches against seasoned professionals such as he'll be facing tonight when he goes against Nate Reynolds?"

Tammy's eyes twinkled. "I'm sure Kyle Temple is up to the challenge. He may be a newcomer to the UWE, but he's ready. I've watched him wrestle. I think Nate Reynolds may be in for a surprise."

"And what about the controversy surrounding Kyle Temple? What is your take on the situation?"

Tammy looked smug. "We've had our own experts look into Mr. Temple's experiences with past life regression, and we've learned some amazing things."

Excitedly, Parnell turned to the camera. "And I believe we have an interview that we can show the folks at home. This is Dr. Nicol Eubankov, a noted psychoanalyst."

The shot switched to a set depicting a doctor's office. Seated at a desk was a near-caricature of a psychologist, complete with Freud-like beard and fake Austrian accent. The man linked his hands on top of the desk and spoke ponderously. "I haf examined this Kyle Temple at length," the man said, laying on the accent thickly, "and haf come to the conclusion that he is indeed the reincarnation of Jesus Christ. He haf spoken at length to me as Jesus, saying things only that Jesus would know." The man went to stroke his beard and then seemed to think better of it, perhaps worried that the thing would come off in his hands.

"Notice that they don't say what Kyle said," Randy pointed out. "Just 'things Jesus would know'. They don't know what they would be, so they're keeping rather quiet about the details."

Debbie agreed. "I haf doubts about this man's veracity."

"I don't know," Jimmy said. "Did you see all the diplomas on the guy's wall? He's got to be pretty smart."

The segment ended and Tammy and Parnell returned. Parnell was nearly jumping with expectation. "And now we'll get to see Kyle Temple for ourselves. Let's take you to the ring announcer."

"Ladies and gentlemen," the ring announced said, his tones grave and solemn, "let us bring to the ring one of the most accomplished wrestlers in UWE history…."

Randy continued to watch, but the sound began to blur into background noise as he thought of Kyle. He zoned out all through the entrance of Nate Reynolds, not snapping out of his reverie until the camera showed Kyle making his grand entrance.

Lights flashed and some pyrotechnics shot off as the music, full of pomp and circumstance, swelled. Amid sparks and flashing colors, Kyle entered the arena.

"Oh. My. God," Debbie said.

Kyle was dressed in a white robe, looking to Randy like something straight out of the book *Bible Stories for Young Readers* he'd had as a kid.

Kyle's hair was brushed to a shine and flowed onto his shoulders. Sandals covered his feet instead of his usual wrestling boots. To top things off, he wore what appeared to be a crown of thorns around his head. Twelve buff guys followed him out, all wearing similar robes.

"Whoa!" Jimmy exclaimed. "He's got disciples! How cool!"

Randy pulled a throw pillow out from behind him and bit into it to keep from screaming.

CHAPTER
TWENTY-EIGHT

DURING the following weeks, Randy assumed his despair would ebb at least a little. He figured the human mind could only deal with so much sorrow before it finally shrugged its metaphorical shoulders and said, "What the hell. Life goes on."

This did not happen.

If anything, the pain Randy felt increased.

Every time the phone rang, Randy sprang to answer it. Never was it Kyle's voice on the other end. His mother called repeatedly, as did Debbie. He even got calls occasionally from Jimmy and Pete. There was nothing from Kyle. No text messages. No emails. Not even a postcard of greetings from sunny Tampa.

One call came when Randy was alone in his apartment with the lights down low. He was sobbing as the phone's jangle nearly made his jump out of his skin. He'd been watching a *Smallville* repeat, and the on-screen relationship between Clark Kent and Lana Lang was reminding him too much of his own situation. It wasn't until he'd managed to dry his tears that he realized he'd just compared himself to Kristin Kreuk.

The voice at first sounded like Kyle's, making Randy's heart do flip-flops. It wasn't until the person on the other end began to ask him just how interested in a magazine subscription he was that he realized it wasn't Kyle. The language that then came out of Randy's mouth would have made Sneed blush. After listening to Randy's tirade, the telemarketer meekly asked, "Does this mean you're not interested in the magazine subscription?"

Randy hung up and continued to sit in the dim room, lost in thought. He thought out whole conversations with Kyle, thinking about what he'd say if he could actually get in touch with him. He planned every word and had a different script ready in his head depending on Kyle's reactions. Randy didn't realize how long he'd actually sat, unmoving, until he saw the sun rising through his living room window.

AS WRESTLEPALOOZA approached, the *Crier* kicked back into gear, putting Kyle back on the cover after several weeks of small articles buried between stories of alien invaders and celebrities who had been proven to be transsexuals. "JESUS" TO WRESTLE CRUSHER PHILLIPS AT WRESTLEPALOOZA was the headline that shouted at Randy at the convenience store the Tuesday before the big Thursday night pay-per-view. He supposed he should be happy that they finally put the JESUS in quotation marks, but he was too depressed to really care. He still hadn't heard from Kyle, and he had been so sure that, with Wrestlepalooza taking place in Indianapolis, arrangements would have been made for Kyle to return to Randy's apartment. So far, that hadn't happened. None of Kyle's friends had been contacted by the newest UWE wrestler, or if they had, they were keeping it from Randy. The silence on Kyle's end was leading Randy to assume the relationship was over. Part of Randy wanted to believe that it was simply that Kyle was being kept too busy to even get in a phone call. But no, that really didn't explain things. Randy had to face it. Kyle had found a new life, and there was no room for Randy in it.

Randy had turned down Debbie's invitations to join her on the weekends to watch Jimmy wrestle. It was best to let that part of his life go. He'd had it with wrestlers, their fans, and certainly with *America's Crier*. From here on out, Randy vowed to date only skinny guys with no interest in sports. It was much safer that way.

Wednesday came and went and there was still no word from Kyle. Randy's mood blackened. Debbie asked him to come with her and Jimmy over to Pete's house to watch the Wrestlepalooza pay-per-view, but Randy refused.

"Like I want to see that," he told her petulantly as they met at lunch that afternoon.

She frowned, looking down at Randy's nearly untouched fast-food lunch. "You may not now," she said, "but I think you'll regret it if you don't see it. Maybe not today—"

"But soon, and for the rest of my life?"

Debbie smiled weakly. "I wasn't going to use those exact words."

Randy's lip twisted. "If I'm Ingrid Bergman, where's my Paul Henreid consolation prize?"

"I never did get that. Paul Henreid was much better-looking that Humphrey Bogart. Maybe they should have traded roles."

Randy squinted his eyes. "If you're going to talk sacrilege, I'm moving to another table. But now that you've brought up *Casablanca*, let's switch topics and discuss movies. I never want to talk about wrestlers, wrestling, boyfriends, Wrestlepalooza, or *America's Crier* ever again."

"I still think we should go to Pete's tonight. We'll have snacks and...."

Debbie didn't finish. Randy had picked up his tray and moved it to an already occupied table where a young mother was trying to get her toddler to finish eating his chicken nuggets. Randy plopped down next to the child and smiled at the woman. "How are you doing?" he asked.

She stared without replying.

IF HE had been totally honest, Randy could have told Debbie that he did want to see the Wrestlepalooza event. He just didn't want to see it with any of his friends, nor did he want to watch it alone. He'd decided to watch the show at the sports bar down the street from his apartment. He'd returned there several times after his drunken visit the night Kyle left, and he'd noticed a flier on the wall announcing a special Wrestlepalooza party for that evening being held at the bar.

Randy arrived early, mainly to ensure he got a good seat at the bar with an unobstructed view of the large screen television but also to get in a little harmless flirting with the bartender. True, the guy was straight and not really Randy's type, but that actually worked as an advantage. The last thing Randy wanted was to flirt with someone who might take the attention seriously. The bartender (Randy still, after several visits, had never learned the guy's name) didn't seem to mind.

Randy paid the cover charge and settled at the bar. He smiled when he saw that "his" bartender was working. There were few patrons as of yet, so the bartender came over to Randy with the attitude of someone prepared for a long conversation.

"What can I get for you, sport?" he asked.

"Is the kitchen open? I sort of skipped lunch today."

The bartender nodded. "What'll you have?"

"Burger and fries?"

"Done." As the bartender disappeared to take his order into the back, Randy gazed at the television. A tennis match was on. Unfortunately, it was women's tennis, so Randy wouldn't have any cute butts to ogle while he ate. The bartender returned with a smile. "Want to get something to drink while you're waiting for your food?"

Randy smiled. "I'll have a cosmo."

"Not one of the specialty martinis?"

"No, I think I'm swearing off of chocolatini, strawberrytini, and pretty much any other kind of tini, for the next millennium."

"Don't blame you," the bartender replied.

The place filled up fairly quickly, making Randy glad he'd decided to come early. All the stools at the bar were rapidly filled, and most of the tables followed. If Randy hadn't been able to sit at the bar, he probably wouldn't have stayed. He couldn't imagine anything worse than sitting at a table in a straight bar alone while couples, frat boys, and rednecks surrounded him. *Okay*, he told himself, *watching the show at Pete's would have been worse. Much worse.*

He started on his third cosmo just as Wrestlepalooza began. A table of frat boy types whooped in excitement and raised their beers in a toast. Randy, unseen by them, raised his cosmo as well. He was surprised that the movement seemed exaggerated and clumsy. Usually three cosmos didn't get him that tipsy. Maybe his lack of appetite lately was interfering with his ability to consume alcohol. Randy made a mental note to start nursing his drinks. The Wrestlepalooza show was likely to go on for several hours, and Kyle's match was bound to be the last one shown. He didn't want to pass out before the big event.

It pained him to think that the action was going on in the Indiana Dome, less than a mile away. Kyle would be there, probably getting ready for his dream to come true. The one true love of Randy's life was within walking distance. Not that it mattered. Kyle could be on the moon as far as their relationship was concerned. It was over. Randy knew it.

Halfway through the show, Randy's head began to ache. The frat boys were loud and boisterous. Every move in the ring brought at least one shout or exclamation out of them, and the cumulative effect of their cries was really beginning to annoy Randy. They reminded him of too many weekends spent in high school gyms watching Kyle wrestle.

Finally Tamalita Edwards came on the screen, accompanied by hoots and whistles from the bar crowd. Randy couldn't hear what she was saying, but he did pick out Kyle's name. It was time for the main event.

Next to her, announcer Ted Parnell looked like he had to pee. He practically danced from one leg to another, excitement oozing from every pore of his skin. Randy squinted just to make sure it wasn't the cosmos causing the announcer to flutter. Tammy was stock still, though, so it must indeed be Parnell. Randy wanted to slap him.

Crusher Phillips was introduced, bringing boos from the bar crowd as well as from the throng seated at the sold-out arena. The big, burly wrestler climbed into the ring and gave the camera the finger.

Randy blinked. He hated the guy already, which of course was what the UWE expected. He felt a twinge when he saw the massive muscles covering every inch of the guy's body. In a real fight, Kyle wouldn't have stood a chance. Randy was suddenly glad for the unreality of professional wrestling. Kyle would probably get a few scrapes and bruises from his night's work, but at least he wouldn't be killed by the Goliath.

Randy downed the rest of his drink as the announcer called out Kyle's name. He felt a sudden apprehension. This was it. This was what he'd tried to warn Kyle against. Something horrible was about to happen. Randy felt it in his bones. He also felt a staggering impulse to piss, possibly brought on by Parnell's antics, but he had to see Kyle's match. The restroom would just have to wait.

The frat boys were on their feet, chanting the word "Jesus" over and over again. Beer was being spilled everywhere, but they were too drunk to actually notice or care.

The television showed the entrance area, and suddenly Kyle's image was there on the screen.

He was dressed in his old black square-cut wrestling trunks, but what astonished Randy more was his face. Kyle had shaved off the beard and moustache. His hair was not only cut short, it was now a dark-brown color. There was no Jesus robe. There was no crown of thorns. The twelve disciples supplied by Tammy still followed him out, but they looked confused and kept their distance from Kyle, as if they didn't want to take any of the blame for his new look.

The bartender was shaking a cocktail without taking his eyes off the screen. "Wow. This is some new gimmick. I thought he was supposed to be their Jesus guy. He doesn't look very Jesus-like to me."

Randy wasn't sure it was a gimmick. He wondered if Tamalita Edwards had even been aware of Kyle's transformation. When the screen went back to her and Parnell, Randy had his answer. Tammy was red with anger and shock, and Randy was sure she wasn't putting on an act. He couldn't hear her over the roar of the audience, both in the arena and the bar, but he could read her lips, which said, "What the fuck does he think he's doing?"

Kyle made his way to the ring, a determined look on his face. The twelve disciples didn't follow, deciding instead to meander around the entrance area. If Randy thought the catcalls accompanying Phillips's ring entrance were loud, the screams at Kyle were deafening. The ring was pelted with soda cups, popcorn bags, and other debris. A close-up showed Kyle's face. Randy thought he detected a slight gleam of alarm in his eyes, but Kyle kept all emotion from his face. Randy felt a swell of pride fill his chest, almost eclipsing the worry in his mind. "Good for you," Randy muttered aloud.

Suddenly pandemonium broke out. One guy in a ringside seat jumped up and scrambled into the ring, totally escaping the large security guard only a few feet away. In seconds others from ringside followed suit. The ring was flooded with people. One of the cameramen obviously tried to get closer for a shot, but the viewing audience was treated to an unexpected view of the arena's ceiling. Another camera angle quickly filled the screen, showing the ring from much further away. There just seemed to be a mass of people. Randy couldn't see Kyle amid the arms and legs that were everywhere. Security guards attempted to pull people out of the ring, but they were overwhelmed. The ring announcer was screaming, but his shouts were indistinguishable from those of the crowd around him. The television speakers just belted out a wall of sound.

The frat boys sat down and grew quiet, not sure of what they were seeing. One of them snarled, "What the fuck?" while another said loudly, "Aren't they going to wrestle?"

Finally the security team got the ring cleared. Left were a confused-looking referee, the ring announcer, and a puzzled Crusher Phillips. Of Kyle there was no sign.

The audience was spilling out of the arena as if a fire had broken out. People were shoving others out of the way. A brief camera shot showed one young man kicking another guy who'd fallen. The exits were jammed as everyone tried to get out at once.

Cameras switched from the ring to Tammy and Parnell and then to the audience and back again. Still Kyle was nowhere to be seen.

In the ring, Phillips shrugged his shoulders and climbed slowly out. He walked deliberately through the dissipating crowd towards the backstage area. The camera went back to Tammy Edwards, who gulped and stammered out, "Well, we're not sure what's going on here…."

Randy bolted from his barstool and hit the door within seconds. He wondered how long it would take him to run the several blocks to the Indiana Dome.

CHAPTER
TWENTY-NINE

DESPITE the fact that it was late in the evening, downtown Indianapolis seemed filled with people. Randy dodged right and left as he ran in the rain, only vaguely aware of the people he was avoiding. They were just shapes to him, obstructions getting in the way of his quest. As he neared the Indiana Dome, the crowds thickened, causing him to slow down. The throng was exiting after Wrestlepalooza's bizarre ending, heading for their cars or out for a drink. As Randy pressed into the crowd, he felt like he knew what a trout going upstream went through. Several people gave him dirty looks as he shouldered past them. He ignored them.

He didn't know how he expected to find Kyle amid all these thousands of people. Hell, the UWE cameras couldn't even pick him out. Still, he knew he had to try. Randy finally made it to one of the Indiana Dome doors. People were still filing out. He shoved his way through. No one stopped him, although a security guard looked as if he was thinking about it. "Left my car keys," Randy told him by way of explanation. The guard nodded. Randy continued to push his way through.

The arena was nearly empty. A few people were still milling about, but most had already exited. Randy had no idea what he should do. Unable to come up with a better plan, he made his way quickly down to the ring. Desperate, he lifted up the skirting. He wasn't surprised to find that Kyle wasn't hiding under the ring. Randy hadn't really thought he would be, but it was the only place he could think of to look.

Dropping the cloth back into place, he turned to find a furious Tamalita Edwards standing behind him. "You!" she shouted, a bit of spittle settling on her lip. "I knew you had something to do with this! I'll have you know that your little boyfriend is fired! In fact, I'm going to sue his scrawny little ass."

Randy grabbed her by the shoulders. "Where is he? Have you seen him?"

She shook him off. "No, I haven't seen the son of a bitch, and if I had, I'd have kicked him in the nuts. He ruined the whole fucking show. The only reason I hired him in the first place was because of the Jesus thing. He had no right to shave his facial hair. Hell, it was in his contract that he couldn't shave! And what happened to his Jesus outfit? Did you know he was going to do this? Did you put him up to it?"

"No, I didn't put him up to it," Randy said, exasperated. "And as for what happened, I'm guessing he had a sudden attack of taste and realized he couldn't go through with your little charade. You're sure you don't know where he is?"

She didn't even seem to hear. "This was the worst Wrestlepalooza ever, and that includes the time Poncho Nolen accidentally set himself on fire. If I get my hands on that little twerp, he'll regret ever being born. He made a joke out of professional wrestling."

Randy frowned. "Is that even possible?"

"I'll rip his nuts off, that's what I'll do. He'll know not to mess with me!"

"Enough with the testicle mutilation!" Randy wailed. "Do you have any idea where he could be? That's all I want to know."

She looked at him blankly. "I obviously don't, otherwise I wouldn't be standing here wishing him ill. If you find him, make sure you tell him that I've fired his ass."

"Gladly," Randy replied. He moved past her, heading back to the concourse area. He quickly checked a few restrooms only to find them empty. He paused for a moment to use one of them. Heading for the exit, Randy saw only a janitor pushing a mop across the floor. No one else was in sight. Randy's footsteps echoed as he made his way back outside.

Where could Kyle have gone? His apartment? Randy's? Did he go to see one of his wrestling buddies like Jimmy or Pete? He had to be somewhere.

Think, Randy, think. Where could Kyle go?

Nothing came to him. Dejected, Randy walked out of the Indiana Dome back to the street. As he slowly made his way to the corner and waited for the light to change, he noticed a somewhat familiar man rushing up to him. He turned for a better look. The guy obviously recognized him, but Randy wasn't quite sure he knew who the guy was.

The man had a grin on his face, and he held out his hand for Randy to shake. "I thought that was you. I was clear down the block when you came out of the Dome, but I was sure it was you. You're Kyle Temple's boyfriend, aren't you?"

"I'm afraid I can't quite place you. Do you know where Kyle is right now? I'm trying to find him."

"We met briefly a while back. I'm Jeff Hardesty. I work for *America's Cr—*"

He didn't finish, since Randy's fist slammed into his mouth. Before he could register what was happening, Hardesty was on his back looking up at Randy, who in turn was looking at his own fist as if wondering where the power had come from. Hardesty rubbed his bleeding lips. "What was that for?" he asked.

Randy's chuckle was hollow. "You have to ask?"

Hardesty paused and then said, "No, I guess I don't."

The light changed, and Randy left Hardesty lying on the sidewalk.

KYLE wasn't anywhere to be found. Randy tried both of their apartments. He returned to the streets and just started wandering, not sure of what to do. He took out his cell phone and called Debbie. She answered on the first ring.

"What's going on?" she demanded. "Where's Kyle? Was that some sort of stunt, or—"

"No," Randy told her, breathing hard. "I talked with Tammy Edwards. She was pretty pissed. There's no way she was party to it. Have you heard from Kyle? Has anyone there?"

"No, we were hoping you knew what was going on. Where are you now?"

Randy stopped and looked around him. "I'm not sure. Not far from my apartment. I just started walking the streets. I can't stay still."

"Maybe you'd better head back," Debbie said, "just in case Kyle shows up there."

"He'd call my cell phone. I can't just sit around and wait. Is Jimmy there? Ask him if there's some place wrestlers like to hang out. Other than the gym, I mean. A bar or something like that."

"A wrestler's bar? You're stretching things a bit, but I'll ask." She took the phone away from her face for a second, and Randy could hear a muffled conversation. When she came back, she said, "He says wrestlers hang out in titty bars a lot."

"Well, I don't think that's going to help me with Kyle. Where...." Randy froze. "Wait. The gym. Sneed's Gym. Kyle could be there. It's the one place I haven't checked."

"Want us to come with you?"

Randy was already walking to the corner, where a taxi was sitting. "No need. Just get the guys to try to think of anywhere Kyle could go. I'll keep you posted."

THE trip to Sneed's Gym was a bust. The gym was locked up tight, and no lights were on inside as far as Randy could tell. Just in case, Randy pounded on the door, but there was no answer. He finally returned to the waiting cab after first checking in with Debbie. They hadn't heard any news, nor had they come up with any bright ideas.

The crack of dawn found Randy on the road, trying to retrace the route Kyle had taken to his mother's trailer. Randy wished now that he'd paid more attention to actual landmarks when they'd driven out there the first time, and spent less time moaning. After several wrong turns, he finally came across some farm building that seemed familiar. He drove on and eventually saw the sign for Clark's Hill. His heart began to race as he turned into the trailer park and found the daisy-painted mobile home.

He paused before knocking on the door, realizing it was still fairly early and that Mary Temple might not be up yet. He listened to see if he could hear sounds of movement from within.

As he pressed his ear to the door, a voice came from behind him. "She ain't there."

Randy turned to see a little girl standing by his car, holding a Kermit the Frog doll by the neck in a strangulation grip. "Do you know where she is?"

"She went to Indianapolis," the girl replied, pronouncing the city as 'Indian apples'. "Her son was wrestling there last night."

Randy felt like hitting himself. Of course Mrs. Temple would have gone to the show. She probably got a hotel room and Kyle was probably staying with her. Even if he wasn't, the UWE would have put him up in a hotel. By not thinking clearly, Randy had wasted the entire night and most of his morning. He patted the little girl on the head as he rushed past her. "Thanks, kid," he shouted as he slammed the car door and sped off back toward the city.

AFTER meeting up at Randy's apartment, everyone took a section of the hotels and motels listed in the phone book and began calling. Pete, Jimmy, and Debbie all used their cell phones. Randy used his house phone. Debbie pointed out that even if they found the hotel that Kyle was staying at, they might not admit the wrestler was staying there. "He's a celebrity now. They might not tell us. Confidentiality and all that."

"We've got to try, anyhow."

Pete suggested they ask for Kyle's mother. "She's not a celebrity. I bet you Kyle arranged for her to stay in the same hotel, so if we find her...."

"Brilliant!" Randy kissed Pete on the forehead, causing the Latino to break out in a wide grin.

Hours of calling, however, resulted in no leads.

THREE days after Wrestlepalooza found Randy feeling beaten and dejected. No one, it seemed, had heard from Kyle. Randy had finally found Kyle's mother at home, but she said she hadn't heard from her son. Debbie thought perhaps she was lying, covering for Kyle, but Randy had believed her. Mary Temple had seemed genuinely worried.

Randy called Sneed. He even contacted Carl Bennett on the off chance that Kyle had been to the former mesmerist for a reading.

Randy thought Bennett sounded strangely like Boris Karloff over the phone. "No, my dear boy, I haven't heard from or seen Kyle in quite some time." A tinny yapping sound came over the phone line. "Quiet, Pepper.

Sorry I can't be of assistance, young man. Kyle was a nice boy. I wish I could help you."

Randy thought about asking how Bennett felt about turning their lives upside down by leaking the story of Kyle's Aramaic speeches to the press, but he instead simply asked, "Well, if you hear from him, could you call me right away?" Randy gave Bennett both his regular and cell numbers.

"I will. I hope you find him."

In desperation, Randy even phoned Tamalita Edwards, whom he tracked down at the UWE headquarters in Tampa. He wished he hadn't.

"That son of a bitch," Edwards screamed into the phone. "No, I haven't seen him. He certainly hasn't shown his sorry ass back here. He didn't use his return plane ticket, that much I do know. If I ever do see him—"

"You'll do something horrible to his testicles, I know," Randy finished for her. He hung up.

While at work on Wednesday, Randy got a call from his father.

"Son, I was just talking with your mother. She's been acting peculiar for the last several days...."

"More so than usual?" Randy asked.

"She's been quiet," his father said ominously. "So I knew something was up. This morning I found her sneaking out of the shed in the backyard. She was acting very guilty. I figured she had some stray cat that she'd found and was hiding it there. You know how she is with strays. At first she wouldn't say anything. She just clamped her mouth shut. Well, then I found her trying to sneak some food out there. I went out there myself, thinking she's got some dog or something. She came right out and padlocked the door and wouldn't give me the key. I could hear someone rustling about inside. Then I heard someone sneeze. Your mother is hiding some guy in our shed. I think it's your boyfriend."

RANDY pulled into his parents' driveway and screeched to a stop. His mother and father were standing by the front door. His father wore a worried look. His mother, wearing a blue dress adorned with her usual string of pearls, looked grim and determined, her arms folded over her chest. Randy's father rolled his eyes as Randy rushed up to them.

"She's got the key," he said, exasperated. "She's hidden it in her bra and won't take it out."

Randy looked steadily into his mother's eyes. "Mom, I know who you've got hidden in the shed. I can't believe you did this without saying anything to me!"

"He made me promise!" Mrs. Stone's tone was unrepentant. "He showed up late that night, after the wrestling show, and asked me... begged me, to let him sleep here. He said he needed some time alone to think. I put that old army cot out there in the shed. I got him a book light and he took some of your old comic books from your room—"

"Mom, give me the key! You can't leave him padlocked in the shed!"

"Your father followed me out! It was the only way I could think of to keep him hidden!"

"The boy's been out there for days, then?" Mr. Stone made a face. "The boy must smell to high heaven."

Mrs. Stone flashed him a glance. "Don't be silly. He showered in the house while you were at work."

"I thought somebody had been using my loofah."

Randy continued to stare at his mother. "I'm getting that key. Either you hand it over or I'm going after it. I mean it. I will. I'm that desperate."

Mrs. Stone blanched. "He's counting on me."

Randy held out his hand. "I don't know why he came to you, but I'll settle that with him later. Right now I just have to talk with him. The key, please."

Reluctantly, Mrs. Stone fished out the key. Both Randy and his father averted their gaze as she rummaged down the front of her dress, finally producing a small key. Randy took it quickly and started around the house. His parents followed.

The large, roomy shed was behind the garage. It was rarely used; as far as Randy knew, it had only ever contained their Christmas decorations and the lawn mower when it wasn't in use. The white wooden doors had the name Stone painted across them in black letters.

Randy held his breath as he turned the key in the lock. He removed the padlock and tossed it aside. Throwing open the door, he said, "Kyle, I know…."

He stopped.

The shed contained boxes marked Xmas and the lawn mower. There was a cot set up, covered with blankets and comic books.

Kyle, however, was missing.

CHAPTER
THIRTY

RANDY'S mother and father sat on the couch at opposite ends, as if physical touch would result in spontaneous combustion. Mr. Stone nursed a glass of Glenfidditch. Mrs. Stone sat stock still, looking ahead with her head held proud. Randy sat across from them in an armchair, rubbing his forehead to try to hold off an oncoming headache.

"You're sure he was in there before you padlocked the door?" he asked his mother for the tenth time.

"Absolutely. I was talking with him just as your father was coming toward the shed. Kyle asked me to bring him some more Spider-Man comics and one of my grilled cheese sandwiches. That boy really likes his grilled cheese."

"He can't have been in there," Randy said, exasperated. "I know it was locked when I got to it. I had trouble getting the damn key to unlock it, in fact. You must have not locked it properly and he came out and locked it after him."

His mother looked down her nose. "I know I locked it. I remember hearing the click."

"Why did he come here in the first place? Why didn't he come to see me?"

"Actually, he came here looking for you," she said with reluctance, as if the admission made her role less important. "He'd already been to your place but you weren't there. He came here to see if we knew where you were. Your father had already gone to bed. I told him we hadn't seen you and the poor boy told me what happened at his wrestling show. He was very upset. He said he wanted to be alone to think. I suggested he stay in your old room, but he said the garage would do him fine. I told him that your father would find him in the garage but there was room in the shed. He said that would be perfect."

"And he's been in the shed since Thursday night?"

"Except for when your father's been at work. Then he used your old room."

Mr. Stone frowned. "But why in God's name? Why wouldn't you say something to me or Randy? You know Randy's been looking for him."

"He said he needed time to think," Mrs. Stone answered calmly. "It was a pleasure to help him out. He's such a nice boy." She looked at Randy. "He's so ashamed of having yelled at you. He told me all about your fight, something you never discussed with me, by the way. He's so hurt. He's almost afraid to see you again, that's how bad he feels about it. He's scared. He thinks you don't love him anymore."

"Would I be searching the whole damn state for the last three days if I didn't?" Randy said. "I just need to see him. We need to be together. You're sure you don't have any idea where he went?"

Mrs. Stone shrugged. "As far as I know, he should be out there in the shed. I know you don't believe in the reincarnation thing, but I think the young man has performed a miracle."

Randy groaned. "Getting out of a locked shed is hardly in the same category as feeding a multitude with only a loaf of bread or walking on water. I have to admit, I'm stumped, though. If the door was really locked, I have no idea how he managed to get out. I just know he's not—"

"You're welcome to your opinion," his mother interrupted archly. "Let me have mine."

Sighing, Randy said, "Well, I'm right back at square one now. I have no idea where he's gone."

"I do hope you'll find him soon," his mother said. "I really wanted the two of you to be here for dinner today." She eyed Randy's T-shirt and jeans critically. "And I'm assuming you're going to go back and change before coming to dinner. The relatives should be starting to arrive soon, and I really need to get to the kitchen and check to make sure Mrs. Pitcairn doesn't need any help."

It took Randy a moment to realize what his mother was talking about before remembering it was Easter Sunday. His mouth fell open. He closed it. Finally, he said, "I knew that. I remembered. I was planning on coming back."

"I invited Debbie and your little wrestling friends to come as well."

That brought a small smile to Randy's face. "I never thought I'd see the day when you'd be having people like Jimmy Murdoch or Pete over for Easter dinner."

Mrs. Stone said, "It's so easy to get so high and mighty when it comes to what one believes. One tends to forget that Jesus traveled with the common folk. The high and mighty wanted nothing to do with him. Getting to know Kyle has reminded me of what's important."

"And that is?" Randy asked.

"Love."

Mr. Stone raised his glass in a toast. "Amen to that." Taking a long sip, he smacked his lips and then said, "You know, I hate to be the one to point out more coincidences. Lord knows you boys have had a hard enough time lately, but you've got to note the oddity in that it's been three days since Kyle disappeared, and we've had to 'roll back' a door with our name, Stone, written on it only to find that he's not there anymore. It's the Easter story all over again, and on Easter Sunday to boot. It's pretty weird."

Randy just stared icily at his father.

"I'm just saying," his father muttered.

RANDY nearly didn't return to his parents' house for Easter dinner. He really didn't feel up to being with a crowd of people, and there were several relatives that would be in attendance that he didn't particularly want to have to deal with. Uncle Fred would be there, for one, and Uncle Fred had the habit of asking unceasing questions about Randy's love life. This was Uncle Fred's way of showing how "cool" he was with Randy's lifestyle. Randy certainly didn't want to talk with anyone, even Uncle Fred, about Kyle. It was still just too painful.

Two reasons made Randy show up. For one thing, he knew he'd never hear the end of it from Debbie if they showed up at the Stones' for dinner and he didn't. The main reason, though, was he hoped—prayed—that Kyle would return to the shed and he could finally talk with him.

He pulled up in front of the house and parked behind Aunt Carol's blue Subaru. As he got out from behind the wheel, he noticed another car parking behind his. Curious, he looked in to see who was driving. His eyes widened as he recognized Jeff Hardesty.

Hardesty got out, holding his hands up in surrender. "Whoa, sport! No fisticuffs this time, okay? I just want to ask you something."

Randy felt his shoulders tense, but he forced his fists to relax. "What do you want? Don't you have alien congressmen to bother or celebrities to out?"

Hardesty grinned uneasily. "Believe it or not, I'm not some evil ogre."

"No, that would be a slur to evil ogres everywhere."

Hardesty apparently decided to let that pass. "Look, the Kyle stories are over anyway. We're moving on to other things."

"What, you've discovered that Newt Gingrich is a leprechaun?"

"No," Hardesty said, "although I might use that. That's pretty good. No, it's just that our readers' attention spans aren't that long. Frankly, if we were to go on with the Jesus/Kyle thing, they'd get bored with it pretty quick. I just wanted to let you know I didn't have any hard feelings." Hardesty rubbed his chin. "For the slug, I mean."

Hardesty stuck out his hand, but Randy just glared at it. "You've got to be kidding. I'd rather shake hands with a boa constrictor, and they don't have hands."

Shrugging, Hardesty dropped his hand. "Suit yourself. I'm heading back to Chicago today. I just wanted to see if you guys were all right, really. That was some performance your boyfriend gave the other night."

"No, we're not all right," Randy replied. "I haven't seen Kyle. Your stupid little stories have caused more trouble than you'll ever know. And if Kyle and I don't get back together...." Randy advanced menacingly on the reporter and continued, "I'll find you. And just remember, this skinny guy can pack a punch."

"It was a lucky shot," Hardesty said without animosity. "But for what it's worth, I hope you and Kyle get back together. You shouldn't let something like *America's Crier* get between you. That crap doesn't matter. I'm just happy whenever I get a real story like Kyle's. Usually I have to make the shit up." Hardesty shuffled his feet. "I guess that's all I wanted to say. I'll see you around, sport." He gave a little wave before returning to his car.

RANDY made his rounds, saying his obligatory hellos to relatives he only saw once or twice a year before finding Debbie and Jimmy. Randy engulfed her in a fierce hug. "I'm surprised you actually came," he said.

Debbie released him with a grin. "I figured you needed cheering up. Pete and his girlfriend are somewhere around here, probably in the kitchen. Liza's been helping Mrs. Pitcairn finish getting dinner ready, and Pete's been stuffing his face with deviled eggs since we got here. He won't have any room for dinner at the rate he's going."

Randy gave Jimmy a brief hug. "I'm glad you could come."

Jimmy was chomping on a peanut-butter-filled stalk of celery. "Glad to be here. Your mom puts on a good spread. Hey, your dad told us about Kyle's vanishing act in the shed. Weird, huh?"

Randy sighed. "I just wish I knew where he was. I'm really worried about him."

"You'll find him," Debbie said with assurance. "He just needs some time to think. He's probably embarrassed that he didn't listen to you in the first place."

"I hope that's the case," Randy said.

Debbie squeezed his arm. "I have faith. You two were meant to be together."

Randy nodded. "Maybe that padlock doesn't work right. You know, like it may seem like it's all closed and everything but it really isn't."

"The seatbelts in my Kia are like that sometimes," Jimmy said. "You think you've clicked them, but then you're driving down the road and out they come."

"I think I'll just pop out back and check the shed again," Randy said. "Just in case he's back out there."

Randy made his way to the kitchen, where his mother was pretending to help Mrs. Pitcairn and Liza with dinner. Pete was in the corner, trying to decide if another deviled egg was in order. "Darling," his mother gushed, kissing his cheek. "I'm so glad you're here. I was afraid you might be mad at me for hiding your boyfriend. Forgive me? It's the holiday for forgiveness. At least I think that's what Easter is for."

"You're forgiven. And thanks for inviting my friends. I really appreciate it."

His mother sighed. "I just wish Kyle was here. He should be, you know. It just feels like the family isn't complete."

Randy kissed his mother's cheek. "Thanks for saying that. I'm going out back. Maybe he's back out there."

"I checked earlier. There was no sign of him."

"Well, I'm going to check it again." Randy hit the back door. Outside, he found the air slightly chilly. It had looked like rain when he'd gotten out of bed that morning, but now the sun was forcing its way through the clouds. Randy looked up, hearing a bird fluttering in the old oak that stood next to the garage.

A branch was swaying wildly. Randy narrowed his eyes. If that was a bird, it was a fucking big one.

Suddenly the branch snapped and, with a strangled cry, Kyle fell out of the tree, hit the top of the shed, and rolled off, finally hitting the ground with a thud.

Amazed, Randy ran over and helped the laughing wrestler to his feet.

"That was gnarly," Kyle said, still chuckling.

Randy clutched Kyle tightly, holding on with all the desperation of a drowning man grabbing hold of a life preserver. The tears started to well as he pressed his cheek against Kyle's face. He said softly, "What the fucking hell were you doing up the fucking tree?"

Kyle broke down and sobbed into Randy's shoulder. Neither of them spoke for several minutes. They swayed on their feet, entwined. In a choked voice, Kyle said simply, "I'm so fucking sorry. I never meant to hurt you. I'm so fucking sorry. I'm so stupid."

Kissing Kyle's cheek, which was wet from both of their tears, Randy said, "You could have called. Sent me an e-mail. Anything. I couldn't bear not hearing from you."

Kyle's shoulders shook from his sobs. "I couldn't. Not after what I'd said to you. I thought you'd hate me forever."

"I could never hate you." Randy held Kyle's face in his hands and then kissed him long and hard. "Now, what the fuck were you doing up in the damn tree?"

"I had to see if you were in the house. I saw Debbie and Jimmy in there, so I figured you were probably in there somewhere. I was going to try to get Jimmy's attention and get him to come out here. I was going to tell him to talk to you and see if you were mad at me. You know, to see if there was a chance you'd talk to me. I was too scared to just knock on the door and do it that way."

"So you tried to break your neck instead? Quite right."

"So you're not mad?"

Randy let his kisses answer. When they finally came up for air, Randy said with a small chuckle, "I saw your show Thursday night."

"You were there?"

"No, I didn't have the guts to go. I was watching the show at a sports bar. When the riot broke out, I ran like The Flash down to the Dome. I looked everywhere for you. Needless to say, I couldn't find you."

Kyle smiled. "I don't know what got into me. The day of the show I suddenly knew I couldn't go on with the Jesus act. Just the idea of putting on that stupid robe and wearing that dumb crown... I just couldn't do it. It felt wrong. I went out and shaved everything off and colored my hair. I wore a baseball cap into the Dome so no one could tell. I knew Tammy would blow a gasket when she saw me. She did come to talk with me before the show, but luckily she didn't ask me to take off the cap, and I managed to keep my face away from her so that she couldn't see I'd shaved. Out in the arena, I knew there would be some reaction to me changing my appearance, but I really didn't think it would start a fight like that. When the crowd went wild, I got scared and hid under the ring for a few minutes. One of the roadies must have left a jacket under there. I put that on and then figured I'd try to just blend in with the crowd and get to one of the exits."

"Wearing wrestling trunks and boots?"

"I didn't figure too many people would be looking down at my legs. There was a lot going on, and anyways I was desperate. I thought I was going to get lynched, if not by the crowd at least by Tammy."

"She did have something like that in mind, although I think she wanted to hang you up by your balls. She has a testicle fixation."

"You talked with her? I'll bet she's pissed. I ruined the whole show."

"I don't know. You certainly made it interesting. So you ended up here? In my mother's shed?"

"I couldn't think of anyone who'd let me stay somewhere and just let me think for a few days without telling anyone where I was. Then I thought of your mother and how much she liked me...."

"She did say you were part of the family."

The tears had dried up, so Kyle took a moment to run a forearm across his nose. He sniffed loudly. "I read all of your comic books."

"I know." Randy put his forehead against Kyle's. "So tell me. How did you get out of the shed?"

Kyle looked puzzled. "I just walked out of it. What do you mean?"

"Mom was convinced she'd put the padlock on. It certainly was locked when I got to it. When you weren't inside, we were all pretty shocked."

Shaking his head, Kyle said, "All I know is that I heard your mom talking with your dad. I thought for sure he would open the door and find me in there. After a while, when nothing happened, I opened the door. No one was there, so I figured I'd go for a walk in the park for a while. I came back here and climbed up the tree to see who all was here for Easter dinner. I guess you know the rest."

So many things were going through Randy's mind that he wasn't sure what he wanted to say first. He finally just looked into Kyle's eyes and laughed. "I love you," he said.

Kyle's face shone. "Ditto," he said.

They heard the back door open and turned to see Debbie, Jimmy, and Pete piling out of the house. Debbie screamed happily and nearly collided into Kyle and Randy. When Jimmy and Pete caught up, they all enjoyed a group hug.

"You dumbass," Debbie said, laughing. "You scared us half to death."

Randy kissed Kyle's forehead and rubbed his now-short hair. "It doesn't matter. All I care about is that I've got him back."

"I don't know if you should be glad I'm back," Kyle replied with a grin. "I'm jobless now. You'll have to support me until I can find work. My dream of wrestling in the big time obviously is a bust."

"Sneed will take you back," Pete said, smacking Kyle on the back. "And you won't have to wear no stupid crown of thorns, either."

Kyle grabbed Randy's face and kissed him hard. "It doesn't matter," he said. "This guy here is all I really care about. He's my real dream."

"And we can put all this stupid Jesus stuff behind us," Randy said. "The coincidences… everything. And that's all they were. Coincidences. Just weird coincidences."

JEFF HARDESTY thought about taking a picture. He was perched on a rock in the neighbor's yard, barely able to see over the fence. His instincts had told him to stick around the Stones' house. Somehow he knew something was about to develop. And sure enough, he'd witnessed Kyle falling from the tree and the tearful reunion of the lovers. It was nice. He really should take a picture. After all, he was a reporter for the *Crier*. He didn't have a conscience. He just lived for bizarre stories. And what could be more bizarre than "Jesus" showing back up on Easter Sunday, of all days?

Hardesty started to take his camera out of its case. He craned his neck and saw the two guys kissing again. They looked so happy.

Grunting, Hardesty put the camera back and stepped off the rock.

There were always aliens to pursue. And predictions by psychics telling of the End of Days to come. And he did have that story of actual mutant turtles living in the sewers of Des Moines to write. The *Crier* really didn't need another Jesus story.

Hardesty began to whistle as he made his way back to his car. He looked up and enjoyed the feel of the warm sunshine on his face. It looked like it was going to be a lovely day after all.

STEPHEN OSBORNE has been an improvisational comedian, a pizza restaurant manager, and a bookseller. Other than writing, his addictions include British television shows, reading mysteries, and (a recent addition) Broadway musicals. He lives in rural Illinois with Jadzia the One-Eyed Wonder Dog.

Visit him at Facebook: http://facebook.com/stephen.osborne2 and Twitter: http://twitter.com/southbendghosts. Contact him at leftyIN@yahoo.com.

PALE AS A GHOST

STEPHEN OSBORNE

www.ingramcontent.com/pod-product-compliance
Lightning Source LLC
Chambersburg PA
CBHW070010260626
47159CB00005B/1745